ALASKA WILD

HELENA NEWBURY

NEW YORK TIMES BESTSELLING AUTHOR

Third Edition

This book is entirely a work of fiction. All characters, companies, organizations, products and events in this book, other than those clearly in the public domain, are fictitious or are used fictitiously and any resemblance to any real persons, living or dead, events, companies, organizations or products is purely coincidental.

This book contains adult scenes and is intended for readers 18+.

Cover by Mayhem Cover Creations

Main cover model image licensed from (and copyright remains with) Wander Aguiar Photography

ISBN: 1541166574

ISBN-13: 978-1541166578

DEDICATION

Dedicated to Tracy, who named the character of Megan, and to all my readers. Thank you for letting me do what I love.

ONE

Kate

I MET HIM at the edge of the world. I'd flown from New York to Seattle, then from Seattle to Anchorage and finally from Anchorage to Nome, the planes getting smaller each time. I'd been in continuous motion for twelve hours. But when I climbed out of the plane and set foot in Alaska, I stopped dead and just stared.

The tiny town of Nome is right on Alaska's Western tip...but I wasn't ready for how that *felt.* I turned in a slow circle as the chill spring wind tugged at my coat. To the south and west lay dark sea that looked so cold, I was sure my hand would instantly freeze solid if I dipped it in. Overhead, the sky was so brutally blue it was almost painful, so huge it made me feel like an insignificant speck. To the east and north was open country: towering mountains and thick forest. No skyscrapers. No highways. Nothing normal.

New York, seen from space, is a cluster of lights so

dense that it becomes one throbbing mass. I'd spent my whole life there. Alaska is a dark void, the points of light so small and so far apart they almost disappear.

What the hell are you doing here, Kate?

I realized I was flipping my phone over and over in my fingers inside my purse, drawing reassurance from its smooth, man-made lines. I headed for the tiny terminal building as fast as I could.

Inside, I could smell coffee and that calmed me a little. Okay, it was nothing at all like an airport back in civilization, but there were things I recognized: an information desk, a couple of screens showing the handful of flights due that day, and a sign pointing to the restrooms. I followed the arrow, relieved myself and emerged from the restroom staring down at the single, forlorn bar of signal on my phone. That's how I walked right into him.

My face *whumped* right into the valley between the big, hard mountains of his pecs. My thighs slammed *one-two* into his, except his were as solid and unyielding as a rock face. One foot wound up between his boots, my groin perilously close to his. I bounced back a little but he didn't move at all, as if he was part of the landscape.

I'm five-two, so I instinctively looked up. That wasn't nearly enough. I had to tilt my head *right* back.

He was staring back down at me and I just froze because....

Because suddenly, all of that *wild* that had made me so nervous outside was standing right in front of me, distilled into six feet plus of muscle and stubble. His eyes were the same brutal, frozen blue as the sky outside. *Alaskan blue.*

I'd never thought about what my exact opposite would be like. Now I knew. Huge, where I'm tiny. Rough where I'm smooth. Everything, from his battered boots to his wide, muscled shoulders were built for *work:* grunting, rock-smashing, tree-chopping work. I stood there in my suit, clutching my laptop bag, and it was as if I was from a different world. He belonged in this place as much as I didn't. I knew, straightaway, that he was born here.

And yet while the landscape outside unnerved me, this man triggered something completely different, an awakening that started at every millimeter of my skin that touched his but rippled in until it hit me soul-deep. There was something about him: animal and raw. Not just wild but Alaska wild. It was new and intoxicating, ripping through me like a hurricane and leaving behind a scalding heat. It was so strong, it was almost frightening.

But somehow, touching him felt...*right.* Like some tiny piece of technology, all brushed aluminum and glossy screen, slotting into a crack in a granite cliff face...and discovering it fits perfectly.

I took a deep breath...and, as my chest lifted, I felt my breasts pillow against the hard ridges of his stomach. I was wearing bra, blouse, suit jacket and a tightly-belted coat and not one of those layers meant a damn thing. I could feel the animal heat of him throbbing straight into me, could actually feel my nipples pull and tighten—

I stepped back. "Sorry." I tried to get myself together but, as soon as I met his eyes again, it was as if every thread of my clothing had been reduced to ash, the particles blasted aside by a scorching wind that seemed to slam me back against the restroom door. I tried to take a breath and found I couldn't. My chest was tight, my eyes wide. The heat inside me went lava-hot, a crashing, scorching waterfall that slammed straight down to my groin. I'd never in my life felt such *want.*

He wanted me.

I looked deliberately away and then back. I tried to reduce him to something ordered, to a description. Six-four. Dark hair. Blue eyes—

It didn't work. The words were boxes into which this man refused to be stuffed. He wasn't *six-four.* He was just *big,* big like the mountains outside were big. His hair wasn't *dark,* it wasn't some color you could pick off a chart. It was as thick and lushly black as an animal's, and grown long and loose enough to brush his collar. He had a couple of days' worth of stubble but it wasn't carefully shaped and precisely trimmed, like the guys back in New York wore it, the *artfully rough* look. This was just a guy who hadn't come near a razor in a few days because he'd been out in the wilds.

He was gorgeous, those blue eyes eating me up from a face that could have been carved from rock, all hard jaw and strong cheekbones. And he was so *big.* If he was heading somewhere and I literally threw myself at him to stop him, my small body hitting his in the chest, he'd just walk on unimpeded with me clinging to him.

It hit me that he still hadn't spoken. I took another half step back. But this time, he didn't let me open up the distance between us. This time, he took a step forward, bringing us even closer. I caught my breath as his broad chest pressed up against me and his blue eyes filled my vision. I could smell icy, fresh water, moss and forests. And beneath it, a scent I knew was *him,* the smell of warm skin and taut muscle with just a hint of something hard and ready and primal.

Every guy at the FBI—which was virtually every guy I knew—wore precisely the same suit in filing-cabinet gray and smelled the same: ozone from the printer, dry-cleaning chemicals and shoe polish. I'd been around indoor guys my whole life. I'd just met my first true outdoor guy.

And as we stared at each other, I saw something else in his eyes, wrapped up together with the lust. Puzzlement. As if this wasn't normal for him. As if he didn't understand why he was so drawn to me and didn't trust it.

And *still* he didn't say anything.

"He doesn't talk," said a voice to my left.

My head snapped around. I saw a guy in his late twenties, not much older than me, a holster on his hip and a big, gold *US Marshals* badge pinned to his shirt.

And that's when I realized that the guy I was pressed up against had his hands behind his back. And then I saw the cuffs and understood why.

I slipped sideways and, this time, the big guy didn't follow me. My legs felt like wet paper: I had to focus just to stay upright. A *prisoner?!* A *criminal?!* And I'd been getting all melty about him. What the hell was wrong with me?

I took a big pace away to put myself at a safe distance. *Except, this isn't really a safe distance, is it?* The cuffs drew his arms back and together, making his biceps and the powerful muscles of his back bulge even through his jacket. *He could just run at me, slam me up against the wall and—*

Stop it!

"You're transporting him?" I asked, trying to make my voice coolly neutral.

The young marshal grinned. He swung a huge, dull green army holdall down off his shoulder and dropped it to the floor with a *wumf.* He had tight curls of sandy-blond hair and looked as if he should be playing bass in a band, not wrangling prisoners. He looked too young. And he was big but the prisoner was *huge.*

I glanced down at my own petite frame. *Not like I can talk.*

"Boone here won't give me any trouble," said the marshal. "Will you, Boone?"

The prisoner—Boone—had finally stopped looking at me and was gazing impassively at the restroom door. It was a relief...and yet, some traitorous little part of me wanted those blue eyes back on me again, no matter what crime he'd committed.

"Local cops picked up Boone last night," said the marshal, talking about the guy as if he wasn't there. "In a little town called Koyuk. Found out there was a warrant out for him and they knew we were flying another prisoner out of here today, so they drove him over and handed him off to us."

I nodded dumbly. It was gradually dawning on me that the marshal was trying to flirt with me. I hadn't picked up on the vibe at first because...well, it's not something that happens to me a lot. And now that it was, I had no idea what to do. I had no procedure for *flirting*. And I'm not good with things I don't have a procedure for.

And it wasn't just me being weird or frosty or all the other things guys at the agency have called me. I wasn't interested, which made no sense at all. The marshal had a nice smile and he was friendly enough. He was exactly the sort of guy I should be dating: we even had something in common, him being a marshal and me being FBI. This was exactly the sort of random encounter that leads to romance, a chance meeting at an airport in the middle of nowhere. And yet something about him left me cold.

And I kept finding my eyes being drawn back to Boone.

"Who is he?" I asked. It felt wrong, talking about him that way, but Boone was staring so resolutely away from me that it didn't feel like I could talk to him directly.

The marshal shrugged. "Just some loser. Vagrant, really. Lives up in the mountains. Hunts for his food. Only comes down into town once every few months and he doesn't speak to anyone when he does. Been around these parts for years, cops had no idea he was wanted until they picked him up for brawling with some guy in a bar and ran his prints."

Brawling. The word fitted Boone. He looked as if he could wrestle a bear. My eyes ran over his broad back, down to his tight waist and hard ass—

I tore my eyes away and shook myself. "Well. Nice to meet you." And turned and headed back out into the airport before anything else could go wrong.

I had a job to do. I'd traveled almost four thousand miles to do it.

I headed straight for the hangers. I didn't even stop as I passed the coffee stand, despite the fact it was mid-morning and I hadn't had my morning cup yet. I'm a New York gal: I *need* my coffee, especially when I've been traveling all night. But this couldn't wait.

I searched hanger after hanger, finding nothing but

male maintenance workers. I needed the one female one. I needed Michelle Grigoli.

Five years ago, she'd filed a police report after being attacked on her way home from work. Attacked in a very specific way, with very specific threats made and a distinctive knife used.

In New York, Chicago and most recently Boston, some bastard had been attacking women in the exact same way. Ten so far, starting eight months ago. I had a suspect and I knew he was the one but I couldn't make it stick because there were no witnesses. He'd always come from behind and blindfolded his victims. He knew I couldn't touch him: he'd smirked his way through his interrogation. The DA had ordered me to drop the case unless I could bring him something new in the next twenty-four hours.

That's when I'd thought to check my suspect's home town of Nome, Alaska. I'd turned up Michelle's spookily similar police report: my working theory was that she'd been the very first victim, while he was still perfecting his technique. And she'd said in her statement that she'd gotten a good look at him. She was the one person who could tie everything together. That's why I'd flown all the way up here, on my own dime and in my vacation time. The bureau chief thought I was crazy. But I wasn't going to let that son of a bitch hurt anyone else.

I rounded an aircraft fuselage and saw a worker in blue coveralls, half-inside an inspection hatch. The head was hidden but the body looked female. "Ms. Grigoli?" I called over the blaring rock music, my heart thumping.

A hand reached out and fumbled for the radio. A small, slender, feminine hand. My heart lifted. I'd been waiting twelve solid hours for this moment. "Can I speak with you a moment?"

The woman clicked the radio off and hauled herself out of the fuselage. She had long black hair pulled back in a ponytail and oil stains on one cheek. I wanted to punch the air. *Yes!*

And then my world fell apart.

"Michelle transferred out of here," the woman told me. "I'm Nicole."

I had to force myself not to yell. "*When?!*"

"Yesterday."

No! Five years since she'd made her statement, two years of investigation and I'd missed her by one day. My chest contracted as if someone was squeezing my heart in an icy fist. If I didn't get to see her today, the whole case was blown. "Which airport did she transfer to?" *Please let it be close. Please let it be close.*

"Fairbanks." When I looked blank, she sighed and took pity on me. "It's a city. East of here."

I thanked her and sprinted back inside the terminal. A few minutes studying route maps gave me a tiny shred of hope. There were flights from Nome to Fairbanks and from there to Seattle. If Michelle made a positive ID, I could be back in New York to slap it on the DA's desk just in time. As long as I got a flight to Fairbanks *right now.*

I ran over to the airline desk. The woman behind it perked up, as if glad of some activity. Even for a tiny airport, I realized, the place was a ghost town. "Hi!" I said breathlessly. "I need a ticket for the next flight to Fairbanks, please. When is it?"

She tapped at her keyboard and chewed on a pencil. "Tomorrow."

"*Tomorrow?*"

"Normally there are a few flights a day. But one plane hit bad weather and had to divert and the other was grounded with engine trouble. There's nothing now until tomorrow."

That explained the empty airport. I thought of my suspect, back in New York. Now he knew we were onto him, he'd slip away, change his name...it might be years before someone pinned him down again. How many more women would he attack in the meantime? "*Please!*" I begged. "I'll take anything. A mail flight. A cargo flight. I don't care."

She saw something on her screen and her face lit up. "Oh!" Then her smile crumbled. "Oh."

"What?"

She shook her head. "Thought there was a flight, but it's a charter. US Marshals."

I remembered the young marshal by the restrooms. *Yes!* "When's it leaving?"

"*Now*. They're waiting for take-off clearance." I ran for the door. She shouted after me. "Wait, you can't just—"

"Sorry!" I yelled and threw open the door to the runway. I managed to flash my badge at a security guy just in time to stop him body-tackling me. Gasping from the shock of the freezing air, I searched for—

There. There was only one plane on the runway. Even smaller than the one that had brought me to Nome. It was turning around, lining up to take off. *Shit!* And it was a good few hundred yards away across the windswept concrete. *This is nuts....*

Then I thought of the photos of the most recent victim. No way was I letting him get away with it. No *way*.

Thanking God I wasn't wearing heels, I sprinted.

As I got closer, I started waving my arms in the air. "Hey! HEY!" I yelled. But the plane continued its turn until it was pointing straight down the runway, ready to go.

As I got closer, the blast from the propellers hit me and I had to veer away from the spinning blades. I skirted around to the front and jumped in the air, waving my arms right in front of the windscreen. *"HEY!"*

The pilot gawped at me through his window. *What the fuck, lady?!* He had one arm braced on the throttle, ready to go, and used the other arm to wave me away.

I shook my head and held up my FBI badge, using both hands so that it didn't get blown halfway down the airfield. Then I stood there resolutely, all five-foot-two of me, and refused to get out of the way.

I saw the pilot sigh...and then his hand cranked the throttle back to idle. The blast from the propellers lessened a little and I ran to the plane's side door.

It was already sliding open. A man in a US marshal's uniform was leaning out, but not the one I'd seen earlier. This guy was pushing sixty, his close-cropped hair mostly silver. He was the opposite of the other marshal: he looked like he'd been chasing down criminals his entire life, mostly outdoors, his skin as weathered and tough as leather. "What in the name of all that's holy do you think you're doing?" he snapped.

Despite his anger, his gray eyes looked kind. "I'm sorry," I told him, still panting from the run. "But I've *got* to get to Fairbanks, right now. I have a suspect who's going to walk if I don't get there." I showed him my badge and gave him a hopeful smile.

He glanced back inside the plane. With his body

blocking the door, I couldn't see who else was in there. When he turned back to me, just for an instant, his eyes looked...*scared.* Which made no sense at all.

"No," he said flatly. "This is a US marshal's flight. No civilians."

"I'm not a—"

"No one who doesn't need to be there. Got prisoners on board." He ducked back inside the plane and started to close the door.

"Please! I'll sit in the front. The back. I'll sit wherever you like. Just let me on board!"

He shook his head, scowling, and slid the door the rest of the way shut.

I shoved my hand in the gap and caught the door. I managed to bring it to a stop a half-inch before it would have sliced my fingers off and hauled it half open. "*Please!*" I begged. He gave me another shake of his head.

Then I glimpsed the young marshal, the one I'd met before, sitting on the far side of the plane. I met his eyes. "*Please!*"

And the young guy grinned. "C'mon, Hennessey. We can help the FBI out. There's plenty of seats."

The old marshal—Hennessey—snapped his head round and glared at the younger guy. But there was something wrong about it. His eyes were angry but they were also pleading. What the hell was going on? Hennessey *had* to be the more senior one....so why did the young guy seem to be giving the orders?

No matter. I wasn't going to say no. I quickly climbed aboard before they changed their minds.

There were eight seats but only two of them were taken. One was occupied by Boone, his wrists and ankles now chained and the two chained together.

Across the aisle from him was another prisoner, this one in a smart suit and white shirt but equally securely chained. I took one of the empty seats a few rows in front of them. The two marshals strapped themselves into folding jump seats facing us. The young one gave me a flirtatious grin. But the old one, Hennessey....

I expected him to scowl at me but I didn't see anger in his eyes. More like frustration...and worry.

He'd looked scared, earlier. I suddenly realized he'd been scared *for me.*

The pilot throttled up and the plane sped down the runway, then soared into the air.

Why did I suddenly feel like I'd just made the biggest mistake of my life?

TWO

Kate

FOR TWO HOURS, I stared out of the window and watched as we flew over nothing at all.

I'd naively thought that Nome, out on the coast, was *nowhere*. But now, heading east across Alaska, we were plunging right into the heart of the uninhabited heartland. Nome was a freakin' sprawling metropolis compared to this.

All I could see were mountains, forest and rivers. It was as if time had stopped a few thousand years ago: no houses, no shops, not even a road. There was a moment, about an hour in, when I looked from horizon to horizon and realized that I couldn't see *anything* man-made, not even a power line, and the feeling was exactly the same as when you try to put your foot down in the swimming pool and discover you're out of your depth.

I reluctantly slipped off my thick wool coat. It was warm enough on the plane that I didn't need it but part of me hated to leave its comforting hug. Part of me wanted to wrap myself up in it as tightly as I could and hunker down until we got somewhere more familiar. What I *really* needed right now was a big, hot cup of coffee. That would make it feel more like home.

It was the knowledge that I was out of touch—*completely*. I live my life meshed into the FBI: emails and phone calls, text messages and Tweets, a constant flow of information that lets me know I'm part of something bigger. Without it, I felt like a fish suddenly separated from the rest of the shoal. In a very big, dark ocean.

The irony is, normally I don't even look out of the window on planes. I *hate* heights and I usually spend flights studiously staring at my laptop, trying to pretend we're still on the ground. But on this flight I had to keep my eyes on the window or I'd catch his eye. The young marshal had been staring at me almost constantly.

I knew I should talk to him and thank him for helping me get on board. I could hear my best friend, Erin, raging at me for not having already arranged a date. And I knew she was right: my last proper date had been six months ago. Most guys—the ones who even notice me in the first place—find me too hard, all stone and iron when I should be giggly and soft.

That's what the FBI does to you. You put up armor to defend yourself, not just from the scumbags you have to deal with but from the backbiting and politics. It's worse if you're a woman and if you're a *small* woman, trying to convince everyone you can do your job as good as them?

It starts to get difficult to let the armor down.

So when a guy like the young marshal showed

interest in me, I should have been all over him. But there was something *off* about him. Something behind that easy, white-toothed grin and those bass-player curls. Something that made my stomach tighten. It made no sense.

And while I could ignore the young marshal, there was something I *couldn't* ignore. I could feel Boone's eyes burning into the back of my neck. And against everything that was right, *his* gaze sent a slow, undeniable throb soaking down through my body. I couldn't even see him but just being in his presence had a physical effect on me. My breathing was faster; my eyes, when I looked at my reflection in the glass, were wide, my cheeks flushed. Calming myself didn't work. Ignoring him didn't work. *He's a criminal! What's the matter with you?* But this was primal, wired in deep. As soon as I thought of Boone, I thought of being—

Picked up and—

Pinned by his strong hands, my blouse ripped open as his lips came down on mine—

"Who's your other prisoner?" I asked the young marshal, finally meeting his gaze. I had to get my mind off Boone before I dissolved into warm, helpless goo.

The young marshal blinked at me. "You don't recognize him?"

I turned to look. Expensive suit. Snow-white shirt. Fancy cufflinks. His chin was shaved as smooth as a pool ball and his black hair must have been cut and styled within the last week. He was as perfectly presented as Boone was rough.

And when I caught his eye, the green eyes that gazed back at me were utterly cold, ruthlessly calculating how I could be useful to him. I didn't let it show but I shuddered inside and turned back to the young marshal. "Nope." I leaned a little closer so that I could whisper over the drone of the aircraft engines. "Who is he?"

The young marshal grinned, apparently enjoying my closeness. "That's *Carlton Weiss!*"

Carlton.

Weiss.

Everyone in America knew his name. I'd just never seen a picture, until now. He was famous for what he did, not what he looked like.

Weiss was a Wall Street fund manager. For over ten years, he'd presided over what he claimed was a unique investment system that let normal people escape the rat race. What it really amounted to was the biggest financial scam in US history. Millions of Americans, most of them in their forties and fifties, had invested billions of dollars. When the scheme was exposed, Weiss had been completely unrepentant, first relying on his lawyers to get him off and then, when that looked like it was going to fail, fleeing...along with all the money. He'd been missing for weeks and most people had assumed he was already on a tropical island somewhere.

"What the hell was he doing in Alaska?" I asked. Across the aisle, I saw Hennessey, the old marshal, stiffen. Was he annoyed that I was talking to his underling or was it something else?

"What you have to realize is, Alaska's very close to Russia. It's only about 50 miles away, across the Bering Strait. Out in the middle, there are even these two islands, Big and Little Diomede, and they're less than three miles apart, but one's Russian and one's

American. We figure Weiss did a deal with someone to smuggle him across from Nome to Russia." He gave me another one of those big, wide grins. "Lucky for us, he got on his high horse about the fuckin—excuse me, the freakin' *wine list* while he was hiding out in a hotel and one of the staff recognized him and called it in. We're taking him to Fairbanks, then down to Seattle. He'll be in jail by tonight." He beamed. "I'm Allan, by the way. Allan Phillips."

I gave him a hesitant smile. He seemed friendly, in a cocky, frat boy kind of a way. And everything he was saying sounded right...so why did it feel so wrong? Why did talking to him feel like inching my head between a crocodile's open jaws? "Kate," I told him. "Lydecker." Then, to change the subject, "What about Boone? Why do the cops want *him?*"

Marshal Phillips shook his head. "They don't. The military do. He got court-martialed and then escaped before they could lock him up."

I couldn't help glancing over my shoulder at Boone's massive, muscled form. He was about as far from my mental image of a buzz-cut solider as it was possible to get. "He's *military?*"

"*Former* military. He's been out in the mountains a long time."

"What did he do?"

The marshal shrugged. "No clue. It's probably in his file, but I didn't get time to read it yet." He nodded down at a couple of blue file folders tucked into the pocket beside his seat. I could just read the name on the front one: *Mason Boone.* "He only got put on our flight at the last minute. We're dropping him off at Fairbanks: there's an Air Force Base there. The military police can deal with him. Now—"—he leaned a little closer—"What's the FBI doing all the way out here?"

That feeling of wrongness again, the gut instinct I've learned to trust. I unfastened my seatbelt and stood. "In a second," I told him. "I need to stretch my legs."

He nodded, looking disappointed, and I quickly turned and headed down the aisle towards the back of the plane, grabbing hold of seat backs each time the little plane bobbed and swayed.

As I moved away from the marshal, the anxiety ebbed away. But as I drew closer to Boone, a whole different feeling started up. He just looked so big, crammed into that tiny airline seat, his shoulders much wider than the narrow seat back. The chains were thick, heavy steel: they should have made him look small. But somehow, they only emphasized the power of that massive, rough-hewn body. *So powerful, he has to be chained down.* I thought of King Kong. He'd been shackled by man and had broken free....

Stupid. He was strong, yes, but even he couldn't break out of *those.* I slowed as I got closer, thinking about what Marshal Phillips had said. *He only comes into town once every few months.* Who could live like that, barely seeing another living soul?

Boone was gazing towards the front of the plane, eyes unfocused. *He must know I'm here.* Was he deliberately not looking at me?

"Don't waste your time," said a low, nasally voice behind me.

I spun around. Weiss was staring up at me with a cold grin. The chains looked very different on him. He was tiny compared to Boone, one of those guys who manages to be skinny but soft-bellied at the same time. The chains put me in mind of a small but vicious dog. He didn't look as if he could break free but he looked as if he might slip right out of them.

"What?" I said.

Weiss nodded towards Boone. "He's a loon."

I glanced at Boone again but he was still staring straight ahead. "Do you even know him?"

"C'mon." His thin lips twisted. "What sort of person would want to live all the way out here?"

I gazed coldly back at Weiss, trying to ignore the fact that I'd been wondering much the same thing.

"Now *you,*" continued Weiss, "you're a New Yorker. A city person, like me. Am I right?"

I shook my head. "I have nothing to say to you." A little part of me was curious, though. His scam had been so big, so elaborate, that the authorities were still in shock. They couldn't figure out how anyone had the sheer gall to pull it off.

"Gotta talk to someone." He jerked his head towards Marshal Phillips. "The Boy Wonder isn't doing it for you. Who's left? The old guy? The hobo?"

I flushed, flustered and confused. This guy didn't behave like someone headed to prison for the rest of their life. And I had some instinctive urge to defend Boone, even though he wore the same chains as Weiss. "None of them stole billions of dollars."

"I didn't steal it. I separated it from people who didn't deserve it. It's not stealing if they're idiots."

I gripped the seat back in front of Weiss's so that I wasn't tempted to hit him. "My parents lost money in your scam," I said tightly. "Twenty-six thousand dollars."

Weiss cocked his head to the side. God, he really

was unrepentant. There wasn't even a flicker of guilt in his eyes. "It amazes me that such stupid people could squeeze out a daughter who'd make it into the FBI. Or is there an affirmative action program for height?"

My fingers tightened on the seat back. I knew he was trying to bait me and there was no way to react that wouldn't make it worse. But I could feel my self-control slipping: he had a way of getting right under my skin—

And then we heard the *chink chink chink* of a chain slowly moving.

Weiss and I looked up to see Boone twisting in his seat to look at us. More precisely, he was staring right at Weiss. And this time, those Alaska-blue eyes said *stop. Stop right now or I will annihilate you.*

Weiss's expression turned sour...but he shut up. He wasn't cowed by my badge or the presence of the marshals, but Boone's physical presence did the trick.

I turned to my savior. "Do you need anything?" I said awkwardly. I glanced at my purse. "I don't have much. A granola bar. A bottle of water."

Boone lifted his eyes to look at me and I caught my breath. Immediately, it was back, a wall of heat that slammed right into me and almost knocked me off my feet. I wasn't used to that from any man. Certainly not from a criminal. Again, it felt as if my clothes were vaporizing, his gaze sweeping over every part of me like a lover's hands: a smooth palm caressing my naked shoulder, strong fingers squeezing my breast.... And yet he spent the most time on my face, just staring back at me in a way that made me gulp. Not just lust. A simpler need. He wanted me, but he wanted...*me.*

I'm wasting my time. Everyone says he doesn't talk.

But, just as I gave up hope, his head lifted a little and his jaw worked. I thought of the Tin Man in Wizard of Oz, all rusted up. I wondered how long it was since he'd spoken.

"....water," he rasped at last. His first two syllables, I was guessing, in a very long time. The accent made me think of the landscape beneath us: rough and hard as granite, but with the syllables smoothed by wind and rain. It had that measured pace you only find a long way from a city. Then, after another few seconds, "I'd like some water. Please."

There was an intake of breath from the front of the plane. I glanced around to see both marshals blinking in surprise. Boone must not have spoken the entire time he was in their custody.

I quickly retrieved the bottle of water from my purse, unscrewed the cap and then held it out to him. He just looked at me and then raised his wrists. He could take the bottle but the hobble chain wouldn't let him get it anywhere near his mouth.

Swallowing, I brought the bottle to his lips. I hadn't figured on how intimate it would feel, watching his lips part and find the neck. That full lower lip, soft and jutting above that stubbled jaw. The hard upper lip, closing around the plastic. Powerful. If those lips kissed you, you'd damn well stay kissed. He stared right at me as I tilted the bottle and the cool water flowed, the muscles of his powerful neck flexing and contracting. *Gulp, gulp, gulp....*

I lowered the bottle. I'd gotten lost in those eyes. Nearly half the bottle was gone. "Okay?" I asked weakly. The blood was suddenly pounding in my ears.

He nodded, eyes never leaving mine for an instant.

I had to move. If I didn't move, something crazy was going to happen. *What's the matter with me? He's a criminal!*

I couldn't face returning to the front of the plane and Marshal Phillips. Something about him still felt off. He felt wrong in just the same way Boone felt right...which made no sense at all.

I kept walking towards the back of the plane but there wasn't that far I could go. A few more empty seats, then a luggage rack where the marshals had stowed their bags. I recognized the huge, dull-green army holdall Phillips had been carrying.

I turned and glanced back at the marshals. Both of them were checking their watches. Hennessey looked at Phillips, who shook his head warningly. *Not yet.*

What were they counting down to? We weren't due to land anytime soon. I checked the window but there was nothing outside even remotely resembling Fairbanks. In fact, there was no sign of civilization at all.

For the entire flight, I'd felt that something was off about Marshal Phillips. Now, that feeling started to join with other things in my mind, a snowball that grew as it rolled. There'd been Hennessey's insistence that I not get on the plane, Phillips's lack of respect for his superior, Weiss's cockiness in the face of imprisonment...and now it felt like something was going to happen. Soon. Within minutes.

At the FBI, I'd learned to trust my gut. And my gut said something was wrong.

I moved so that my body was in front of the luggage rack and put one arm overhead, pretending to stretch out my shoulders. With the other hand, I unzipped marshal Phillips's holdall just enough to see what was inside.

I frowned. Backpacks. Three of them. I poked one and felt softness inside, as if they were full of fabric. I started to relax. I don't know what I'd been expecting to find, but it wasn't this. Maybe it was changes of clothes for the prisoners or something.

But wait: why three bags? There were only two prisoners.

The backpacks had openings at the top. I hooked a finger inside and pulled out a corner of the fabric, rubbing it between my fingers. Thin, white, silky material, carefully packed.

They weren't backpacks. They were parachutes.

Phillips and two others were planning to bail out.

I'd stumbled right into a prison break.

THREE

Kate

I ZIPPED THE BAG CLOSED, finished my fake stretch and walked back to my seat on legs that felt waxy and numb. I gave Phillips a quick smile and then stared out of the window again. The whole time, my mind was in overdrive, my heart thumping as I put it all together.

Weiss. This had to be about Weiss. He had billions of dollars hidden away, probably in offshore accounts. When he was caught, he must have bribed Marshal Phillips and together they'd planned this escape. No wonder he was so cocky: he knew he wasn't going to jail. And the third parachute must be for Hennessey: he was in on it, too. The only thing I couldn't figure out was: why all this complexity? Why not just let Weiss go back in Nome, where he could sneak over to Russia? We'd traveled hours in the wrong direction.

I watched both marshals out of the corner of my eye. They were almost constantly checking their watches, now, and looking out of the windows to gauge their position. I only had minutes left.

I dug in my purse, found my phone and powered it on. But when the screen lit up, there was no signal. I couldn't call the FBI. I couldn't call anyone. I was completely cut off. And the two marshals were armed. I'd left my handgun back in New York. *Shit.*

A little voice inside me said: *why not just sit tight?* In a few minutes, they'd bail out and it would all be over. The pilot would fly us on to Fairbanks, I could tell the police what had happened and they could begin the hunt. But out here, in this vast wilderness, Weiss could easily slip away. Weiss would walk free and the marshals would buy new identities and retire rich.

No. No way. So what if he was a white collar criminal? He'd stolen from millions of families.

I grabbed paper and pen from my purse, then eased myself casually out of my seat and wandered up to where the pilot sat. I could feel Phillips's eyes on me as I passed him, but he didn't stop me. The pilot looked round in surprise as I gingerly sat down in the empty co-pilot's seat. From his expression, he still hadn't forgiven me for running out into his path on the runway.

"I just felt sorry for you, sitting all alone up here," I said, trying to sound as air-headed as possible. "But what a view! Do you ever get used to it?"

The pilot looked at me like I was crazy but muttered something about how it was even better in summer. I wasn't listening. I was frantically writing on the paper in my lap.

PRISON BREAK, I wrote. *MARSHALS INVOLVED. RADIO FOR HELP.* I pulled out my FBI badge, put it next to the note and then shoved the whole thing into his line of sight, using my body to shield what I was doing.

He read it. Looked at me once in disbelief, then a second time in panic. Then he nodded and keyed the radio. “Tango two-five for Fairbanks International,” he said quietly.

There was a metallic click. The pilot froze, looking at something behind me.

I looked up at our reflection in the windshield. Marshal Phillips was standing right behind me and his gun was leveled at the back of my head.

FOUR

Boone

Moments Earlier

Breathe. Just breathe.

It started as soon as they put the chains on. The cuffs the sheriff had put on me back in Koyuk hadn't been so bad. But these heavy, clanking chains...they were impossible to forget about. I couldn't imagine myself somewhere else, like I'd been trained to do. I was someone's prisoner again. And the plane was too damn small, the air too stale and warm. I tried to focus on the landscape outside the windows. Freedom was out there. But having it so tantalizingly close only reminded me that I was heading to Fairbanks and then to the deepest, darkest cell the military could find.

Just. Breathe.

Because if I lost it, I'd go into what I call *lockdown*. I'd retreat into myself, just like I had years before, and

I'd lose the ability to feel or think. Then I really would be helpless. Then my mind would be imprisoned, too.

There was only one thing that kept me going: her. She was the one tiny breath of air in the cabin, the one point of light in the darkness. *Kate Lydecker.*

Every time the chains got too much, I closed my eyes for a second and I was back in the airport, her warm body *wumf*-ing against mine in slow motion. And what a body. Just the right combination of soft and firm. She was just a little thing: hell, the top of her head was only up to my shoulder. It was difficult to believe she was an FBI agent...until you saw how determined she was. The way she'd stood in front of our plane had made me shake my head in silent awe. I pitied the person she was chasing.

I hadn't been able to stop looking at her, the whole time she sat at the front of the plane. In her crisp blouse and smooth gray suit and with those soft lips pursed in thought, she looked like she came from some other world where everything was modern, sleek, and perfect. *What the hell is she doing in Alaska?*

Then that prick in the suit had given her a hard time and something had risen up inside me, caveman-strong. I hadn't even met her before that morning but the idea of someone hurting her made me *mad.*

She'd offered me water. As if she actually gave a shit about me. I hadn't spoken to anyone in months but, for her, I'd forced myself to string a sentence together. I think I even remembered a *please.* And she'd leaned over me, putting that bottle to my lips, and as I drank I soaked up the sight of her.

Her eyes were deep brown, hard and yet always with just a little cautious warmth. She wore her mahogany hair pulled back into a severe little braid, maybe to look more imposing, but all it did was make her sexier. I've always liked long, loose hair on women but on her, the bouncing braid just drew my eyes to all that soft, exposed skin around the back of her neck, all the places that are normally hidden. Just as her pant suit, with its white blouse, made me focus on the little triangle of skin below her throat, on that hint of collarbone. Her skin looked so damn smooth. I wanted to just slide my big, calloused paw under that blouse and over her bare shoulder and find out *how* smooth, then pluck her bra strap off her shoulder and...*damn.*

With this woman, everything she did to cover herself up just made me want to undress her more.

Stupid. My chest tightened. That part of my life was long done with. I was on my way to jail for a very long time.

I closed my eyes and drew in a long breath, hearing the chains rattle and clank. And then a sound I wasn't expecting: the click of a gun being cocked. I looked up to see Marshal Phillips with a gun to Kate's head.

Aw, hell no.

Some instinct made me glance across at Weiss. He was grinning. That's when I realized what was going on.

I tensed, about to rise...then looked down at my chains. *Shit!* I couldn't do a damn thing. Not like this.

For a second, everyone was frozen. Kate was staring coldly at Marshal Phillips. The pilot was looking between the two of them, white-faced. Hennessey was watching the whole thing with a face like thunder.

The radio suddenly blared, startling everyone.

Phillips's finger twitched on the trigger and he must have come within a fraction of an inch of blowing Kate's head off. But he caught himself just in time.

"Tango two-five, this is Fairbanks International," squawked the radio. *"Go ahead."*

Phillips was still panting from the shock. Hennessey got up and took charge. "Tell them everything's fine," he barked to the pilot.

The pilot swallowed and asked the control tower how the weather was looking in Fairbanks. They told him to expect cloudless skies and he thanked them and signed off.

"Just keep us heading for Fairbanks," Phillips told the pilot. Then he looked at Hennessey. "Get the chains off Weiss."

Hennessey glared at him, as if he didn't like being ordered around. He was the senior marshal but, apparently, Phillips was in charge...and the young guy was loving the power trip. Hennessey walked over to Weiss, took out a key and started to undo the padlocks. Weiss grinned as his chains fell away.

"You're a *marshal,"* grated Kate. "How can you do this? How much is he paying you?"

"Shut up!" spat Hennessey. "It's not like that."

"Take a seat," Phillips told Kate, and shoved her forward. She stumbled and I tensed again, the protective rage boiling up inside again. I didn't want to see anything happen to her.

Kate sat down beside me. Even with everything that was going on, just having her that close sent a surge of hormones through me: dammit, but this woman did a number on me. I tried to rationalize it, told myself that it was months since I'd even seen a woman; years since I'd been really close to one.

Maybe it was just that, like a parched man in a desert reacting to his first sip of water.

But that was bullshit. There was something about her, something that made me crave more and more of her. Her skin, her eyes, the way her breasts lifted *just so* as she breathed, pushing out against that demure white blouse. The way she pressed her lips together—*there, like that.* Dammit. Like she was a mouse determined to stand up to a cat, no matter how big and fearsome. Even that gleaming mahogany hair looked hard: by drawing it back tightly, she'd formed it into protective armor. But if I could just release it, I knew it'd be so soft....

It was a long time since I'd touched anything soft. My hands were calloused from swinging axes and working wood.

The last of Weiss's chains rattled to the floor and he stood. He and the two marshals moved to the back and started strapping on parachutes. So that was the plan. But why go to all this trouble? If the marshals were on the take, why not just quietly disappear back in Nome? It didn't make sense.

For a few minutes, I listened to the men behind me. Weiss didn't know how to put on his parachute and was getting testy with the marshals. "I'm paying you enough," he snapped at one point. "You're meant to take care of all this stuff!" He reminded me of a wealthy, entitled tourist on a safari.

Then I froze. Beside me, Kate had placed her hands on the armrests and was taking quick little breaths. Her heels came up off the floor so that she was poised on the balls of her feet. She was preparing to push off and—

Jesus, she was going to run at them. She was going

to try to take them on, unarmed. Was she *insane?*

I stared at her, trying to communicate with my eyes. *Don't do it! Just let them go!* In another few minutes, they'd jump. We could fly on to Fairbanks and it would all be over. But she wasn't looking at me. Her gaze was fixed on the seat back in front of her, that sweet little jaw determinedly set. God, she had some crazy sense of justice! She was trying to do her duty as a damn FBI agent.

She lifted herself infinitesimally out of her seat and then sank back. I realized she was psyching herself up. *One, two, three* and she'd run at them. That was *one.*

She doesn't stand a chance. One of them would shoot her before she ever got close.

Unless I helped her.

She lifted herself again, thighs tensing under her suit pants. That was *two.*

Let her, a vicious little voice inside me said. *She's part of the system. You don't owe the system a damn thing. Not after what it did to you.*

But I owed *her*. She'd been decent to me. I wasn't going to let her die.

Three. She lifted herself, already turning to run—

My hand slapped down on hers, clamping it to the armrest.

FIVE

Kate

MY HEAD SNAPPED AROUND. I found myself staring up into Boone's eyes and I caught my breath, pinned there. That icy, Alaskan blue was burning up with anger and concern.

And then he spoke in a low rumble, the words vibrating up as if from a thousand feet beneath the surface. "*Release me.*" That accent again, as *outdoors* as I was *indoors.*

I couldn't breathe. My eyes went from his face to his chains and back.

His hand squeezed mine and that...did something to me. I can't explain it. His hand was so big, it just swallowed mine up completely, warm and dry and *strong*. "I can help you," he said. "But not with these on."

I stared at him, feeling my shoulders slowly rise and fall as I panted. I was jacked up on adrenaline, heady with it. I'd been a split-second away from running at the marshals when he'd stopped me.

Release him?! He was a prisoner, a wanted man. My eyes flicked to the prisoner files at the front of the plane. *I don't even know what he did!*

He was much bigger than me. He was a fugitive in custody. Taking off his chains would be insane...and absolutely against procedure. I *always* follow procedure. That's why the FBI suits me so well. I like being part of something structured and organized and controlled.

Except—

Except I was alone, cut off from all contact, thousands of feet in the air, facing two men with guns. There *was* no procedure for this.

And when I stared into Boone's eyes...I felt like I could trust him.

That's insane. You don't know anything about him.

But that didn't stop it being true.

I felt myself nod. His hand squeezed mine again and a rush of heat went through me. *Oh, Kate...what the hell are you doing?*

Movement behind us. Marshal Hennessey walked past me, close enough to touch, heading towards the pilot with a small bag of tools. And jangling on his belt were the keys for Boone's chains.

Now or never.

I sprang out of my seat and grabbed his shoulders. He started to twist around, looking at me disbelievingly, one hand reaching for his gun. There was no fear in his eyes. Once he saw it was me who'd grabbed him, his eyes actually narrowed in frustration. He probably thought he could just shake me off and keep walking.

I'm used to that. People have been

underestimating me my entire life.

I hooked my foot around his ankle, preventing him from stepping back and catching his balance. And then I used my body weight to haul him up and back at just the right angle—

What do you do when you're smaller than all the other kids and everyone's kicking sand in your face?

You learn judo.

Hennessey came crashing down, falling across Boone's lap. Boone got the idea immediately, snatching up the keys and going to work while using his elbows to keep the marshal pinned.

Behind me, I heard Phillips curse and start towards us. Unless I could delay him long enough for Boone to get his chains off, we were finished. As Phillips marched down the aisle towards us, I ducked low and grappled him, my shoulder against his hip...but I didn't have the element of surprise, this time, and he planted his weight and grabbed *me,* one strong arm encircling my waist and holding me bent over. I pushed hard, forcing him back, but this time *I* was the one off-balance. Then his other arm encircled my neck in a choke hold and squeezed, cutting off my air.

"You should have listened to Hennessey and stayed off our plane," he said mildly.

I thrashed and struggled but the narrow aisle left me no room to maneuver. My vision started to narrow, the world growing dark.

And then there was a sound I'll never forget, a metal waterfall as pounds of heavy chains all slithered to the floor. Phillips's hold on me loosened as he looked up in shock. Three footsteps, quick but so heavy they shook the whole plane. The sound of a punch and Phillips was suddenly flying backwards through the air.

I staggered away from him, straightened up...and saw Boone standing next to me, still lowering his fist. He was glaring down at Phillips, now slumped on the floor, his eyes burning with a cold rage. Free of his chains, he looked even bigger and wilder, his massive chest rising and falling as he panted like a beast. He had Hennessey's gun in his other hand—he must have been too worried about hitting me to use it up close. He glanced at me and the deep undercurrent of concern I saw there made me go warm inside. I'd been right to trust him.

For a split second, I relaxed. That was a mistake.

Weiss darted forward and drew the gun from Phillips's holster, pointing it at us. Boone immediately raised his gun and the cabin went utterly silent as the two faced off against each other. *Shit!* I hadn't even been thinking of him as a threat. He was a white collar criminal. He wasn't meant to be violent!

"Let's make a deal," said Weiss.

Boone silently shook his head.

"Just think for a second," Weiss said, his voice syrupy and patronizing. "You're a wanted man, on his way to jail. Come with us and you can walk away."

My breath went tight in my chest.

"There aren't enough parachutes," said Boone, his voice level. "There are only three, right? One for each of you." Oh God..he was thinking about it!

"You can have his," said Weiss immediately. And nodded at Phillips.

Phillips's face twisted in rage. "You sonofabitch!"

Boone went quiet. I stared at him in horror. *Of course he'll do it. He's going to jail if he stays on the plane.*

"I'll pay you," said Weiss. "A hundred thousand dollars to put the gun down right now and come with us." He had the easy tone of a man who's used to buying his way out of things. When Boone hesitated, he pressed. "You're *on the wrong side!* You're one of us, not one of them!"

I saw Boone's stern expression weaken. His eyes flicked to the window and the mountains outside.

And then his eyes went to me, just for an instant. And he looked back to Weiss and leveled the gun with new ferocity. "I'm *not* one of you," he growled.

I saw Weiss falter. And then he smirked. I turned and followed his gaze just too late.

Hennessey brought the wrench down on the back of Boone's head and he staggered forward, conscious but dazed. Hennessey grabbed the gun from his hand and went to stand beside Weiss, both of them pointing their guns at Boone and me. We froze.

"Easy," Hennessey told Weiss. "Let me handle this."

"Fuck that," said Weiss. "They've made us late. We're going to miss our jump point." And he leveled the gun and fired.

The whole cabin echoed with the explosion. My eyes screwed shut and every muscle in my body went rigid as I waited for the pain to hit.

But nothing happened. My eyes opened. Had he shot Boone first and I was next? But Boone was standing there blinking in shock, just as I was. Had Weiss *missed?*

Then I felt the world tilt and slide. For a second, I thought I *had* been hit, maybe in the head, and this was the start of death. Then I staggered into Boone, his warm body huge against mine, and I realized the world really *was* tilting. The plane was gradually twisting over on its side.

My head snapped around to the front of the plane and I saw the pilot, slumped forward in his seat, and the blood on the windshield. Weiss hadn't missed at all.

Weiss and the marshals were now backing towards the door, their guns trained on us. And suddenly I understood.

They'd never intended to just jump out and let us continue to Fairbanks and raise the alarm. The plan was to crash the plane...with Boone and me on board.

SIX

Kate

MY HEART started to slam in my chest. The floor was tilted over at almost forty-five degrees, now: we had to cling on to the seat backs to stay upright.

"Go finish up in the cockpit," Weiss told Phillips. "Hurry!"

Phillips got to his feet, shaking his head in anger. "You were going to give him my *chute?* Leave me here to die?!"

"Things change," Weiss told him. "Get over it."

Phillips scowled, grabbed the tool bag from Hennessey and ran off to the front of the plane. There was the sound of banging and then he returned carrying a metal box.

"Toss it," Weiss told him. Phillips slid open the door and outside air rushed into the cabin. We were low enough that there was enough air to breathe but it was so cold it felt like my lungs were freezing and the roar of the wind was deafening. Phillips hurled the box out and I followed its sickening curve down until it was just a speck.

Oh God. This is really happening. They were going to leave us there, the pilotless plane would plunge into the rocks and we'd be killed. I glanced at Boone. *Why didn't he take the deal?*

Weiss and the two marshals checked their parachutes a final time. I tried to think of something, anything, we could do. But the only way out of this had passed hours ago, when I'd forced my way onto the plane. I caught Hennessey's eye for a second before he looked away guiltily. He might be working for Weiss but he seemed a lot more reluctant than Phillips. No wonder he'd tried to stop me getting on board. He knew I was signing my own death warrant.

A noise started, a rising wail that I'd only heard in movies, the sound of a plane picking up speed as it dives. By now, the windows on one side of the plane were almost completely filled with ground and the other with sky. The plane was almost standing on its wing and it was losing altitude fast. "We've got to go," said Weiss. "Right now." And he took a deep breath...and jumped.

I watched in disbelief as he fell away from the plane. Seconds later, his parachute bloomed into a huge white canopy. Hennessey was next. He hesitated at the door and gave me a troubled look over his shoulder. "Sorry," he muttered.

For a second, anger flared inside me, pushing back my fear. Was that supposed to make it better? To ease his conscience? He'd still taken Weiss's money. "Go to hell," I said bitterly.

His eyes narrowed...and he jumped. A second later, I saw his chute open. The wail was rising in pitch and volume, a banshee's howl that made it difficult to think. The plane was still tipping, rolling onto its back as it descended.

Only Phillips was left, now. He backed towards the door, his gun still pointed at us. "You should have taken that bastard's deal," he told Boone grimly.

I heard Boone draw in a shuddering breath, as if he was trying to control his anger. One big, warm hand settled on my shoulder and squeezed it gently.

And then Phillips jumped and three parachutes were floating down towards the ground.

And we were in a plane with no pilot. Going down.

SEVEN

Kate

FOR A FEW SECONDS, I just stood there, clinging onto the seat backs, staring at the slowly descending parachutes. Already, they were thousands of feet below us. And below *them*—

I made a mistake and looked down.

I hate heights. When we have meetings up on the top floor of the FBI building in New York and everyone else is admiring the view, I stare fixedly at my notes. I don't especially like flying but, when you're up and the cabin crew are pushing reheated food at you, you can almost convince yourself that the sky outside the window isn't real.

As I stared out of the open door, reality came back sickeningly fast. We were thousands of feet up...with no way to get down. I staggered back on legs numb with fear.

And then the plane's roll sped up. I grabbed for a seat back and missed, falling backwards, then tumbling as the plane rolled fully onto its back. I screamed and landed hard on the ceiling that had now become the floor. The plane began to angle down and I rolled....

Right towards the open door.

I tried to grab hold of something but this was the ceiling: there were no seats to cling to, just smooth white plastic. The rectangle of blue and white came closer and closer, opening up to swallow me. *Oh Jesus God no please no!* The wind enveloped me, sucking at my clothes and I screamed so hard my throat hurt—

A big, warm hand grabbed my wrist. I looked up to see Boone stretched full-length along the aisle. He was all that was holding me inside the plane. I looked down and immediately wanted to throw up. One leg was actually outside, hanging out into thin air.

Boone hauled me towards him as if I weighed nothing, just a smooth, effortless *lift*. I managed to get to my knees and together we crawled towards the cockpit. Both of us had had the same idea: our only hope now was to pull the plane out of the dive. It was tilting further and further down each second. By the time we reached the cockpit, we were slithering down an almost vertical slope.

The pilot was still in his seat, slumped over the controls. Boone hauled him out and took his place and I climbed into the co-pilot's seat. We were angled so steeply down, I had to brace myself against the instrument panel or I would have wound up falling right through the windshield.

Ahead of us, the ground filled our view. I couldn't see sky anywhere. *Oh Jesus.*

"Please tell me you were in the Air Force," I croaked. "Please say you know how to fly."

But he was looking at the controls with the same

incomprehension I was. I could feel the panic taking over. *We are both going to die.*

And it crossed my mind again: *why didn't he take the deal?* I hadn't had a choice, but he had.

The ground was close enough now that I could see individual trees. I looked in desperation at what was in front of me. A thing like a steering wheel. A *lot* of dials, one of them spinning madly. More switches and knobs than I could count.

I gripped the wheel the way the pilot had. It turned under my hands but that was no good. We needed to go *up*.

I had a vague memory of people pulling back on the wheel in movies. Did it move that way, too? I pulled and nothing happened. But then...wait, it *was* moving. It was sliding towards me, millimeter by millimeter. I'd expected it to be like a car, where you're just guiding it, but this needed strength. It felt like I was hauling a truck full of rocks up a slope. I grunted, giving it everything I had.

Then, suddenly, it got easier. Next to me, Boone had grabbed his wheel and was hauling it back towards him. The view through the windshield started to change. We were pulling out of it.

But not fast enough. As the horizon came into view and we leveled out, the ground started to rise, too. We were heading up the side of a mountain, and it was steeper than we could climb.

"Buckle in!" said Boone, letting go of the wheel and grabbing his own seatbelt.

I grabbed for my own belt, fumbling with the buckle. A forest rushed up to meet us.

And then everything went black.

EIGHT

Boone

WATER. That was the first thing I was aware of. Water was running down my face.

Except it wasn't running *down,* towards my neck, like it should. It was running from the back of my neck along my cheeks, winding its way through my stubble, collecting on my lips and nose and then dripping from there.

I opened my eyes and saw branches. It took me a few seconds to figure it out.

The plane had come to rest nose down in some trees and I was maybe thirty feet above the forest floor, facing straight down. Only my seatbelt was keeping me in my seat.

I could hear heavy rain. That explained the water. But how was it hitting me in the back of the neck?

I twisted around. *Oh.*

There was nothing but sky above me. The back of the plane wasn't there. The cockpit had snapped off in the crash just a few feet behind my seat. Beneath us, the remains of snapped-off trees, some viciously sharp, stood up like stakes. We'd have to be careful climbing down.

I looked across at Kate. Just like me, her seatbelt was the only thing keeping her from falling out of her seat and down into the trees below. She was slumped forward in her seat, unconscious. But she was breathing.

I released a breath I hadn't realized I'd been holding. It caught me by surprise: it had been years since I'd worried about another person. She looked so small, hanging there, so fragile....

"Kate?" I said gently.

She stirred slightly. Groaned in pain, which made my chest close up tight in a way I couldn't explain. There was something about her, beyond her looks. She might be small but on the plane she'd thrown herself headlong into the fight, all because she didn't want to see those bastards get away. She wanted *justice*. Childish, sure. But it reminded me of when I used to believe in things, too.

"Kate?" I said, a little louder.

She started to properly awaken, her arms and legs flailing weakly as she tried to figure out her surroundings. And as her weight shifted, suddenly the whole cockpit fell.

For a few sickening seconds, we were in freefall, accompanied by the rustle of leaves and the creak of branches giving way beneath us. Then there was the crash of shattering glass, a violent jolt and we stopped. I looked down....

What had stopped us was one of the snapped-off trees. The metal at the edge of the windshield was caught precariously on the trunk. But one of its branches—

My stomach twisted.

One of its branches, its end a jagged, splintered spike, had crashed straight through the windshield and was three feet from Kate's chest. If we moved again, it would go right through her.

NINE

Kate

I OPENED MY EYES and stared at the branch and its knife-like tip. The vibrations from the fall were still dying away, the branch swaying like a cobra about to strike. *Oh Jesus.* A cold sweat broke out across my back.

"Don't move," intoned Boone. "Do not...move."

I sat there frozen, taking long, shuddering breaths, until everything came to a complete stop again. Then I carefully looked around and took it all in: Boone, strapped in next to me, the missing fuselage behind us, the ground far below.

I swallowed and closed my eyes. I *really* don't like heights.

"You hurt?" asked Boone. There was still that hesitation before he spoke, as if he was having to dig the words from way down deep, but it was reducing a little each time.

"I don't think so," I said weakly. I slowly opened my eyes and tried not to look at the ground. But that left me looking at the broken-off branch, primed to stab straight through my heart.

"Okay," said Boone slowly. "This is what we're going to do. You're going to take off your seatbelt—"

"I'll fall!" I tried to keep the panic out of my voice but failed.

"No you won't." His voice was like iron. "Because I'm going to reach over and grab you. As you slide out of your seat, I'll pull you over to me."

"Grab me *first!*" My voice was going high and tight with fear.

"I can't." I could hear the frustration in his voice, the anger at not being able to help me. "I'm going to have to lunge across to reach you. When I move, we'll likely fall again. We have to do it at the same time."

Oh God. I looked across at him. Those blue eyes were like the sky reflected in a glacier, ice as hard as rock. Determined to save me.

I looked down at the branch. If he moved too slow. If he mis-timed it. If I slipped out of his grip—

"Kate?"

I glanced his way again, my heart thumping in my chest.

"I *will* catch you," he said.

And something in his voice made me believe him.

I reached down and felt for the buckle of my seat belt. Hooked my fingers under the release.

"We'll do it on three," said Boone. He sucked in a deep breath and extended an arm, ready to lunge. "One."

I deliberately didn't look at the branch. I looked at his arm, his tanned wrist twice as thick as my own.

"Two."

Every muscle in my body tensed.

"Three!"

I hooked my seatbelt open and fell.

Boone lunged towards me, arm extended.

The whole cockpit shifted again and plunged down, the branch spearing up towards me—

Boone's hand closed on my wrist and I was wrenched sideways in mid-air. The branch whipped past me, close enough to touch—

The cockpit came to a stop as the branch buried itself in my seat back, right where I'd been sitting. I swung, dangling from Boone's outstretched hand. He was panting. I was panting.

"Got y—" he started.

I screamed as his seat belt gave way and we both plunged. And instant later, we stopped again. I looked up. He had me by one hand. With the other, he was clinging onto the arm of his seat. I could see the muscles standing out hard on his back from the effort but he wasn't letting go. *"Got you,"* he said again, breathlessly. And this time, there were no more surprises. I hung there weakly, face upturned to the heavens, and just let the rain soak me as my heart slowed to something approaching normal.

***

It took a full twenty minutes to climb down the tree to the ground. That may not sound like much, but when you're clinging to the rough bark of a tree trunk, high above the ground, twenty minutes is a lifetime. When my feet finally touched the dirt, I wanted to lean down and kiss it.

Boone had taken a moment to dig around under the pilot's seat and had found a box of flares. He'd also twisted off a jagged shard of metal he said he could use to make a knife. Both of us were soaked to the skin and, now that we were safe, the cold was really starting to set in. It must have been around noon and it was spring, but it was ferociously cold.

"We need to find shelter," muttered Boone. Even he was hugging himself, his jacket and plaid shirt plastered to his chest.

But I hardly heard him. Something in the trees had caught my eye. I stumbled forward. The trees grew too far apart to provide much cover from the rain and it coursed down my face, making it difficult to see. My shoes squelched, they had so much water in, and I'd started to shake. But I kept putting one foot in front of the other, my eyes fixed on what was before me. I was willing it to change.

Our plane had crashed near the edge of the forest. I slowed to a stop as I passed the final few trees and the view opened up in front of me.

I was on the edge of a mountain. Below me, rocky cliffs which fell hundreds of feet, then a thick carpet of forest. Far off in the distance, I could see a river. More mountains. And absolutely nothing else. Just wilderness, as far as the eye could see.

I was in the absolute middle of nowhere.

The rain ran down through my soaking hair, running in little waterfalls down my face and off my chin, each drop chilling me a little more. I squeezed my eyes shut, trying to remember the route map I'd glimpsed in the airport. We'd been roughly midway between Nome and Fairbanks when we crashed. That area of the map was just a big, blank space. No towns. No *anything*. I'd lost my purse in the crash but it didn't matter: I knew there'd be no cell signal way out here.

I felt the panic start to rise inside me and took a long, shuddering breath. *Oh Jesus. What are we going to do?!* We had no food. We had no water. We were probably hundreds of miles from the nearest person.

A voice behind me said, "Kate?"

I whipped around and stared at him, my eyes wild.

He looked at me. Looked at the view. "It's okay," he said at last.

I shook my head. "No. N-No, it's *not.*" Suddenly, I was close to crying. I was shaking with cold and I was shaking with shock and I was shaking with holding back panicked tears, and all three were mixed together.

He stepped closer, close enough that he towered over me. I looked up into those big blue eyes. "It'll be okay," he promised. That accent again that matched the landscape.

I didn't fit here. But he did.

His palms cupped my shoulders, warm even through my soaked suit. A few strands of hair must have come loose from my braid because his thumb found them plastered to my wet cheek and he pushed them back out of the way. *"It'll be okay,"* he said again.

And I believed him.

"But we've got to get warm," he said. "We've got to get out of this rain." A hand slid from my shoulder to my back, guiding me. "C'mon."

He pulled me into step beside him, his arm settling around my waist. Not knowing what else to do, I let him lead me across the forest floor, picking our way between trees and over logs. I felt ridiculous, next to him. One of his big strides would have equaled two of mine, but he kept it slow so that we stayed together, the side of my body pressed against his. He kept looking at me, checking on me, and I realized he was worried about me. That maybe I was more than just scared and cold, that maybe I was in some sort of...shock. All I knew was that I felt numb. Stumbling along beside him, my face running with water and maybe tears, it felt like it was all happening to someone else.

He led me to a cliff face: at the bottom, there was an overhang which formed a shallow cave. He pushed me inside and then, a hand on my shoulder, he guided me to sit. He could be surprisingly gentle, for such a big guy.

I instinctively checked around for bugs—I *hate* anything that scuttles—then sat on the bare rock hugging my knees. After so long in the rain, being out of it felt amazing. I rubbed my face again and again, trying to get rid of the sensation of water running down it.

Meanwhile, Boone had collected armfuls of dry branches and twigs from the corners of the cave. He piled them up expertly and struck one of the emergency flares from the plane. A second later, the fire roared into life, bathing us with orange light. When the warmth hit me, it felt so good I actually cried out. I hadn't realized how cold I was.

It was only as I started to thaw out and calm down that I realized how out of it I'd been. I looked up to find Boone watching me carefully.

"Better?" he asked.

I nodded. Then, "Sorry."

"For what?" He went quiet for a moment,

regarding me from under his heavy brows. I kept thinking about what Marshal Phillips had said: how Boone barely talked. He must have said more to me, in the last few hours, than he had to another living soul in the last few years. At last, he said: "You just got a little spooked. Most people wouldn't be doing half as good as you are."

Hunched over the fire, with his long hair and the flickering light throwing shadows across his massive body, he could have been some barbarian from a thousand years ago. He matched the landscape outside, where nothing had changed in all that time. I'd wandered into his world.

When he stood, unfastened his jacket and peeled it off, I didn't really think anything of it. The plaid shirt beneath the jacket turned out to be a cut-off, showing the thick swells of his shoulders and biceps. But then he began to unfasten *that,* revealing a triangle of hard, tan flesh beneath a soaked white t-shirt. As he popped the buttons one by one, that triangle turned into a valley and then into a deep, shadowed cut between two huge mountains of muscle. I swallowed as the shirt came off completely. Dime-sized pink nipples topped those swells of muscle: God, each pec seemed as big as my head. Hard and yet soft, warm and solid–

Then he grabbed hold of the hem of his t-shirt and hauled the wet fabric up over his head.

I quickly looked into the fire, my heart suddenly pounding. I could feel him looking at me but I didn't dare look up. I didn't need to see him. The image of his body was burned into my mind: shoulders that looked even wider, now he was topless, cantaloupe-big muscles that narrowed and then flared to the *next* bulge and the *next,* my eyes were rising and falling as if on a rollercoaster until they hit the broad, veined, expanse of his forearms. His chest was so broad...the way those twin swells curved out, you'd need both hands to explore even one side. When he bent over his back, too, was heavy with muscle. There wasn't an ounce of fat on him but I figured he must be twice my weight. He was the *solidest* man I'd ever seen. And now I had to sit there and try not to think about him leaning over me, pushing me back onto the bare rock, as he brought his lips–

"You too," he said.

I looked up. Oh God, he had his hands on the belt of his pants. "What?"

"You need to take your clothes off too."

It took a second or two for that to process. "*What?!*"

He drew in a breath. "You're freezing. You need to warm up."

"I'm warming up," I said. My voice came out as a squeak.

He shook his head. "The wet cloth is sucking out all your body heat. You need to strip off, dry off, dry your clothes, then put it all back on."

I gaped up at him and a war started in my mind. On one side of it was shock and outrage and even a little amusement, that he actually thought I'd strip off in front of him. On the other were the messages coming in from every part of my body: my numb feet, the frozen muscles of my back, my head that throbbed from being cold for so long. They told me that he was *right.* The fire was comforting and I could feel the warmth on my face and hands but it didn't penetrate my sodden pant suit. I was getting colder, not warmer.

"Kate," he said. And deep in my brain, a whole flurry of green lights went on as I heard him say my name. It felt *good.* Like everything else he said, it seemed to come from way down deep, escaping from under layers of granite. And he said it firmly: an admonishment, a chastisement. *Stop being silly.* That did something else to me: along with all those green lights, a trail of cherry-red ones blazed into life, ones I never even knew existed, flaring and pumping out shameful heat in a line that led straight down to my groin. Something about that firmness short-circuited me in a way no New York guy had ever managed. But there was a softness there, too. That concern I'd seen in his eyes, mirrored in his voice. He was worried about me.

I spend every waking moment showing how tough I am. I don't *get* many people worrying about me. I swallowed and looked away, suddenly flushing, and then looked breathlessly back at him.

"Kate," he said again. "Take off your clothes."

TEN

Boone

AS THE WORDS sank in, she looked up at me, her expression unreadable. God, she was as good with people as I was bad with them. She should have been a damn poker player: I had no clue what was going on in her head. *What do you expect? She's FBI.* She spent her life negotiating and interrogating.

And I was a big, clumsy lunk who'd said maybe five words in the last year, until today.

Our gazes were locked on each other, neither of us willing to look away. She didn't want to do as I said; I wasn't going to let her freeze to death.

Little rivulets of water were still creeping down her forehead from her soaking hair, tracing the shape of her cheekbone just like I wanted to with my thumb. Her jaw was set, her full lower lip pouting just a little as it pressed against her upper, droplets of water gleaming like jewels.

I'd never understood what the word *imperious*

meant. I did now. She looked like some medieval warrior queen, ready to lead her people to victory. Fearsome...and beautiful.

The look she had, with everything pulled back and buttoned up and locked down tight...that only made it better. I had this overwhelming urge to just *release* her: not just her clothes and that braid of dark hair but *her*. Because sometimes, when she looked at me, it felt like all that restraint was just there to keep something wild and powerful and scalding hot under control.

I wanted to have her. I wanted to push her down on that hard rock floor, peel those wet pants off her legs and her panties with them, fill my hands with those high, pert breasts and just—

I got that. I understood that. Hell, I couldn't even remember when I'd *seen* a woman in the last year, let alone be close enough to one that the scent of perfume and warm female skin filled my senses. She was gorgeous. Of course I wanted to fuck her.

But I wanted to kiss her, too. And that, I didn't understand. I'd left all those parts of me behind, years before, when I'd come home to Alaska. I knew I'd never have that life again. Yet whenever I looked at her, I felt this deep, irresistible *pull*—

Get a hold of yourself. I had to get her down off this mountain and then slip back into hiding. Things could go back to how they were before I made that fateful trip to Koyuk and got arrested. But first, I had to get her warm.

"I'm not doing this to see you naked," I told her.

And prayed she couldn't tell that I was lying.

ELEVEN

Kate

I could tell he was lying.

Not all the way. If he'd said, "I'm not *just* doing this to see you naked," it would have been the truth. I knew on some level that he was right: if I didn't shed the wet clothes, I was in serious trouble. But in the flickering firelight, I could see the lust in his eyes. It shot through me like an electric charge, setting off little powder kegs of *how dare he* and *I don't even know him* and *he's a fugitive.*

But the charge wound its way right down into my depths, hissing and sparking, and when it reached my groin it triggered a huge, silent detonation that filled my whole body with heat. *He wants me.*

Not in the way men in the FBI wanted me, with their toying and planning and careful seduction, where only half of it was about me and half was about bagging themselves a female agent. Boone wanted me the way men have wanted women for millions of years, hot and deep and primal. After the way he'd looked at me in the airport and on the plane, I'd been sort of ready for that from him. What I wasn't ready for was my own reaction. He was some mountain man who hunted and climbed mountains and slept under the stars. He was *meant* to be primitive. But I wore a damn suit. I'd thought that meant all the primitive stuff was long gone.

It wasn't. That part of me had always been there, lurking deep, only ever teased by the men I'd met as they danced intricate dances around it. Now I'd met a man who tapped right into it and it was rushing to the surface like black, hot oil.

He wanted to see me naked. And I liked it.

I stood and shrugged off my suit jacket, the fabric so sodden it had gone shiny. For a split second, I looked at it, thinking about the laundry care instructions and how I should be careful not to ruin the shape—and then I caught myself and just wrung it out, water splattering to the cave floor. I bent and laid it right by the fire and then—

As I rose, I caught his eye. Saw his gaze flick down. I followed it.

My blouse had gone translucent and my white bra wasn't much better. The dark shadows of my nipples were clearly visible through the fabric, especially with the cold turning them into hard, puckered nubs that pushed out through the material.

I swallowed and stood, turning away from him. But as I stood, I crushed my thighs together. My fingers worked their way down the front of my blouse. How had he done this with his shirt so easily? Had he been able to feel me watching him the way I felt him now?

I reached the last button. *I can't.* But already, the fire felt better now that the heat was only coming through one layer of fabric. It would feel *amazing* on my bare skin.

My bare *naked* skin.

I peeled my blouse off my shoulders and down my back, shuddering at the touch of the wet cloth. But immediately, I felt the heat lick my back. I wanted to turn around but that would mean....

It's just like wearing a bikini, I told myself.

I looked down at the sodden, almost transparent fabric. I thought of Boone's eyes. It wasn't like wearing a bikini.

I stepped out of my shoes. Unfastened my pants. They were cut loose on the leg but the rain had plastered them to my thighs and calves and I had to drag them off inch by inch. The whole time, I could feel Boone's gaze on my bare back. Right on the clasp of my bra, as if he was trying to burn through that last offending scrap of clothing.

I wrung out my blouse and pants and laid them next to the fire, too, still with my back turned to Boone. I was very aware of the way my panties were clinging to the cheeks of my ass...but even more aware of what they'd look like from the front.

Be confident, I thought. I planned it out, the way I plan everything. A neat, quick turn, then I'd drop and sit down on my ass, knees together and up, breasts pressed against them as I hugged them. Very little would be on display. *Yes. I'll do that.*

I turned around–

He was standing there watching me, his hands still on his belt. As if he'd been standing there the whole time. As if he was transfixed.

And I just stood there in my underwear, watching him watching me, and forgot how to move. Every inch of my skin was damp and super-sensitive. One moment, the forest breeze would blow through the cave and hit my flesh and it would goosebump; the next, the breeze would drop away and the fire would warm me, sending throbs of heat deep into me. It should have made me gasp and twist and shudder but I didn't move. I felt as if I'd been turned into a statue by his gaze.

He held my eyes for a second before he moved down over my neck and shoulders, down to the breasts I always tried to hide at work, to squeeze and compress under jackets because I didn't want it to be about me being a woman. Suddenly they were there, exposed in tissue-thin, wet fabric, his gaze like a lover's hands as it caressed them. I swore I could feel him lifting them, squeezing them, his thumbs grazing my nipples....

Down. Down over my stomach, down past the hollow of my navel, down to where my hips flared and the fire lit my pale thighs with streaks of orange and gold. His eyes followed every line, every curve.

And then his gaze was going back up, up to—

I caught my breath. I could feel him there, his eyes locked right on that translucent triangle of white fabric between my legs, on the dark shadow of hair and the hint of lips—

I sat, hugging my knees. How long had I stood there? A second? A lifetime? I inched closer to the fire. It was much, much hotter, like this: I could feel it evaporating the water from my skin and slowly pushing back my bone-deep chill. But inside, a different heat was swirling. I felt almost heady: shocked and appalled and...*proud?* I stared into the fire, my breathing gradually slowing down. I must have been damn near panting the whole time I was standing there and I hadn't even realized it.

Then I heard the rattle of a belt buckle. I'd forgotten that he was undressing, too. I kept staring at the fire as he kicked his boots off and then lowered his pants. But the flames were moving, flickering, and beyond them I could see gray jockey shorts, soaked through and clinging, outlining a hard ass and–

I quickly looked down. And tried not to think words like *thick*. Or *long*.

I waited for him to sit. But he lifted his hands and I saw his shadow on the cave wall hook his thumbs into the waistband of his jockey shorts and–

I didn't consciously move my gaze, but suddenly I was looking up, right at him–

The shorts fell around his ankles.

My heart was a bass drum in my chest. My face flushed and prickled but, with every passing second, the heat soaked inward to my core. Him naked, me as good as. Me sitting, eyes upturned towards him, him towering over me and, between his legs–

God. *Stiffening*. *Rising*. Thickening and swelling as he looked at me, the balls beneath it so full and heavy–

I dropped my gaze and stared so hard at the fire, the light hurt my eyes. I only looked at him when he was safely sitting, the flames between us hiding everything below his chest. Then I let out a long breath, the dangerous, scalding heat inside retreating.

But it didn't disappear. It stayed there, just under the surface.

We sat there in silence as our clothes and bodies dried. He seemed comfortable to just sit like that, gazing at me across the fire. To me, it was maddening.

I'd never spent so much time in another person's presence and not filled it with chatter.

But as minutes turned into hours, my mind started to change. All of the banter and jokes, the little games and double-talk that filled the dates I'd been on...it all started to seem ridiculous. Smoke and mirrors to hide the real reason for us being there, the one that Boone could communicate just fine with his eyes. I started to relax. And as my body warmed, sitting there with my thighs pressed together, looking at his naked chest...it wasn't uncomfortable at all.

By the time our clothes were dry, though, reality had started to set in. He wanted me. I wanted him. But that didn't change the mess we were in. Shouldn't we be talking about how the hell we were going to get out of here? And it didn't change who we were. He was a fugitive, for God's sake, and I was an FBI agent.

I had to say something, anything, just to end the silence that was getting way too comfortable.

"Do you really not talk to people for months at a time?" I blurted. It was the first thing that came into my head.

He nodded. Not proud of it, not ashamed of it. As if that was just how it was.

I tried to imagine living like that...and couldn't. I met his eyes across the dancing flames. *Why did you run,* I wanted to ask. What prison sentence could possibly be worse than this self-imposed exile? At least in prison you can have visitors. At least a sentence would eventually come to an end. Had he been planning to hide in the mountains forever?

He looked quickly away, then stood and started pulling his clothes on. "We should move," he muttered.

That threw me completely. I'd gotten used to sitting by the fire. "Move?"

"Down off the mountain. We've still got a good few hours of daylight left."

I blinked. "Wait...no. No, we're meant to stay with the plane. Rescue crews will come looking for it."

He shook his head. "They won't find it. 'Least not for a few days. You remember that box the marshals threw out of the plane?"

I nodded.

"That was the emergency transponder."

All the warmth from the fire seemed to seep out of my body. There was no telling where it had landed, if it had even survived the fall. Certainly, it was nowhere near us. The rescue crews would go to the wrong place.

I shook my head stubbornly. *Procedure.* Procedure would keep us alive. "We should still stay here. That's what they always say, in the event of a plane crash. The wreckage is easier to find. And we have shelter, here, and—"

He squatted down beside me. By now, he had his pants and boots on, but he was still topless, the smooth muscles of his shoulders gleaming in the firelight. I was suddenly very aware of my near-nakedness.

"We need to move," he said.

But I shook my head again. It wasn't just about following the rules. That was part of it. Following the rules, being part of the system—that's what I *did.* But it was more than that.

Heading off into the wilderness scared the crap out of me. The plane wreckage was the last scrap of civilization I had and I wanted to cling onto it with both hands.

He looked down at the ground as if trying to figure out how to deal with me. *Endless months of solitude and then the first person he has to talk to is a scared, shaken female.*

Maybe I wasn't the only one out of my comfort zone.

He raised those big blue eyes to me. And in the firelight, the combination of *hard* and *soft* I saw there made me catch my breath. *Soft* because he wanted to look after me. And *hard* because he was going to do it whether I liked it or not.

"Look," he said. "Right now, it's about six degrees. But up here, once the sun goes down, it'll drop below zero. And we already used up all the dry wood I could find. Once the fire goes out, we'll freeze." He looked out of the cave mouth, towards the edge of the mountain. "We need to get *down*. For every three hundred feet we go down, the temperature will go up a degree. By nightfall, we can be somewhere we can survive, somewhere there'll be animals to hunt."

"Tonight," I echoed weakly, hugging my knees tight.

"We can bed down and carry on in the morning."

Bed down. I pushed that thought away. I had enough filling my mind already. "But where are we going?" *Please say there's a town. Please say there's a town only a few miles away....*

"My cabin."

"How far's that?"

"Not far. Forty, maybe fifty miles."

I felt my eyes bug out. "*Forty miles?!*" If we'd been in a car, it would have sounded like nothing at all. But on foot...I thought about how far a five mile run seemed. How far a marathon was. *Forty. Miles.*

"It's our best chance." He looked around. "If we stay here, at this altitude...we're going to die."

I looked away, my mind whirling. Then I looked down at my clothes, lying by the fire. He must have gotten the message because he stood up and walked around to the other side of the fire. He grabbed the rest of his clothes and turned his back to finish dressing, giving me privacy.

I quickly stood up and pulled on my pants, blouse and suit jacket. It felt ridiculous, putting on a suit for a cross-country hike, but it was all I had.

Boone held something out. "Here."

It was his jacket. I hesitated, staring at his bare arms, exposed by his cut-off shirt. "Won't you freeze?"

He shook his head.

I pulled the jacket on over my suit and it was *glorious,* still warm from the fire and thick enough to keep the chill out. "Thanks," I said with feeling.

The jacket's size drowned me a little, since it was made for him. It even smelled of him a little, of wood smoke and clean air and the outdoors. It brought home to me the craziness of what I was about to do.

I glanced at Boone. "Give me a minute." Then I stepped out of the cave. I needed space.

The rain had stopped. The air outside was shockingly cold but it helped me think. *Forty or fifty miles. With him.* The cave had been comforting, even intimate, but it had felt temporary. In my mind, we'd been killing time until we were rescued. This was different. This was putting my faith in him. *He's a criminal!*

I started to walk, making a wide circle through the trees, always keeping the cave in sight so that I didn't get lost. Being an FBI agent is about balancing gut instincts and cold, hard facts. Up until now, I'd been letting my instincts rule the day. For some reason, I trusted him. But now it was time to take stock and get real.

Technically, I should be arresting him and trying to get him into custody. Instead, I was thinking about letting him lead me deeper into the wild. What if he was lying about what was best for us? He was a wanted man: he sure as hell didn't want to be around the crash site when the authorities showed up.

What if going off into the wilds with him was the most dangerous thing I could do? Yes, he'd saved my life. But on the plane, a temporary alliance made sense. Now, our needs were opposed. I wanted to get back to civilization. But if we got there, it massively increased his chances of going to jail. At a word from me, the first cop we saw would arrest him. And if I *didn't* do that, I'd be aiding a fugitive.

The best thing, from his point of view, was to make sure I never got home.

My stomach twisted. Had years of being an agent made me paranoid? Or were my instincts about him wrong? I went back and forth in my head.

He saved me.

He's a fugitive.

I...like him.

He's strong enough that he could kill me with one good punch.

He didn't take the deal and bail out with Weiss.

He's wanted by the military. For something so bad, they were going to lock him away for so long, that he gave up a normal life to run from it.

I climbed over a fallen log...and stopped.

Before me, lying on its side, was the rest of the plane. I could visualize now how we must have come in, skimming the treetops, the cockpit breaking off and tangling in the branches and the rest of the plane slamming into the ground. It had hit so hard, parts of it were buried in the ground. My stomach twisted. If the plane hadn't snapped in two, we both would have been killed.

I stepped gingerly inside. There was no sign of my purse or my coat—everything loose probably fell out of the open door or was lost when the plane broke up. And I couldn't see anything else useful....

And then I stopped. Right at the front of the cabin, just before where the cockpit had snapped off, were the folding seats where the marshals had sat. And next to one of them was a pocket holding two blue paper files.

"Kate?" Boone's voice.

I darted forward and grabbed both files.

"Kate?" He was closer, now.

I didn't have time to check names so I folded both files together into halves, then quarters, then stuffed the whole thing into the front of my pants and covered it with my suit jacket. The whole time, my heart was thumping in my chest. If I was wrong about him and he saw me....

"Kate?"

I whirled around. He was leaning in through the door.

We stared at each other. "Find anything useful?" he said at last.

I shook my head. "Nope."

"Ready to go?" But the question his eyes asked me was, *do you trust me?*

The file, with its answers, felt red-hot against my body. “Sure,” I said.

And we set off.

TWELVE

Boone

I felt...*free.*

Some of it was having the chains off. Some of it was being out of the claustrophobic plane. And some of it was being back in the mountains, far from people, far from anyone who'd put me back in a box.

Except for her.

I tried to push that thought away. She'd been nothing but good to me. I could do my part, get her to safety and, in return, hope that she wouldn't send the authorities after me. As far as she knew, I was just a criminal. She didn't know what they wanted me for. As long as it stayed that way, everything would be fine.

"How do you know where we're going?" Kate asked.

Kate's voice was a world away from my own Alaskan rasp. Boston or New York or something, definitely *city*. It spoke of cocktail parties and business meetings, quick and efficient and yet softly feminine. It was like my ears were being caressed by wisps of goddamn silk. I'd spent four years avoiding people but I could have listened to that voice all day.

I stopped and pointed down the mountain and along the valley. "River's about forty miles that way. My cabin's not far beyond it."

"So you've been this way before?" she asked hopefully.

I shook my head. "Not exactly. I don't normally go this high. The hunting's better down near the river and in the forest. But I've passed close by here, on my way to Koyuk." I nodded behind us. "That's about forty miles the other way."

"You *walk* eighty miles to get to a town?" She shook her head in disbelief. "That must take *days!*"

"Four or five."

"But where do you sleep?"

I frowned at her, bemused, then nodded at the landscape. "Out here."

She just stared at me like I was crazy and then walked on. God, she was so far out of her element, it was untrue. The ankles of her pant suit were already caked with mud and torn by thorns and we'd barely gone two miles. At least she wasn't in heels. But it went deeper than her clothes. She was looking around at the landscape as if it was the surface of the moon instead of...you know, *normal.* She was hating this.

And me? A twinge of guilt went through me as I realized I was loving it. I actually had to stop myself smiling. It made no sense. Sure, this was the world I was used to but I didn't go around grinning when I was out hunting. And this was a long way from an ideal trip: I had no supplies and, for the first time ever, I had a civilian to worry about. More stress, not less. So why was I—

It was her.

It was watching her walk along ahead of me (always ahead. However we started out walking, she always drifted into the lead, like a puppy determined to prove itself). It was the sway of her ass under that damn pant suit. It was the way she was so *naked,* under all those clothes—

I cursed myself. *That doesn't even make sense!* But it was true. I looked at the back of her suit jacket and all I could think about was the white blouse underneath and the white bra beneath that and the soft, pale breasts beneath *that,* the nipples I'd glimpsed like tight, pink pencil erasers, surrounded by delicate areolae....

She was covered from head to foot, more demure than any Victorian lady. Yet somehow she was sexier than any model parading around in her underwear. The more she wore, the more I wanted to take it off her.

And that braid.

That. God. Damn. *Braid.*

Before the end of the first hour, I'd been hypnotized by it. It bounced against the soft, pale skin of her neck, focusing my attention on it as clearly as if some sniper had put a red laser dot there. My eyes were locked on that soft indentation at the bottom of her scalp, where gossamer-thin wisps of hair gleamed against her neck. I wanted to bury my lips there. I'd already imagined every possible angle I could kiss that part of her: I'd smelled her fragrant skin, had the hair tickle my nose, felt the braid silky-smooth and heavy against my fingers as I lifted it out of the way.

That braid was *her.* It summed up everything

about her, all her gorgeous femininity pulled back into something practical and efficient, twisted tight and knotted in place. I wanted to unknot it. I wanted to free all that hair and see it cascade down her back just like I wanted to free the heat I could feel inside her. But before I did that, I wanted to grab hold of that braid and use it to gently but firmly tug her head back and cover her mouth with mine. I wanted to use it to guide the kiss as I took ownership of those imperious, pouty lips. I wanted to plunge my tongue deep into Kate Lydecker and–

"So you do know where we're going?" asked Kate, turning to look over her shoulder at me.

For a second, I couldn't speak. I just stared at her lips.

"Mason?"

I blinked. No one had used my first name in a long, long time. I'd almost forgotten I had it. "Yeah," I said. I tried to keep my voice level but I could hear the throaty rasp in it. "Yeah. I know where we're going. As long as we keep heading north, we're good."

"But how do you know which way is north?"

That threw me. I cocked my head to the side and frowned at her, trying to understand the joke. Then I realized that she was serious: she had no clue.

She must have seen the surprise in my eyes because her face grew dark. "I put an address into the car's GPS." She raised her chin defensively. "That's how I navigate. That's how everyone navigates!"

I nodded. But she'd gotten it wrong: I didn't think she was dumb and I wasn't mocking her. The only thing I was feeling was a big, unexpected swell of that protective instinct I got whenever I was near her. She was screwed out here, without me. And I realized that's why she was touchy. She wasn't used to having to rely on someone else.

I took hold of her wrist, trying not to think about how good her smooth skin felt against my calloused palm, and showed her how to figure north using the sun and her watch. She was a fast learner. When we walked on, I saw her trying it herself a few times to make sure she had it. And the weird thing was, I'd enjoyed teaching her. I'd been just fine on my own for years but now, sharing this stuff with her....

Now, those years felt lonely.

My eyes locked on that braid again...and then I caught myself and stopped in my tracks. For a moment, I'd gotten caught up in it, in some fantasy of me and her, happy together.

As if I could have that. As if I could have a normal life. I looked around at the mountains. *This* was my life: out here on the edge. Walking. Hunting. Maybe one night in five sleeping in an actual bed in a ramshackle cabin, the rest under the stars. Hell, even going into Koyuk, my one contact with civilization, was now too dangerous. I was back on their radar. I was going to have to withdraw even more. Who'd want to share that life? Certainly not a woman like Kate.

Her braid swished back and forth, bouncing off the soft skin of her neck.

And I clamped down on my feelings and walked on after her. I'd get her to safety. Then I'd say goodbye. That was the only sensible thing to do.

So why did it feel so wrong?

THIRTEEN

Weiss

"Goddamn it," I muttered, rummaging through my pack. "Seriously? Fucking energy bars?" I waved my hand at the back of the 4x4. "We've got plenty of space. Would it have been too much trouble to bring some real fucking food?"

The lead mercenary—I couldn't remember if his name was *Sergei* or *Stepan:* they all looked the same, to me—shrugged as if trying to make an irritating insect fly away. "When you get to Russia, you have all food you like." His English was better than my Russian but that wasn't saying much.

In front of us, the two other 4x4s stopped. "We're here," said Sergei, and quickly got out as if he didn't want to spend any longer with me than necessary. *Prick.* He could at least be civil. I was paying him enough.

I jumped out...and sank almost up to my ankles in thick, sucking mud. When I looked down, my handmade Italian leather shoes had all but disappeared and the mud and water was soaking the cuffs of my pants. *Great.* I hated Alaska.

When I caught up with Sergei, he and the others were looking at the wreckage...but only half of it. The damn thing had broken up. It took us another few minutes, with the marshals, me and the three Russians spread out and searching, before we spotted the cockpit jammed in some trees, high up off the ground.

I let out a long sigh of satisfaction. "Okay. Get the bodies and burn it all.

Sergei climbed up to take a look at the cockpit while the others started unloading the three body bags from the back of one of the 4x4s. I didn't know who they were: Russians, I guess, or some unlucky homeless guys they'd found in Alaska. Didn't matter. As long as they were the same sex, height and weight as me and the two marshals.

In minutes, the bodies were loaded into the tail section and strapped into seats. Then the Russians started pouring jet fuel over them.

That's when Sergei climbed down from the cockpit. "We have problem," he said as his boots hit the ground.

"The pilot's not there?" I asked.

"Pilot is there. Other two are not."

I stared at him. "Did they fall out of the door, after we jumped?"

Marshal Hennessey shook his head. "I watched that plane the whole way down. No one fell out."

All of us looked around at the forest. *Shit.* "If they're alive," I grated, "we have a very big problem."

The Russians spread out into the trees, guns drawn. They moved silently, even in their heavy boots and military gear. The guy I'd paid in Russia had said they were all former *Spetsnaz*, Russian special forces. The sort of men who knew thirty different ways to kill you even *without* a gun.

A few minutes later, the shout went up. They converged on a spot, then came jogging back.

"You found them?" I asked.

Sergei shook his head. "We found remains of fire. Two sets of footprints. They are heading down mountain."

"God*damn* it!" I yelled. Then I rounded on the marshals. "You should have just shot them!"

"We already have a pilot with a bullet in his head," snapped Marshal Phillips. "You should have stuck to the plan! It was meant to be a blow to the head, so it looked like it happened in the crash! You really want *three* bodies with bullets in, when they investigate this thing?"

"They're out there!" I snapped, getting in his face. "If they tell someone we're alive—"

"They won't!" Marshal Hennessey slid his body between us, hands up to calm us. "They're at least a few days from the nearest town. We can be in Russia by then."

I shook my head. "That's not good enough. This is meant to be *perfect.*" I jabbed my finger at the wreckage. "This isn't just about getting out of the country. I have to have died in that crash!"

That's the thing with stealing $4.6 billion. You can't just walk away, even if you go to another country. They'll never stop hunting you.

Not unless they think you're already dead.

I pointed at the Russians. "You have guns. They don't. We're in 4x4s. They're on foot. We'll hunt them down and bring their bodies back here and burn them with the rest, then carry on with the plan."

The men looked at each other.

"*Did I stutter?*" I bawled.

Sergei shook his head. "Mountain too steep, even for 4x4s. We will have to skirt round, cut them off. Could take days."

I made for the 4x4s. "Then let's get moving." As I climbed into my seat, Hennessey appeared beside my door. I knew what he was going to say before the old gray bastard opened his mouth: *this isn't what I signed up for*. He'd said the same thing when he first found out we were going to kill the pilot. *Fuck him.* I slammed the door so hard the glass rattled.

This whole week had just gotten worse and worse. It was bad enough that I'd had to flee to Russia in the first place. Just because I'd separated fools from their money, just as every con man in history had done. I'd simply done it on a bigger scale.

But Russia hadn't sounded so bad, the sort of country where money can buy you anything: a palace to live in, fast cars, bodyguards...even women. Except getting there had meant going up to Alaska and hiding out in that god-awful town, Nome, while the Russians made their preparations to smuggle me across the Bering Strait. And just as I was about to leave, that bitch of a manager at the hotel restaurant had called the cops. Then I was left in a cramped, cold jail cell for two days while they figured out who should take me south. That was their mistake. It meant the people I was paying had time to organize my escape. It wasn't difficult for them to figure out which US marshals would be assigned to move me, or to convince them to spring me.

But then *he'd* got on the plane, that big, muscle-bound idiot. He was basically a hobo, for God's sake, scratching an existence halfway up a mountain. Who'd have thought he'd suddenly try to play the hero?

And then there was her. I clenched my jaw. Miss Prissy of the FBI, with her pert little tits and her hot little ass all wrapped up in suit and attitude. The two of them together had jeopardized my entire escape. How *dare* they?

I was going to enjoy hunting them down. I might even ask to put the bullet in Boone's head myself, when the time came. And that bitch Lydecker? My cock hardened. I might keep her alive for a while, just so I could teach her a lesson.

Sergei swung himself into the driver's seat. "We are ready," he said sullenly.

I took hold of the grab handle beside my window, ready for a rough ride. "Then let's go hunting."

FOURTEEN

Kate

SOMETIMES IT FELT like we weren't making progress at all. We seemed to move sideways as much as we moved down, zigzagging back and forth. But then I'd look up and catch my breath as I saw how far away the trees above us were.

Looking up was good. Looking down wasn't.

The descent was getting steeper and steeper. There was a moment when I looked below us and realized for the first time that, if I slipped and fell, it was steep enough that *I wouldn't stop.* I'd just keep bouncing and rolling until I went over the edge of a vertical cliff.

I had to close my eyes and count to ten to keep from throwing up. In some ways, it was worse than when we were on the plane. The heights here were just low enough that I could see every detail of the ground I'd hit.

But the drop didn't seem to faze Boone at all. He belonged here in exactly the way I didn't. And every time he took the lead, I'd find myself watching the motion of his shoulders as they swung back and forth, the tanned globes of his muscles revealed by the cut-off shirt. His legs were no less solid, his hard thighs seeming as thick as my waist. The guy was big everywhere. Enough strength and power to pick me up and just—

Kiss me?

Kill me?

I was going crazy, not knowing whether I could trust him or not. My fear of him was smacking up against a deep, physical pull the likes of which I'd never felt before.

After two hours, my thighs were burning from the descent. When they started actually shaking, threatening to give, I finally caved. "I need a break," I told him.

Boone nodded and stopped. I caught his guilty expression. He'd been ready to carry on all day, oblivious. "Sorry," he muttered.

I sat down on a rock and rubbed at my aching quads. Boone sat on another, rooted in his pocket and brought out the jagged shard of metal he'd broken off the wreckage. He picked up a fist-sized rock and started to hammer at it, using the larger rock as an anvil. The muscles of his back stood out through his shirt, as big as any medieval blacksmith's.

"What are you doing?" I asked.

"Making a knife."

I nodded sagely, as if making weapons out of junk was what I did on my weekends. My stomach rumbled. I'd never been so hungry in my life. I was dreaming of bagels with salmon and cream cheese and a big, steaming cup of fresh coffee....

My eyes fell on another boulder, this one as big as

a compact car. There was nothing to eat or drink but there was one thing I *could* finally do, now we'd stopped. "There's, um...something I have to take care of," I told him.

He looked at me expectantly.

"It's been a long journey," I explained.

He just looked at me.

"I have to pee, okay?" I said, exasperated.

He nodded quickly and looked away, staring out across the landscape.

I went behind the rock and crouched down. I double checked he couldn't see me...and then I took out the files. I stared at the printed cover of Boone's for long seconds. It felt like I was digging into his past, uninvited...but I had to know. I opened it up.

Mason Joshua Boone. Holy—He'd been a Navy SEAL?! His service record had been reduced down to a bullet point list. Iraq. Afghanistan. Operations that were just codenames and numbers. *Eight confirmed kills. Twelve confirmed kills. Target successfully extracted. Target eliminated.*

And then I came to the main section of the file: the reason for his court martial. He'd been in Afghanistan, sent to extract a group of civilians, when—

It felt like someone punched me in the stomach and then crushed my insides in their fist.

He'd entered the house of an Afghan family and—

There were photos. Bodies lying in pools of blood. One was of a little girl who couldn't have been more than five. I clapped my hand over my mouth to stifle my scream.

They'd been unarmed. He'd killed the entire family in cold blood, then gone MIA. When he eventually returned to base, he was flown home, court-martialled and found guilty. It was while they were preparing to move him to a military prison that he'd escaped. That was four years ago.

I stared at the photos. Everything my training had been telling me since I'd first met Boone had been right: he was a fugitive who should have remained in chains. And every instinct I'd had about him had been completely, terrifyingly wrong.

"You okay behind there?" Boone's voice.

I snapped the file closed, almost panting with fear. "Almost done!" I called out. But I didn't stand up. I crouched there, staring at the boulder, imagining Boone on the other side.

I could hear a noise that set my teeth on edge. Metal grinding on rock.

He was sharpening his homemade knife. *Oh Jesus....*

I was alone in the mountains with a convicted murderer. He knew how to survive out here and I didn't. And now he was armed. I looked down the mountain. Should I run? Try to take him by surprise? But he was only a few steps away from me. He'd catch me easily. I needed to wait until I could get a head start.

I tucked both files back into my pants, made sure my jacket was covering them and stood up. Boone was looking right at me. He'd torn a strip of cloth from his shirt and wrapped it around one end of the metal shard to make a handle. The blade of the thing looked wickedly sharp. "Ready?" he asked.

I swallowed. "Sure," I said. "Let's go."

FIFTEEN

Boone

Something was wrong.

I could feel the change in her. The way she looked at me. The way she walked an extra step away from me. *Did she know?*

No. Impossible. I was being paranoid. Hell, what did I know about reading people, especially women? She was probably just scared.

I was still feeling guilty for not stopping for a break sooner. She must have been exhausted but she'd carried on until almost ready to drop, just because she didn't want to admit it. Goddamn, but she was stubborn...in a way I couldn't help but admire.

We'd been following a natural path down the side of the mountain. But now the path narrowed to a rock ledge that hugged the cliff face. It was little more than a foot wide with the cliff on one side and a sheer, two hundred foot drop on the other. I couldn't see too far ahead because the ledge disappeared around a corner. It looked doable, but it was risky and hellishly exposed: the breeze tugged at my shirt and I could hear birds calling to each other as they swooped past. I'd spent enough time in the mountains in Afghanistan that heights didn't bother me anymore. But to Kate, I knew it would be terrifying.

She stopped beside me, saw the ledge and drew in her breath.

"It'll be fine," I told her. "If it was on the ground, you wouldn't even think about it. Just hug the rock face and shuffle along."

She looked back at me with huge, terrified eyes. Just from the drop or was something else going on?

"I'll go first," I told her. I climbed onto the ledge, faced the cliff and put my palms on the rock. There really wasn't a lot of room. Behind my boot heels, there was no more than two inches of rock, then nothing but air.

I started to shuffle, keeping both feet on the rock at all times. The trick was to go slow and steady, and to keep your eyes forward. When I'd made enough room for Kate, I beckoned her forward.

She stepped onto the ledge. Glanced down—

"No!" I told her. "Look at the cliff."

She swallowed and focused on the rocks a few inches from her nose. She spread her hands wide, like me...but the left one shied away from my right, as if she didn't want to touch me.

Something *was* wrong. She'd stopped trusting me. I should have trusted my gut and asked her what was up. But this wasn't the place to debate it.

I started to shuffle along with Kate following beside me. We'd almost reached the corner. I stepped over a bird's nest—and then froze. The bird's nest had been hiding the fact that the ledge petered out just beyond. At the corner itself, there was no ledge at all.

Very carefully, I leaned and looked around the corner. The ledge picked up again on the other side. We could step around and over the gap...if we were very, very careful.

Taking a deep breath, I swung one leg around the corner and felt for the ledge. Found it. Then the heart-stopping moment when I had to shift my weight and swing myself around with only my grip on the rocks for support. There was a little bit of an overhang so I actually had to push out from the cliff a little to avoid whacking my head. For a sickening instant, I was pretty much balanced on one foot—

And then I was round. For a second, I just stood there as the adrenaline aftershock sent cold sweat down my spine. Even with my experience, that had been *scary*. I was going to have to be real careful, getting Kate round. At least she'd have my hand to hold onto.

I leaned back around the corner. "Okay," I said in what I hoped was a reassuring voice. "It's not as bad as it looks. Take my hand. You'll be okay."

She shuffled closer, approaching the bird's nest. Both hands gripped the rock.

"Okay," I said. "Now give me your hand." I reached out for it.

At the last second, she pulled it back. And now she was looking at me with big, uncertain eyes.

"Kate?" I asked. "What's wrong?"

I saw her swallow. She looked back along the ledge as if thinking about going back. Then towards me and the corner. She made a little movement forward, as if about to go herself, without my help.

"*Kate!*" I was sweating now, terrified. I'd never had

this before, this sickening churning in my belly. I'd never known what it was like to be afraid *for* someone. "*Give me your hand!*"

But she didn't. She clung to the rock face instead. Swung one leg around as I had done. Shifted her weight—

And that's when she stepped on the bird's nest with her back foot. It slid off the edge and her foot went with it.

And she fell screaming from the ledge.

SIXTEEN

Kate

ALL OF THE AIR came out of my body in one long, ear-splitting screech as I dropped into space. My palms scraped down the rocks I'd been clinging to and then even they were gone. I was free-falling, the wind clawing my hair and clothes upward as I plunged. There was no time to think and I was beyond thought, anyway. I was reduced to animal instinct, grabbing at the air as if it could support me—

My knee clipped something and pain shot up my leg. The impact tipped me forward and—

Something whacked hard into my chest and I *grabbed.* Instantly, one shoulder exploded into pain as the full weight of my body pulled on it.

And I stopped.

My eyes were shut tight. I could feel air all around me. The only part of me that was touching anything solid was my right hand.

I opened my eyes.

My right arm was stretched above me. My hand

was clinging to a rock the size of an apple, the same one my knee must have hit on the way down. And high above that I saw Boone, staring down at me from the ledge. I'd fallen at least fifteen feet.

"*KATE!*" yelled Boone. "*DO NOT MOVE!*"

I hung there panting. I was swaying slightly and every tiny side-to-side movement hurt my shoulder more. For once, my tiny size was a benefit. If I'd been any bigger, I probably wouldn't have been able to hold my own weight.

Boone was lowering himself down off the ledge, feeling for footholds and handholds. "I'm coming!" he yelled. "Just hang on!"

Just hang on. And don't look down. Don't even think about down. Don't think about the fact there's nothing but air beneath your feet for two hundred feet. Don't think about how much your shoulder hurts or how sweaty your hand is getting–

Boone picked his way down the cliff to my side. When he was next to me, almost close enough to touch, he stopped. "That's as close as I can get!" he said. "Reach out to me!"

I turned to look at him. He had his hand outstretched towards me. All I had to do was reach out with my free hand and I could grab him. But–

But what if he'd come down to finish me off? I'd take his hand, let go of the rock...and then he'd simply drop me. Exactly as I'd feared he would on the ledge.

"*Kate!*" he snapped. "Take my hand!"

His blue eyes were burning with frustration. Incomprehension. *Why won't you trust me?*

And then I saw his eyes flick downward. And his expression changed.

I looked down at myself. Because I was stretched

out, my jacket had risen up, well clear of my belt. And tucked into my pants, in plain view, were the prisoner files.

SEVENTEEN

Kate

I locked eyes with Boone. I saw so much there. Hurt. Anger. Regret.

My hand slid a few millimeters on the rock. I was losing my grip.

Boone stuck out his hand again. "Kate," he said in *that* voice. "*Take my hand.*" He drew in a shuddering breath. "I swear: I didn't do it."

I stared into his eyes. Of course he'd lie. Of course he'd try to convince me to let go, especially now he knew I knew. Every bit of training I'd ever had told me to trust the facts, not my gut. *He's going to grab you and pull you and, as soon as you've let go, he'll drop you.*

My hand slipped a little further.

Boone stared into my eyes. "*Please!*"

I took a deep breath. And grabbed for his hand.

His grip closed on me, warm and dry around fingers that had gone clammy with fear. And then he was pulling me towards him and I had no choice but to let go of the rock and—

For a second, I was dangling from his hand, two hundred feet up. It's impossible to express what that felt like. My legs, which had been instinctively scrabbling for purchase, went limp. All of me went limp. I was connected to life only by the warm hand that clasped mine. I was *his.*

And then, his muscles bunching, he lifted me, and I was pressed face-first against the cliff face. His hand pulled mine to a handhold, his feet kicked mine to footholds, and I grabbed and clung, eyes squeezed tight shut. He pressed in behind me, his entire body pressed against my back, holding me there, his lips at my ear. He was panting just as hard as me, panting in fear. Scared that he almost lost me.

The facts were wrong. My gut had been right.

"Take a second," he gasped. "Just take a second. Then we'll climb up."

I nodded weakly. His face was pressed so close to mine that his stubble stroked my cheek. When we could both breathe normally again, I tentatively opened my eyes and we started up, with him nudging my hands and feet to each rock in turn. I couldn't have done it without him, without that protective warmth against my back.

At last, I grabbed the edge of the ledge and hauled myself up. First, I lay full length. Then I managed to get to my knees and finally to my feet. This time, I held his hand as we stepped around the corner. Twenty feet further on, the ledge widened into a path. As soon as it was wide enough, I slumped down, my back against the cliff.

His big body slumped down next to my small one. And then he told me what happened in Afghanistan.

EIGHTEEN

Boone

It was all my fault. That's all I could think. If I'd been any other guy, if I'd been anything other than a fugitive, she would have trusted me. And if she'd trusted me, she would have taken my hand on the ledge and she would never have fallen.

I nearly lost her.

The thought made a big, cold ache open up, right in the middle of my chest, like the mountain wind was blowing right through me. I barely knew her. And yet the idea of something happening to her scared me right down to my bones, scared me as much as the thought of going back to jail.

Maybe even more.

And unless I got her to trust me again, she'd die out here. One thing the Navy taught me: in the wilds, if you can't put your faith in the people you're with, you're dead.

It was four years since I'd told anyone my story. I'd sworn that I'd never tell it again because reliving it stirred up all the anger I'd let settle down to the bottom of my soul. And there was a bigger problem, too: reliving it would put me dangerously close to reliving what happened immediately afterwards. Not only did that scare the crap out of me: if my mind went back *there,* she was as good as dead because I'd lock down and just sit there, glazed-eyed and useless, leaving her vulnerable out here. I knew I was already stretched thin: when we'd been on the ledge, I'd gotten that itchy, antsy feeling like I used to get when there was a sniper around. Which was nuts: there wasn't another living soul for miles. And if I was starting to lose it, that really wasn't a good time to revisit the past.

But I didn't have a choice. I looked across at her, drinking in her beauty, drawing strength from seeing what it was I had to protect. Then I looked out over the landscape and began.

"A group of civilians had been captured," I said. "My SEAL team were sent in to get them back. It was deep, deep in the insurgent-held half of the city so we went in at night: the idea was to go in and sneak them out without anyone knowing we were there."

I paused. "Only our information was bad. We ran into way, way more resistance than we were expecting. We got the civilians out but we couldn't get to our extraction point. The streets started swarming with insurgents. Felt like the whole city wanted us dead. We were using NVGs—"—I looked across at her—"Sorry, night vision goggles. But they'd gotten wise to that and were throwing road flares that made it so bright we couldn't see, and someone had tossed a smoke grenade and...."

I drew in a deep breath. I could smell the tang of

the smoke, feel it in my lungs. I was back there.

"Somewhere along the way, we get separated. Just me and one civilian, a young guy called Hopkins from one of the big military supply companies. It's just me and him, skulking through back alleys, trying to reach the alternate extraction point, which is a rooftop. I have to give him my sidearm so he can watch our back."

I still had my eyes open but I couldn't see the landscape in front of me. I could see a confusing mass of walls and doorways, all rendered in night-vision green. "We somehow make it almost to the extraction point. We just have to get up onto the rooftops and sneak across them and wait for the chopper. So we pick a house that looks abandoned: the door's broken in and we can't hear anything."

My voice slowed. "We sneak inside. Nothing. We climb the stairs. Nothing. We finally start to relax. We just have to wait until we hear the chopper, then we'll climb up through the roof hatch and they'll pick us up. We have to be quiet because we can hear insurgents searching for us right outside, but we figure we're in the clear."

I stopped for a moment. The sun was still well above the horizon as I sat there with Kate. I let the sunlight bathe my face. *You're here. Not there.* A little mantra I repeat when I'm close to slipping back. It usually works well, in the daytime. Not so well at night. But now it wasn't working at all. I was back in a stone-walled room...and one side of it was moving.

"See," I said in a tortured voice, "when we'd come up the stairs, we'd thought it was a small room, only half the size of the downstairs. We figured that's just how the house was built—they're laid out all sorts of ways, when they're packed in so close together. But we were wrong. We suddenly hear something, *really close,* right on the other side of the wall, only it's too loud and too near to be in the next house." The words were bursting out of me, now, like black oil erupting out of the ground when the drill hits it. "And that's when we realize it's not a wall: it's a sheet, painted to look like a wall. And there's people right on the other side of it."

"Hopkins," I said, my voice tight, "He doesn't even think. He just assumes we're about to be overrun. He raises my sidearm and opens up, empties the whole magazine into the sheet. Puts fourteen holes straight through it. And then the screaming starts. And someone staggers forward, pressing up against the sheet, and falls and they rip it down with them and we see—"

I broke off, my lips pressed tight together. "They'd been *hiding,*" I said. "They slept behind that sheet each night, so the house would look abandoned if anyone searched it. When we'd come in, we'd woken them up and they'd been waiting there, terrified, praying we'd leave peacefully. Until one of their kids woke up and made a noise." I closed my eyes. "Mom. Dad. Six children. All dead."

I heard her soft moan of horror from off to my side. My stomach twisted: that night was toxic, the events tainting everyone who heard them. She'd never forget the image she had right now in her mind's eye. It should have made me stop but there was something in the sound that gave me the strength to carry on: not just horror, but sympathy. She was imagining how much worse it must have been to be there, to know that you were partially responsible.

"Things happened fast after that," I told her, opening my eyes and staring at the sinking sun. "The insurgents outside hear the shots and start piling into the house. At the same time, we hear the chopper, right overhead. Hopkins is just standing there, gaping at what he's done, so I push him towards the roof hatch and tell him to go, while I hold them off."

I could feel the fear crawling over my skin, a million freezing insects preparing to swarm. *This* memory was threatening to trigger *that* memory, the one I couldn't control. I pressed my lips together and shook my head. "I'm firing down the stairs when I hear the roof hatch open and Hopkins climb out. The chopper's thundering away, right above us, the downwash blasting through the hatch, blowing everything around: I can barely see. But I run over and climb up to the hatch and—"

I broke off, seeing Hopkins's face in my head. When I restarted, it was with difficulty. I was dangerously close to the brink, close to falling into a place I wouldn't return from. *I have to stop.* But I needed to finish this part. "Hopkins is crouching there on the roof, looking down at me...and he just shakes his head like he's sorry. And then he swings the hatch closed."

"*What?!*" Kate gripped my arm.

Her touch gave me just enough strength to continue. "By now, insurgents are flooding up the stairs. I hammer on the hatch but it won't move—he's put something heavy on top of it. And I can hear the chopper flying away—"

I stopped, as suddenly as if someone had thrown a switch. I couldn't go on. I wasn't sure if I could ever tell her the next part.

So I skipped forward, side-stepping a huge, painful chunk.

"I was MIA for a while. When I finally made it back to base, I found that Hopkins had told them that *I* shot the family."

For the first time, I looked at Kate. Her face was ashen. "And they *believed* him?"

"Turns out, Hopkins's dad owned the supply company. Multi-billionaire. No way was he going to let his son go down for something like that. He put pressure on the military to buy Hopkins's story. And it was easy to blame me: everyone thought I was dead. By the time I showed up, everything was set in stone. They brought me back to the US, there was a court martial...and I was found guilty. I was going to jail for a long, long time. So as soon as I got a chance, I ran."

And that was it. That was my story—or all of it I could tell. I found I was looking into Kate's eyes, trying to read her thoughts—

I realized I was trying to tell if she believed me. I hadn't done that in years. I *knew* no one believed me. I'd had that beaten into me. I'd stopped caring.

But I cared what *she* thought.

Kate shook her head. "That's—Jesus, that's the worst thing I've ever—*That's* why you're out here? That's why you're—" She looked around at the mountains, at the tiny speck of humanity we represented. *That's why you're all alone.*

I nodded and looked down, suddenly unable to meet her eyes. The tension was too much.

A moment later, her small, elegant hand slid on top of my big, clumsy one and gripped tight. I still couldn't look at her.

"I believe you," she said.

My head snapped up and I was looking right into those rich brown eyes, lit up with more warmth, more trust, than I'd ever seen. God, she was beautiful. But I almost glared at her, I wanted to believe it so much. *Don't you be lying to me.*

She stared right back at me, resolute.

She did believe me. She really did.

NINETEEN

Kate

I DIDN'T WANT to get my hopes up too much but it seemed like we were past the worst of the descent. The cliffs had transitioned into gentler slopes, with grass mixed in with the rocks. Boone had been right: it *was* warmer, the further we descended. It became almost comfortable.

And then we entered the forest. By now, the sun was almost setting and Boone was talking about finding a place to spend the night. Just the thought of that made my heart race. *Out here. Alone with him.*

So much had changed in just a few minutes, up on the cliff. My trust in him had done a complete one-eighty and not just because of what he'd told me. That had been the explanation but the way he'd saved me when I fell was the proof. I believed him. I'd watched his face so carefully as he told me about Afghanistan. No way was he lying.

Which meant that, somewhere out there, a lying, moneyed prick called Hopkins had gotten away with manslaughter. He thought the law didn't apply to him. And, meanwhile, Boone had spent four years in self-imposed exile, his service to his country forgotten, his record forever tainted. No wonder he kept away from people, away from civilization. It was about more than just hiding. Boone had lost all faith in the system.

He was in the lead at the moment. I looked down at the huge footprints his boots were leaving and my much smaller ones within them. He was the right size for this vast land and I was comically, *terrifyingly* dwarfed by it. And nothing seemed to bother him: cold, heights, even hunger. I was *starving*.

I let my eyes track down his body. The shafts of sunlight coming through the trees painted stripes across the hulking muscles of his back. They wrapped around the heavy bulges of shoulder and bicep, stroked their way down into the small of his back, then bent outward again over the twin globes of his hard ass—

I was uncomfortably aware that the sunlight was doing exactly what I'd like to do with my hands. He was just so...*big*. Powerful and raw in a way that was a million miles away from the guys I knew at the FBI. And now that I trusted him....

He's still a fugitive. And he'd be living out here forever, unless....

Unless I could get him justice.

I was so distracted, I walked right into Boone's back. It was like we were back at the airport again...except, this time, when I felt that hard body against me, I had a sudden urge to just stay there, wrap my arms around him and—

I jumped back as he turned around. *Don't be stupid!* We were still stranded, still in danger. And I couldn't just—With a guy I barely knew—

I met his gaze and saw the same flicker of helplessness there, the same *pull* I was feeling. A wave of heat washed over me. He wanted me, in the most basic, primal way possible.

But then he looked away for a second, and when he turned back it was as if the lust had been locked behind bars, contained...for now. "Here."

He was holding something out. A stem of berries. My jaw dropped open. *Food!* I hadn't eaten since my flight from Seattle and my stomach felt like it was trying to devour itself. Just the thought of food had me salivating and the berries looked juicy and ripe.... "Thank you," I croaked, and grabbed the stem—

And as he released it, I saw something I hadn't seen before. Just for a second, a hint of a smile pulled at his mouth. Like he enjoyed making me happy.

Then he quickly turned and walked on.

The berries were delicious, exploding into little gushes of tangy juice and sweet flesh as I crushed them in my mouth. Boone stopped to pick a few for himself and, as I'd been doing all day, I drifted ahead of him on the path.

He kept giving me those looks...but he didn't say anything, didn't acknowledge the attraction. *Maybe I'm wrong?* I mean, it was obvious why I was attracted to him, but why would he be into me? I didn't have big boobs or eye-catching blonde hair, I sure as hell didn't have long legs and I didn't even know how to dress sexy—I spent almost all my time in a suit. And I knew I could be work-obsessed and stubborn....

And yet...no, I hadn't imagined it. He looked at me like—I flushed—like he wanted to push me up against the nearest tree and rip my clothes off. But more than that.

He looked at me like I was something special. That made me flush in a whole different way.

So why the silence? Was it because, after four years on his own, he didn't remember how to flirt or make small talk? Was it because I was FBI? Because, when we got back to civilization, we'd be on opposite sides? Or was it—

I blundered through some undergrowth and found a huge, brown shape right in front of me. By the time I stopped, I was almost close enough to touch it.

That's a—

My brain rebelled. It was so far outside my experience, I couldn't accept it. *Of course it isn't.*

That's a—

Oh Jesus God.

The bear rose silently up on its hind legs, towering over me. And roared.

TWENTY

Boone

I REACHED KATE just as the bear roared. The sound echoed around the entire forest and we were close enough that we could feel the hot blast of air on our faces.

I froze. "Don't move," I told Kate. "Absolutely *do not move."*

A brown bear, and a big one. Probably fresh out of hibernation, looking to regain some weight after using up its fat stores through the winter. Bears won't usually attack people. Not unless you surprise them. That's why every hiker knows to make a lot of noise as you walk so they know you're coming. Except we'd both been so wrapped up in our thoughts, we'd done the exact opposite.

And from the look of her, she was a female. The cubs might be close by. *Shit. Shit, shit shit.*

Kate was close to panic, her shoulders rising and falling as she sucked in air. Her weight shifted infinitesimally as her instincts all told her to *run.*

"Don't," I told her. "She's faster than us. If we run, she'll chase us down."

The bear took a step towards us. Kate was in front. It'd go for her first, falling on her with claws and teeth, locking its jaws around her head–

That deep-down urge to protect her welled up and I moved before I was even aware I was going to do it. I put my hands on her waist and swung her around, so that my back was to the bear and she was in front of me, facing the way we'd come. Then I hugged her in close, her back to my chest, and curled myself over her, wrapping her in a protective cocoon. Behind me, the bear let out another roar, so loud it made my ears ring. My sudden movement could be interpreted as a threat. Any second, I could feel the bear's claws sink into my shoulders–

But at least it would be me, not her.

Kate was shaking, her whole body trembling. Her delicate ear was right by my lips. "If she takes me, *run,"* I told her. "Run and don't look back."

I felt her whole body go tense. She found my hand and gripped it tight.

There was a ground-shaking thump as the bear fell to all fours right behind me. It was now so close that I could feel each hot exhale on the back of my neck. I closed my eyes, waiting for the bite.

A wet nose brushed just below my hairline. There was a sniff and a snort, a low growl....

And then heavy footsteps, getting slowly quieter.

I kept her wrapped up in my arms for long minutes, first in case the bear was just circling around, then because she was still shaking, and then just *because.*

When I eventually released her and turned her to

face me, her cheeks were white. She looked over my shoulder, then all around. "It's okay," I told her. "She's gone."

But she was still panting. I recognized it because I'd felt it myself, the first time I'd come face-to-face with a bear. That special kind of terror that comes when you remember man isn't the top of the food chain, once you take away his weapons.

She needed comforting. That's what I told myself. So it was okay to just—

I put my hands on her shoulders and then smoothed them down her back, like stroking a cat. I had no idea of the words to use. I couldn't remember the last time I'd had to comfort anyone. "Shh," I said awkwardly. "It's okay."

My palms swept down into the small of her back and, as I had to reach further, that kind of pulled her inward, toward me. She took a half-step forward and her leg slipped between mine. My hands slid back up...but she didn't step back.

She looked up at me, eyes huge. And suddenly my hands were on her cheeks, thumbs rubbing across under her eyes as if brushing away invisible tears. My fingertips touched the edges of her hair, the start of that tight, pinned-back efficiency....

I leaned down. I felt my lips part and saw hers do the same. Saw her breathing quicken—

What am I doing?

I quickly drew back. One more thump of my pounding heart and I'd have kissed her. If we kissed, I wasn't going to be able to stop. I'd *undo* her, every button of her prim outfit, every strand of that tightly-drawn back hair. I wouldn't stop until she was naked and gasping under me, right here on the goddamn forest floor....

And *then* what? When we reached safety, there were only two outcomes: I hid away up here and she lied about where I was, risking her career. Or she turned me in to the cops.

Either way, I'd never see her again. And I couldn't take that. Being this close to her, hearing that silken voice, smelling her soft perfume...that was driving me crazy. But getting even closer and then losing her...that would be worse.

"Come on," I said, turning away. "Let's find a place to spend the night."

TWENTY-ONE

Kate

BOONE PICKED OUT A SPOT where we could camp, a clearing well off any animal trails where bears might roam. Then, while I collected wood, he stalked a bird. I caught little glimpses of him through the trees: I couldn't believe how someone so big could move so silently, creeping almost in slow motion, testing each step for noise before he committed his weight. Then, when he drew within arm's length of his target, he suddenly moved too fast to follow: there was a flash as the knife blade caught the light and then the bird was dead in his hands.

I got him to show me how to build a campfire: if we were going to be out here for a few days, I didn't want to be completely reliant on him. He patiently showed me how best to stack the wood, then lit it with one of the road flares. I wasn't sure about eating the bird, at first. But when Boone roasted it on a sharpened stick, the smell made my mouth water. We feasted on the rich, gamey meat, fragrant with wood smoke, and it was amazing.

As the sun sank below the horizon, the dark seemed to close in around us. That's when I realized that *dark* in Alaska isn't like *dark* in New York. A city never really gets dark: it's almost as alive at night as in the day, with people and traffic and lights. The forest, though...that became a different place at night. One that made you realize why man invented fire, and why he huddled inside caves when the sun went down. I couldn't see anything outside the little circle of warm light the fire threw out. But I could hear.

"Snowy owl," said Boone listening. Then, "That's a moose."

And then a different sound cut through the night. A sound that reminded me of a dog, but that turned into a long, drawn-out howl that no dog could match. The other animals went instantly quiet.

Boone's eyes met mine. He didn't need to say what it was. Even I'd heard wolf howls, in horror movies. It sounded distant, though–

An answering howl came back, from much closer to us.

"Don't worry, they won't bother us," said Boone quietly. Then, "You'd have to be injured, and run into a pack–"

I nodded quickly. I wished he'd left it after *they won't bother us*. "Everything's so different," I said, looking around at the darkness. "Alaska's so...*big*."

He looked around in surprise, as if he'd never thought of it that way.

"Maybe not to you," I said. I glanced down at myself. "You're the right size for this place."

He frowned at me as if I was wrong. As if I *wasn't*

too small. That lit an unexpected warm glow inside me. "Why'd you come?" he asked.

He was speaking more, now, his voice coming more easily each time, but it was still a little awkward. He still sounded like a man who was used to *doing,* not talking. But even with that awkwardness, I could hear something in his question. He wanted to know why I'd come...and he was glad I did. The warm glow expanded.

"Because I'm stubborn," I said. And I told him about my suspect back in New York and coming here in my vacation time and then trying to get to Fairbanks to chase down the witness. I looked around at where we were and shook my head. "*Stupid.* If I'd just stayed at my desk...."

"I'm glad you're stubborn," he said, his voice a low rumble. "If you hadn't been on that plane, I'd be dead. Couldn't have gotten out of those chains on my own."

"I keep thinking about the pilot," I said, staring at the fire. "I just can't believe...Weiss killed him like it was nothing. He was happy to kill *us* because we were in his way." I looked off into the distance towards where I thought Nome might be. "And now he's going to get away with it."

Boone poked at the fire. "He's got money," he said. "If you've got enough money, the law doesn't apply." His voice wasn't bitter. Bitterness must have come years before, in the first few months of his exile. By now, the injustice of it had eaten deep into him like acid, leaving deep, ragged scars. I wondered if they could ever be healed.

I stared at him, the flames lighting that gorgeous, strong jaw in oranges and yellows, like he was a stone statue cast into hell. I'd spent my whole life believing in the system, believing in justice. I couldn't imagine what it must be like to have your faith in it utterly destroyed.

I finally said what I'd been thinking for hours. "Mason...you have to fight," I said quietly. "You have to clear your name. When we get back, I can help you."

He shook his head.

"I can try to get you an appeal—"

"*No.*" His eyes were blazing, furious...but it didn't feel like the anger was directed at me.

Why won't he even consider it? I couldn't figure it out. But I knew I had to tread carefully, so I changed the subject. "How do you even find your way, out here?" I asked. "What if the sun's behind a cloud? What if it's *night?*"

He met my eyes and I saw the anger slowly fade away. And then, for the second time that day, I thought I saw him smile.

"What?" I asked.

He leaned a little closer and reached out his hand. His finger and thumb touched my chin and I melted. *Oh God. Is he going to—*

He pushed, tilting my head up to look at the sky, and I gasped.

It hadn't occurred to me to look up. In New York, there's nothing to look at.

Out here, the sky was a sparkling carpet of light, a million tiny points set against a backdrop of blues, purples and pinks. I hadn't known there *were* that many stars.

For the rest of my life, when I looked up at the sky in a city and only saw a muddy, orange-tinted glow, there'd be something missing.

"Holy *shit!*" I breathed. I just sat there for a second, drinking it in, as the fire crackled.

"Recognize anything?" His low voice came from off to my side.

I stared up at the stars. "Not much," I admitted. Then, "Is that the North Star?" I pointed.

I heard him inching closer. And closer. I didn't look, didn't want to take my eyes off the sky. And then he was behind me, leaning in, his big arm stroking along the length of my slender one. When he reached my hand, he gently took it in his and moved it to the side. "*That's* the North Star."

I swallowed. The night was getting cold but his big, warm palm was cupped around my knuckles, his heat soaking into me. "What else is there?"

He moved closer, close enough that his body brushed my back. I guessed that he was on his knees, behind me. "There's the Great Bear."

"Where?"

He put his head alongside mine, so he could see what I saw. Still, I didn't glance at him. If I looked at him, I might spook him. It seemed crazy, the idea of little me spooking the big, muscled military vet. But that's how it felt.

"*There,*" he said. And drew it with his finger.

"That's a *bear?*"

And he chuckled, a sound like huge, warm rocks grinding together. "You have to use your imagination."

I wondered how long it had been since he'd chuckled. I suddenly didn't want this to end. "Show me something else."

He went silent. I wondered if I'd pushed too hard.

Then his legs slid either side of mine until he was

sitting right behind me, his chest warm against my back, his groin pushed up against my ass. Suddenly, I could barely breathe.

"What star sign are you?" He asked. He was so close, I felt each syllable as a hot little blast on the back of my neck.

"Libra," I said, my voice catching. My back was so warm, with him pressed there.

"Very appropriate," he murmured. He pointed. "There. We're almost too far north but you can just see it." He drew the shape of the scales for me in the sky.

"It's beautiful," I said. I twisted my head a little, gazing around at the sky. "The whole thing's beautiful."

And I felt my braid brush his cheek, and I froze.

And he froze.

And I felt those blue eyes on me, tracing down the side of my face and down my neck. He didn't say anything but his gaze rode the aftershock of my words.

Beautiful.

I felt him come closer and closer, until his lips must have been a half-inch from my cheek. And then he slowly exhaled: a long, drawn out sigh of frustration. And I felt his body change, every muscle going tight in anger.

He wanted to. *Oh, God,* he wanted to, with an intensity that made me melt inside. But he couldn't.

And for the first time, I started to feel the shape of something. Maybe it was learning how to read people at the FBI. Maybe it was all the time we were spending together. But there was something going on with this man, deep beneath the surface, something that went beyond the injustice that he'd suffered.

"Can I ask you something?" I said, my voice quavering.

I felt him nod.

"Why'd you run?" I paused a second, then continued. "I mean, I know they found you guilty. Okay, you think it's useless to fight it and appeal. But...why run? I mean, living like this, all the way out here...you can't have a life. You can't have *anything*. Why not take the jail time? At least then, eventually, you could be free."

He was silent for a long time. I felt the tension build and build in his body, his chest pressing hard against my back as he took in long, slow, furious breaths. Anger that was turned inward. Anger at himself, at something he saw as a weakness.

"I couldn't let them put me back in a box," he said at last.

And then he surged to his feet. My back was suddenly cold.

"We should get some sleep," he told me.

TWENTY-TWO

Kate

BOONE WALKED AROUND to the far side of the fire and began to lay down. So we were back to that: him on one side, me on the other, like in the cave. But for the first time, I had a hint as to why. Something more than us being on opposite sides of the law. Something deeper and much more painful.

I slowly sank to my knees, looking down at the ground, then flinched as I saw a beetle scuttle across, right where I was about to lie. *Urgh.* By now, Boone was curled up on his side, his big form wound around the fire like a sleeping panther. I lay down facing him, my body more like a nervous cat.

I couldn't get comfortable. It's weird how wrong it feels, to sleep without anything *on* you, without a blanket or a comforter. And the temperature was dropping rapidly. God knows how cold it would have been if I'd stuck to my guns and we'd stayed up at the crash site. Down here, the cold wouldn't kill us...but that didn't mean I'd sleep well. My front was warmed by the fire but my back was freezing. I could feel all my muscles slowly chilling: by the time I woke up, they'd have set like concrete.

"Cold?" Boone's voice. I couldn't even see him, through the fire.

"I'm fine," I lied. And pulled the jacket he'd given me tighter around me. It did absolutely nothing to help. A few moments later, I gave my first shiver.

A huge, dark shape rose up on the other side of the fire. Heavy footsteps moved towards me. I felt him staring down at me. Then: "I could keep you warm. If that's okay."

I looked up at him. His face was in shadow, unreadable. Was he playing games? No. One thing about Mason: he was refreshingly free of all that.

I nodded.

He started to step over my body to get behind me. But when one foot was either side of me, when he stood over me like a colossus, he paused.

I was staring into the fire but I knew he was staring down at me.

I knew because I could feel every single stitch of my clothing being scorched from my body.

There was no doubt about how he felt about me. He wanted to grab me as much as—I flushed—as much as I wanted him to. But he was keeping that lust contained.

Just barely.

He stepped fully over me and lay down behind me. Then he shuffled closer and I gasped as his hard body pressed against mine. He was so big, he covered my back completely. His shins pressed against my calves and feet. His thighs pressed against my hamstrings. His groin nestled against my ass. When he inhaled, I felt his chest fill and press against my back. And when I shifted my head a little, I felt my braid press against his collarbone.

"Better?" he asked.

I nodded. Now my back was warm. But the fire was dying down and a chill wind was blowing through the trees and numbing my front.

"Still cold?" he murmured after a while.

I hesitated. Then nodded.

Three beats of my heart.

"Lift up," he told me, tapping my waist.

I pressed into the ground with my shoulder and ankles, hoisting my hips up off the ground for a second. I wasn't sure what he had in mind.

His arms reached around me and unzipped the borrowed jacket. He stripped it off me and then I heard him putting it on. *What? Now I'm colder!*

His arm hooked under me. His other arm hooked over the top of me. He dragged me back towards him, until we were pressed *tight*. Then he closed the sides of his jacket around me and zipped me in with him, his arms crossing to hold me in a hug.

It was the warmest, the safest, I'd felt since I'd gotten on the plane. No, wait. Scratch that.

It was the warmest and safest I'd felt in years.

His heat spread through me, melting me, until I wanted to just soak right into him. I could feel his slow breath stirring the loose hairs which had broken free of my braid.

And I slept.

***

I woke what must have been hours later. Long

enough for the fire to have died to a glow. Long enough that my body was comfortably lethargic from sleep.

I opened my eyes and found myself looking into another pair. A pair that glowed yellow in the darkness. A pair that floated only a few feet off the ground.

I stayed absolutely still as the wolf stepped out of the darkness.

I went cold, my chest tightening. But with Boone holding me, I wasn't scared. He said the wolves wouldn't bother us and I trusted him.

And he was right. The wolf didn't come any closer. It just stood there, white and gray fur lit up by the fire. It was beautiful and wild. Utterly untamed.

But I realized it wasn't what had woke me up.

Boone was muttering behind me, almost in my ear. That's what had attracted the wolf's attention. At first, I thought he was talking to me. It took me a few minutes to realize he was talking in his sleep.

It should have been cute. The muscled giant, mumbling about sex or some ex-girlfriend, giving me juicy secrets to tease him with the next morning. But it wasn't like that at all.

His arms had gone rock hard around me, every vein standing out. And the words weren't sultry confessions of love. They were guttural pantings and pleas.

He was having a nightmare.

I unzipped the jacket to give me room to move, then twisted around in his arms until I was staring at him, our faces only a few inches apart. His forehead was creased with worry, his face shining with sweat despite the cold. As I watched, his mouth twisted into a grimace. *Wake him? Don't wake him?*

He drew in a shuddering breath, his face contorting, and I felt my stomach twist in response. I couldn't watch him suffer. He'd put his body between me and the bear. He'd risked his life on the cliffs to come down and grab me.

"Mason?"

He didn't seem to hear me.

"Mason?"

This time his face twisted and his breathing became labored but he still didn't wake.

"Mason?" And I reached out and brushed his cheek.

His eyes snapped open faster than I would have thought possible. But they didn't seem to see *me*. His hands grabbed my waist and he rolled us over. My back hit the ground: I *oof*ed as the air was knocked out of me. Then he was on top of me, straddling me, and something was in his hand. Something that caught the light.

The homemade knife stabbed down, aimed straight at my heart.

TWENTY-THREE

Kate

I SHOULDN'T have had a chance. I was smaller than him, weaker than him. he was operating on pure, murderous instinct.

But I have instincts, too. Ones my dad helped me hone on a judo mat in our backyard, for hour after hour after hour. My wrists came up and crossed, braced under his forearms, before I was even aware of it.

The knife jerked to a stop, the point just pricking the front of my blouse. But Boone simply increased the pressure, leaning into the move, forcing the knife downward. I pushed up against him, giving it everything I had. But the knife pushed slowly down. The point made a neat little cut through the fabric of my blouse and sank between my breasts until its tip was millimeters from breaking the skin. I groaned and *heaved,* terror lending me strength, but he was way, way bigger than me.

"*Mason!*" I sobbed in desperation. "It's *me!*"

He growled and pressed and I felt my arms weaken—

And then his eyes opened wider and he rolled off me, panting. His face went white under his dark stubble. "Oh Jesus," he was saying. "Kate? *Kate?!*" I heard the knife land as he tossed it aside. Then he was on me again, this time grabbing at my blouse, tearing open the top to check me.

We both looked down. My chest was heaving with exertion and fear but there was no blood.

Boone slumped in relief beside me.

"What the hell was that?" I asked when I could breathe again. I was scared and my voice was still ragged. It came out more aggressive than I wanted it to.

Boone met my eyes for an instant. I've never seen anyone so eaten up with guilt. Then he shook his head and stood up.

"Mason?"

He walked around to the far side of the fire and lay down, facing away from me.

"Mason?"

I knew he wasn't asleep. But he wasn't talking, either.

I slowly lay down, never taking my eyes off him. I should have been terrified of him. I should never have trusted him again.

But this wasn't him. This was something inside him, the thing that tried to rule him. This was why he'd kept pushing me away. Maybe it was even part of the reason he was up here.

My heart seemed to unfold as I stared across the embers at that huge, strong back. I thought of him out here on his own, every night, haunted by those nightmares. *He shouldn't have to deal with it on his own.*

And lying there in the darkness, staring at him, I made up my mind. *He doesn't have to.*

I was going to help him beat this thing.

I couldn't sleep. I reached behind me and felt the ground. There was a warm spot where Boone had been lying but it was fading fast. And without his arms around me, the dark forest seemed to close in.

After an hour of tossing and turning, I sat up, dug under my clothes and pulled out the prisoner files. Setting Boone's aside, I opened up Weiss's. I wanted to know the bastard who'd gotten us into this mess.

I thought I knew what I'd find. A working-class con man who'd worked his way up, scamming bigger and bigger fish until he managed to pull off the ultimate white collar crime.

But I was wrong. I was so, so wrong.

Carlton Weiss had been born in New Hampshire to Suzanna and Martin Weiss, one of three brothers. The mother was a lawyer. The father ran one of the biggest transport companies in the northeast. The family was *rich.* A happy, well-adjusted, wealthy family.

Except for Carlton.

There was a psych evaluation from all the way back in high school. The counselor had reported aggressive tendencies, extreme arrogance, even raised the possibility of something more serious that might be developing. She strongly recommended follow up. But there was a note written beneath the report: *family declined further treatment.*

Carlton's dad hadn't wanted his son being marked out as disturbed.

The next piece of paperwork was from Carlton's

first arrest, while he was still a teenager. One of the maids who worked for the family had reported that he'd assaulted her in a bedroom. The police had brought Carlton in...but that was it. No charges, no nothing. I suspected Daddy had paid the woman off. If some dutiful cop hadn't insisted on filing the paperwork instead of burning it, there never would have been any trace.

Carlton returned home as if nothing had happened. His first life lesson: the rules didn't apply to him.

The other two brothers went to Harvard to get their MBAs. Carlton didn't make the grade and wound up at NYU. There were a string of discipline reports there for drinking and later drug use. He was finally kicked out in his senior year for running a scam where he'd claim to be acting as the middleman for a group of professors, promising students they could buy a guaranteed passing grade on their finals for one thousand dollars apiece. He'd fooled over a hundred and fifty students into parting with their money and wound up keeping most of it—no one wanted to come forward and admit they'd paid him, and risk expulsion themselves for cheating.

The experience made him bolder. He hadn't graduated but he'd finished college with more money than any of his friends. And now he'd seen his path in life: separating what he saw as idiots from their money.

While the other two brothers followed their dad into the family business, Carlton disappeared for a few years. There were reports of him operating in Paris, London, Chicago and Boston. His name was linked to a number of other slimy financial scammers. I suspected that was his training period: he'd found a handful of people to mentor him and he was learning everything he could. He also popped up in The Bahamas and Switzerland. He was learning everything he could about offshore accounts and hiding money.

There were two more arrest reports, one for sexual assault and battery, one for rape. My insides filled with freezing water as I thought about how close I'd been to him on the plane. Again, the charges were dropped. Once, the woman changed her mind. I wondered if she'd been paid off or threatened.

Once, the victim disappeared.

There was a psych report, too, from when he'd been brought in on the rape charge. A psychologist had spent an hour in the room with him and had noted sociopathic tendencies. *Weiss shows no regard for others,* he'd written. *Almost total lack of empathy or remorse.* He'd also believed Weiss to be suffering from narcissistic personality disorder. Even on the photocopied paper, I could see the deep, outraged depressions the psychologist's pen had made as he wrote, as if he wished he could be branding the words onto Weiss's face as a warning. *Believes the role of others is to serve him or provide him with money or sexual satisfaction. Willing or unwilling.*

The warning signs the school psychologist had noted had developed into full-blown psychosis. All the pieces had fallen into place. Weiss had the experience in scamming people and the knowledge of how to hide the money. He had a burning resentment that he was considered the black sheep of the family and he was convinced his destiny was to become as rich as them, or richer. And he had the utterly cold, sociopathic mindset to get there. That's how he'd pulled off the biggest financial scam in US history: *he'd simply believed he had the right.*

Now I understood how he'd killed the pilot so easily. How he'd been willing to discard Marshal Phillips the instant it suited him. Did the men he had working for him know he was out of his mind?

I got colder and colder, thinking about it. It wasn't just that a man like Weiss existed. I work for the FBI: I'm not naive about what monsters are out there. But when I closed the file and put it next to Boone's....

One of them was innocent and had been forced into a life of exile.

One of them was guilty and was about to begin a life of unimaginable luxury.

The system I'd dedicated my whole life to had completely failed.

I slipped the files back into the top of my pants and lay down, staring at Boone on the other side of the fire. My instincts had been right about him from the start. He was a good man. We needed more guys like him around. Instead, he was up here in the mountains and it was Weiss who got to be around people. I shuddered.

There was only one note of comfort, one thing that let me sleep. By now, Weiss would be well on his way to Russia. He was a long way from me.

TWENTY-FOUR

Weiss

I GAZED DOWN at her sleeping body. The drone was four hundred feet up but the camera made her seem close enough to touch, the night vision system turning the darkness to noon. She was on her side, arms and legs tucked in tight against the cold. Her blouse was open down to her bra, either unbuttoned or ripped, and I could see the curve of one smooth, firm breast.

Bitch.

I couldn't believe they'd made it all the way down the mountain. We were still on the far side, having had to take gentler slopes that the 4x4s could traverse. We might not even have found them, if it hadn't been for the drone. The Russians had brought it over with them in case they had trouble finding us after we bailed out. Now it was going to let us track Boone and Kate until we could catch up with them.

Track them...and watch them. I touched the screen, tracing all the way from Kate's shoulder to her hip. She tensed in her sleep, as if she could feel me.

I'd been watching her all evening. It amused me, seeing her shivering cold and trying to make a meal out of some animal Boone had caught. I was sitting in the back of one of the 4x4s, the heater running, drinking the Russian's vodka. The mercenaries had griped when I'd grabbed it off them, saying it was for them. I'd told them I'd see that they got $10,000 extra when we got to Russia and they'd shut the hell up.

For a while, I'd thought Boone had been going to fuck her. But all he'd done was spoon with her, fully clothed, and then when I next checked they were sleeping on opposite sides of the fire. Maybe he couldn't get it up. Or maybe her legs were closed as tight as that irritating braid.

They'd both get it. They owed me for delaying my escape to Russia. Boone could pay in blood. And Kate?

I was rapidly developing plans for Kate.

TWENTY-FIVE

Kate

"It's so...*quiet,*" I said.

We'd left the forest and were trekking across flat, grassy scrubland towards the river. It was easy going, after the mountain, even though my shoes definitely weren't designed for hiking. But it was eerily silent. Aside from the occasional bird call and the soft sound of the wind, there was nothing. I'd never realized how noisy cities are: even in a quiet suburb, there's always the background rumble of traffic.

I glanced at Boone as we walked. "Seriously, doesn't it drive you just a little bit crazy?"

He looked at me. Looked at the landscape. Shook his head.

"Shouldn't we be trying to make a noise?" I asked. "In case of bears?"

Boone glanced around at the knee-high grass. "Pretty sure a bear would see us coming," he rumbled.

He was even less talkative than normal and I knew why: he didn't want to talk about his nightmare, or how he'd nearly stabbed me. I did. But I knew that, if I wanted to help him, I had to feel my way carefully. Small talk would be a start. But Boone didn't *do* small talk.

I wasn't giving up, though. He'd saved my life more than once. I had to try.

When we reached a stream, Boone stopped. He looked behind us, then all around.

"What?" I asked. "You hear something?"

He just stood there, legs braced, gazing around. Sometimes, he put me in mind of an animal, up on his hind legs, ears pricked up. He finally shook his head, like it was nothing. But his expression didn't say *nothing*. It said he hadn't been able to find it.

The stream wasn't big but the water would be near-freezing. There were a couple of rocks which could be used as stepping stones: if we were careful, we could stay dry.

Boone went first. Thanks to his longer legs, getting to the first rock was just a long stride. For me, it meant almost doing the splits. I stretched out my front leg as far as I could...and Boone grabbed my hand and helped me pull myself across. I landed next to him, the two of us pressed up together on a rock no bigger than a coffee table.

"Tell me about Koyuk," I blurted. "How'd you get caught?"

He stared down at me, breathing hard from hauling me in. He gave me a tiny shake of his head.

But I just stared up at him determinedly. He wasn't ready to share everything—fine. But he could tell me *this*.

Those blue eyes narrowed, frustrated...and then, as he kept staring at me, I saw his expression change.

His eyes were still on my face but...they kept flicking down—

I looked down. I realized I was breathing hard, too, my chest rising and falling. And my blouse was still gaping open from when he'd ripped it.

I looked up into his eyes and the lust I saw there made me catch my breath. It was so raw, so primal, like the ripped blouse was just a hint of what he wanted to do to me, as if my clothes, right now, were just a hindrance. Then he looked away and glanced back at me, angry. *Remember how that happened,* his gaze said.

He thought he was dangerous. He thought he needed to stay away.

I shook my head. *You're wrong.*

"Koyuk," I said quietly. "Tell me."

He turned away and looked towards the next rock. This one was pretty close: he'd barely even have to stretch. "I go there sometimes for supplies. Things I can't make myself. It's okay. Small. The people don't bother me." He shrugged. "Got into a fight. Someone called the cops."

He stepped to the next rock. He extended his hand back behind him so I could take it, but he didn't look around at me. He'd hunched over slightly, his huge back like a rock face between us.

I stepped out, grabbed his hand and hauled myself across. This rock was even smaller: I was pressed right up against his back. "How?" I pressed. "How'd you get in a fight?" Was it something bad? Something he thought would make me hate him? It didn't matter. To help him, I had to know him.

He was looking towards the far bank. It was going to need a jump, even for him. He bent his knees a little, readying himself–

I grabbed his arm. "How'd you get in a fight?" I asked again.

He looked around at me, his blue eyes furious, now. Denying what I could feel between us. Telling me to leave it alone.

I've never been very good at leaving it alone. That's why I joined the FBI. I stared right back at him.

"I heard a noise," he said at last. "Coming from one of the houses." He looked away. "A scream."

I waited. In the middle of all that vastness, we stood like statues, together on one tiny rock.

He looked away. "I saw a guy leave, and he left the door open behind him a little, so I looked in." His lips tightened. "It was his wife. He'd taken a steam iron to her face. So I chased after him. Caught up with him as he went into the bar." He paused. "He won't do it again."

That's why he'd been reluctant to tell me: because it was something that might make me like him. I wanted to hug him. Hell, I wanted to throw myself against that big, strong chest.

He looked down at me and must have seen something in my expression. One big hand came down on my shoulder.

I held my breath.

He shook his head. "I'll make sure you're safe, Kate," he told me. "That's all. Don't forget what I am."

Then he turned and leapt across to the far bank, out of reach.

I caught myself. *He's right.* Assuming we even made it back to civilization, we had zero future. He was a fugitive and I was FBI. He was headed for jail or, if I didn't turn him in, back to the wilderness.

Either way, I'd never see him again. *Stupid! What were you thinking, Kate?*

A sudden heat flashed across my face, a kind I hadn't let myself feel for a long, long time. At work, I never wanted anyone to get the idea that I was weak. It's hard enough being a woman in the FBI, never mind a small one, without that. I'd sometimes dig my nails into my palms so hard they left deep, red marks rather than cry. There had been times, working cases involving kids, where I'd walked two blocks during my lunch break, just so I could find a nice private diner with a bathroom where I could let it all out.

Now, though, I was standing out in the middle of the stream, with nowhere to run. Boone was watching me with that same, stoic expression...but I could see in his eyes that he felt guilty, that it hurt him to push me away. That made it even worse.

I turned my face into the breeze so that it would cool it. Then I gathered up all my strength, took the one step run-up the rock allowed and *leaped,* putting every bit of anger and frustration into it. And short legs or not, I sailed right past his goddamn hand and made it onto the bank—just—stumbled a little and then marched on.

For a few seconds, there was silence behind me. I got a good few steps before he shook off his shock and walked after me. That gave me a little burst of pride.

We were following an animal path, little more than a break in the grass, and in places it was completely overgrown. He let me lead for a minute or so, but I could feel it building in the air. He knew he'd hurt my feelings. "Kate?"

I couldn't turn around. He was right. I was wrong. It would never work, between us. The heat in my face came back, worse than before.

"Kate?"

He was closer, now. So I sped up. I thumped my feet hard into the grass with each step but it didn't relieve the pressure that was building inside, ready to burst out as tears. He was going to force me to turn around and then he'd see—

He was right behind me. "Kate!"

I ruptured inside and half-turned, still walking. "*ALRIGHT!*" I snapped. "I get it!" Tears sprang to my traitorous eyes. *Shit!* "I was being stupid. We're not—"

His eyes were as icy as he could make them. But I could still see the warmth inside. And then his expression changed in a split second and he lunged forward and grabbed my hand and *wrenched,* throwing himself back at the same time. My arm snapped taut so fast it burned and then I was flying through the air.

TWENTY-SIX

Kate

BOONE LANDED HARD on the path on his back. An instant later, I slammed down on top of him. All my senses were reeling. I could smell the fresh, clean scent of him, feel the warmth of his body. He was panting. I was panting. His chest lifted me as it rose and fell.

I crooked my head back so I could look into his eyes. *What. The. Hell?!*

His hands clamped around my waist and he half sat-up, bringing me with him. Then he lifted me as if I were a doll, shifting me to the side so he could look down the length of my body. Checking me over. "You okay?" His voice was strained with fear. "You hurt?"

I shook my head, breathless and still bemused. My chest was still pressed to his, my breasts pillowed against the hard slabs of his pecs.

He sank back to the path, closing his eyes. He let out a groan that turned into a tiny chuckle.

I'd heard that sound before. It was the laugh I'd

heard when we reunited a parent with their missing child. When the body releases all its fear and just slumps, defenseless, because it's back with someone—

Someone it really cares about.

I swallowed and looked away. Then I started to get up.

He grabbed me. Our eyes locked. I was suddenly very aware that I was poised over him, straddling him, with my blouse gaping open. My cleavage was practically in front of his face.

I tried not to stare at that full, soft lower lip. I tried not to think about how it would feel if he just leaned down and kissed me right now.

"Slowly," he warned. "Don't move any further on the path."

We rose together, his hands on my waist. Part of me was trying to work out what the hell he'd seen. Part of me was thinking about how good those hands felt.

We looked along the path, our breathing slowing to normal. "See it?" he asked.

I shook my head.

"Yeah," he muttered. "That's why they're so evil."

He picked up a stick and took a couple of small steps forward, back to where I'd been when he'd grabbed me. Then he crouched and used the stick to part the grass.

Metal. Little triangles pointing up at the sky, sharp and brutally strong. They were attached to a thick band of steel. He cleared away more of the grass. The teeth ran in a big oval, and in the center was a bar and a set of powerful springs.

A bear trap. I'd only ever seen one in old movies.

I'd been about to put my foot right in it.

It took me a few seconds before I could speak. “People *use* those? They just leave them....” I trailed off.

“It’s on an animal trail. Designed to catch the bear when it comes down to the stream to drink.” He stood, turned the stick vertically and then brought the end of it down onto the sprung bar, just as my foot would have done.

The trap moved so fast, I couldn’t see it. The sound was like nothing I’d ever heard, a dead sound, the steel so heavy and thick that it didn’t resonate. The teeth slammed into each other with a snap but then the sound just *stopped.* That would be the moment. That would be when the pain hit.

Boone slowly moved the stick aside. It was just a stump now, the lower piece on the path, the ends shattered into splinters. “It’s designed to break the leg,” he said bitterly. “So the bear can’t walk away, dragging the trap. It has to stay there until the hunter comes.”

I wanted to throw up. That would have been my leg. My bones shattered, my arteries cut. Lying there on the path with no hope of rescue. I would have died out here.

“Is it even legal?” I asked at last.

“Out here, not everybody cares.” He poked the trap. “Some of these traps are fifty years old, passed down within families.”

I looked around at the landscape. Just as I thought I had a handle on it, Alaska hit me again with how utterly different it was. And then I remembered that *he* hunted. “Do...do *you* use—”

He shook his head. “I catch rabbits. Deer. I do it quick. Don’t like them to suffer.” He picked up the trap, walked a few steps towards the creek and then hurled it. I heard it splash.

As he passed me on his way back, he caught my eye and his step faltered. All that effort he'd made to push me away and all the effort I'd made to convince him I was fine with it. And it had nearly gotten me killed.

He stood there and just stared at me. His eyes were almost angry but not angry at *me*. Angry at the world, that it had put me in front of him: something he couldn't shut out and ignore. He put out his hand and slowly cupped my cheek and I melted into his warmth, pressing my face against his fingers. He looked down at me as if I was the most frustratingly irresistible thing in the world.

He gave a tiny nod of his head. An admission that things had changed. An admission that he felt it, too.

He lowered his hand but, instead of going on ahead, he fell into step beside me. We walked for a few minutes in silence, both of us feeling our way. At last he muttered, "What about you?"

"What about me...what?"

"I told you how I wound up out here. How'd you wind up in the FBI?"

I blinked. I hadn't expected it to go there. Didn't want it to go there. But I'd asked him enough questions. If I wanted him to open up, I couldn't be a closed book myself.

I looked ahead along the path. We were coming out of the scrubland and back into forest. I focused on the trees. "My sister," I said. "Marcy. I was eight and she was six. One day, she never came home from school. Didn't get on the bus. Just...gone. We had an amber alert, the police, the whole nine yards."

I felt him looking across at me. "And the FBI got

her back?"

I focused very hard on the trees. "No," I said. "They didn't."

It's funny. I think of Marcy a lot at work. I think back to the memories and the anger burns white-hot. I use it to power me, when it's four in the morning and I'm still digging through files for clues. I use it to blast through the layers of arrogance and bullshit, when I'm interrogating some guy who's twice the size of me. I use it to forge armor of iron and steel for when the guys at work put me down because I'm a woman....even though wearing that armor can make it very cold.

But when I talked to Boone, the anger didn't flare up. It hurt but I didn't have to turn it into anything. I could feel the shape of it. I could feel what was inside it: the cold and emptiness.

"For the first few days, there was a lot of activity. Houses got searched. Posters went up. But after...I don't know, a week? There was this creeping sense that...*that was it*. We'd got used to seeing the same cops, the same detectives...but gradually, they started to be pulled off for other assignments. They used to call every day with an update, then it became once every two days, then once a week."

I kept walking towards the trees. My legs were starting to ache but moving kept me focused, kept me in the *now* and not back in that house, coming home from school every day to find my parents' faces a little more gray, a little more resolved.

"The local police gave up," I said. "The state police gave up. There were no leads. But I was just a kid. I didn't understand things like leads and evidence. I just wanted answers. I knew she wasn't coming back but I knew someone had taken her and I wanted them caught. I wanted justice. And I wanted to know what happened." I shook my head. "It was like...it was like I'd got to the end of a book, my favorite book ever, and the last page had been torn out. And I knew it was going to be a sad ending but I *had to know.*"

Beside me, Boone changed course to walk a little nearer, his body towering over mine. I could feel him looking down at me with that look I'd seen on the plane, that fierce, protective gleam in his eyes, like he'd happily kill everyone who'd ever hurt me. I didn't dare look at him. Already, the trees ahead were growing blurry.

"Six months after it happened, the posters were still all over the neighborhood. Because no one wanted to take them down, you know? But they were frayed at the edges and the ink had run. You could barely even tell it was her anymore. Everyone had given up hope."

I felt my expression change. My lips pressed together and then formed a grim, sorrowful smile. "But there was this *one guy,*" I said. "FBI. Special Agent McKillen. He didn't give up. He was there right from the start and he just kept going and going, pulling at these tiny threads no one else could see. When they pulled him off it, he kept working the case in his own time. And finally, *finally,* he put it all together."

"He kicked down the door of a house in Boston and arrested a guy, and when they took the house apart, they found the bones of three little girls, all from different cities. And one of them was Marcy." My chest ached–it didn't normally hit me like this, but sharing it with Boone was different. It hurt, but for the first time in years I felt the release, too, just like when they'd found her.

I blinked and the trees ahead went swimmy and then sharp again. "That's why I joined the FBI," I said. "Because people shouldn't get away with things like that. We need to bring them down, even if it takes forever. There's got to be justice. Otherwise, what's any of it worth?"

For the first time, I dared to look at him. His face was stony. "You think that's bullshit, don't you?"

"Justice wasn't so good to me."

"That was the system," I told him. "Not justice."

We plunged into the forest. This time, we made sure to walk loudly, crashing through the undergrowth, in case there were any bears around.

I tried to keep my voice casual, keep it light. "What we talked about before," I said, "the charges against you—"

"No."

I glanced sideways at him. "I could help you," I said. "We could appeal. Force Hopkins to take the stand, get all sorts of character witnesses for you—"

"*No.*"

I stepped in front of him, so he had to stop. "It's not *right,* Mason!" I pointed behind us. "You've got an entire life waiting for you, back in civilization! You don't have to be out here!"

"And what if you're wrong?" he growled, scowling down at me. "What if you bring me in and they crush the appeal? Or the appeal happens and we lose? They put me back in a box and—"

He took a long, shuddering breath as if trying to bring himself under control. "I've made my peace with it."

"Bullshit," I said viciously. "It's eating you up inside. Hopkins is living free and you're living like *this.*"

"At least I'm alive!" he snapped. He stared at me for a few seconds. "Didn't you wonder why nobody else spoke up for me? Why all the SEALs in my unit let me get court martialled? They're all *dead,* Kate. The unit got wiped out while I was—" He went silent for a moment. "While I was MIA." He shook his head at me. "Character witnesses? There *are* no character witnesses. No one's going to believe me."

And he pushed past me and stalked on through the forest.

TWENTY-SEVEN

Boone

Goddamn it!

I knew she was right. Sure, there were no character witnesses and sure, an appeal was a long shot, but of course it was worth the gamble. Of course it was worth risking twenty years in jail when the alternative was *my whole life* spent in exile.

Unless you were me.

Unless there was something inside you just waiting for the cuffs to go on and the door to close so it could rush up and own your mind. That was the real reason I couldn't turn myself in. Even if the appeal *worked,* I'd still have to do time in a cell until it happened. She didn't understand what that would be like. And she couldn't. Even if I could find some way to explain it to her, just telling her would put me back there, would open up the door in my mind that I kept tight shut.

And there was another reason, too. I didn't want her to see me like that. I didn't want her to think of me that way. I didn't want her to know I was broken.

And hell, now it was making me paranoid: out in the scrubland, again I'd sworn I could feel someone watching us.

I listened to her behind me, to those soft, feminine footsteps. I didn't dare turn around and look at her because the feelings were getting too strong. Damn it, when I'd seen her about to step in the trap I'd felt fear like I'd never known, worse than if it had been *my* leg. When she'd been lying on top of me, those soft breasts spilling out of her ruined blouse, her thighs straddling mine.... I closed my eyes for a second, remembering the feel of her waist in my hands.

My footsteps slowed.

No.

My hands came up, fingers flexing.

No.

There was a tree right next to me. I was going to turn around, grab hold of her waist again and ram her up against it. I didn't care anymore. Those lips were mine. That blouse was coming off. *I'm going to kiss every inch of her body—*

No!

I stopped. My hands tightened into fists.

"Mason?" Her voice like silk. She was incredible. Brave. Smart. I felt it all tugging at me: everything I'd given up when I fled out here: not just sex but *being* with someone.

I'd thought I was okay. I'd told myself I didn't need any company but my own. I'd been wrong, so wrong.

She was right behind me, now. Her voice grew even softer. "Mason?"

I couldn't go to New York. I couldn't make a life even in a small town. Everything was computerized, now. The first time I visited a hospital, the first time I rented a car or tried to open a bank account, some computer screen would turn red and the cops or the military police would descend on me in minutes. The only place I had a shot was right here in Alaska.

And this was no place for someone like Kate.

Hell, it was even worse than before. After four years, I figured I'd dropped off the radar. But now the military knew exactly where I was. And when the authorities found the crash site and discovered I didn't die in the crash, the military would come looking. I'd have to hunker down harder than ever. I might not be able to risk going to a town for six months or more. Maybe I could manage that, but Kate?

"Mason?" she asked. "What is it?"

It didn't matter how much I wanted her. It didn't matter how much I needed her. If I wanted to do the best thing for her, I had to get her to safety...and then let her go. And the closer I let her get, the more painful that moment would be when it happened.

"Nothing," I grunted. "Just getting my bearings."

She stepped in front of me, making me look at her. "You figure it out?"

I nodded, unable to speak. And continued on.

***

We hiked through the forest for the rest of the day. I managed to find some more berries to eat. Then, around noon, I stabbed four small fish as they swam past my feet in a creek and cooked them on a flat stone over a fire. It wasn't much but it would keep us alive until I could get us to the cabin.

The sun was setting when we neared the river. But

even before I could see it, I knew something was wrong. The sound was too loud, too wild. We broke through the final few trees and I cursed.

The river ran through a gully, here, the water twenty feet below us. And instead of being a calm flow it was a raging, white-topped beast. As I watched, a tree branch washed past, flashing by us in seconds.

"We have to cross *that?!"* asked Kate.

"It's not normally this fast and deep. I always cross in the morning—you can wade across, then. It gets worse in the afternoon: the sun melts the snow during the day." I looked across the river. "*Dammit.* My cabin's only a few miles from here."

"So what do we do?" She looked down into the gully. There were no rocks, like at the stream. "Do we swim?"

"God, no. It's mainly melt water. Ice cold. Swimming, we wouldn't make it halfway across even without the current. And it's too strong: it'd smack us into a rock." I looked downstream. "Come on. Let's take a look further down."

But things were no better half a mile downstream. If anything, the river was deeper and fiercer.

Then I found the log.

A tree had toppled, right at the edge of the gully. The trunk made a bridge across. Kate looked at the tree, looked down at the water and went green. "You're not serious?"

I weighed it up in my mind. The trunk was thick and, when I thumped it with my boot, it seemed sturdy. It wasn't going to move. If I'd been on my own, I would have climbed across it without a second thought. But I knew Kate hated heights.

On the other hand, I didn't want her to have to

spend another night in the open. It would be dark soon and we'd left it too late to find a good spot to camp. What's more, I knew where I was: my cabin was less than two miles away. If we got across the river, we could spend the night in comfort. And however irrational it was, however much I knew it must just be paranoia, I still kept feeling like there was someone watching us. All my instincts were screaming at me to get my woman somewhere safe and warm.

My woman?!

Idiot.

I turned to Kate. "It's your call," I told her. "We can climb across and get to the cabin tonight or we can camp one more night and wade across tomorrow when the river's down."

She took a long look at the log. Then she looked around at the darkening forest. The temperature was dropping: it was already colder than the previous night. She pulled her borrowed jacket tighter around her.

"Let's climb across."

TWENTY-EIGHT

Kate

"I'll go first," said Boone. "To make sure it's solid."

"You're not sure it's solid?!" I started to second-guess my decision.

"It feels solid. But just in case it's rotten in the center. If it takes my weight, it'll take yours."

He straddled the log like a horse, then began to shuffle out over the water. I made the mistake of looking down into the gully and my stomach twisted. The light was fading fast. The water was just roaring, glossy blackness, only visible when it crashed against rocks and turned to white foam.

Boone reached the center: God, he was so far away! He bounced up and down a few times and I saw the log flex just a little. I drew in a horrified breath.

"Seems okay," he said. "I'm going to keep going."

I dug my nails into my palms as he shuffled further and further away. He'd almost disappeared into the darkness when he swung his leg over and climbed off. Safe.

"Piece of cake!" he yelled.

I looked down at the river. "Don't do that!"

"Do what?"

"Be all reassuring!" As I stepped towards the log, I felt sick. I'd changed my mind. It was higher and darker and the river was louder than I'd thought. *We should have camped.*

"Kate?" he called. "I can come back. If you've changed your mind, it's okay."

I opened my mouth. But as soon as I did, I felt every guy who'd ever patronized me waiting with baited breath.

I closed my mouth again. And climbed onto the log.

"You'll be fine," called Boone. I could just make him out as a silhouette on the far side. "Just keep two hands on it and use your legs to shuffle along." Then I saw him slap at his leg.

"What was that?"

"Nothing. A bug."

I took a deep breath and shuffled out over the water. The light was going fast, now. The log was black, the water was black. I could barely see where I was putting my hands. But the wood did feel solid. I told myself that, if the log was sitting on the ground, I wouldn't think twice about it. It was plenty strong enough and wide enough. *Just forget the water's there.*

Except...I couldn't forget it. The further out I shuffled, the more the crashing of the water surrounded me. The air felt different, too, wet and freezing cold with spray, as if the river was reaching up to grab me.

"You're doing great," called Boone. "Nearly

halfway."

I tried to make it mechanical: reach forward with my hands, shuffle forward with my ass. Reach forward with my hands, shuffle forward with my ass. Reach for—

I screamed and pulled my hand back, heart pounding.

"What?" yelled Boone.

I'd put my hand on something and it had moved. "I don't know!" I yelled, my voice high with panic.

But I did know. My mind was just trying to deny it. It had been small and hard-shelled and it had scurried under my palm. A stab of fear shot up my spine.

I stared at the log, but there was no detail, just a silhouette. I couldn't see where to safely put my hands.

"Kate?" yelled Boone.

I was taking big, quick panic breaths through my nose, now, my eyes searching the log. And then, as my eyes adjusted to the gloom—

The surface of the log was moving.

I choked back a scream.

They were pouring out of a hole. Little shiny-shelled beetles, thousands of them. The log was their home and Boone's passage had woken them up.

I tried to shuffle backward but I didn't dare put my hands down. I humped my ass back but it was too slow, too slow—

"Kate! Be careful!" Boone yelled.

And then the beetles reached me. They spread out as they hit my spread thighs. Some ran over my knees and up my legs. Some went straight over my groin and up over my pants to—

Oh Jesus tiny legs scurrying up inside my flapping

blouse, over my stomach *they're on me they're on me—*

"*KATE!*" Boone was climbing onto the log. "*HOLD ON! HOLD ONTO THE LOG!*"

They were surging up my body, inside and outside my blouse, over my breasts and collarbone, heading for my mouth. I slapped with both hands, tearing at my clothes, twisting around so I could climb back the way I'd come—

"*KATE!*"

I felt my balance go, my legs sliding on the wood—

And then I was falling.

TWENTY-NINE

Kate

IT WAS SO DARK, I couldn't tell how far away the water was. I could just hear the roar as it waited to consume me.

Then I plunged in and it was so brutally, unimaginably cold, it didn't even feel like water. It felt like I'd been driven into solid ice, shards of it scraping and clawing at my body, biting right down to the bone. Water at freezing point isn't liquid: it's pain.

It was in my mouth, in my lungs. I was a good swimmer. I knew to kick for the surface and I kicked...but every movement drove more cold into my muscles, making them scream. I kicked harder, desperate, trying to reach light and air....

But when I broke the surface, it was just as dark as underwater. And the air was filled with spray that blinded me and crashing waves that smacked me in the face, making it impossible to breathe. I couldn't get my bearings. I couldn't see *anything*. But I knew I was moving: I could feel myself spinning around, rising and falling with terrifying speed.

The river had me.

And then the sound of the river changed. Right ahead, the water was smacking against something, the steady roar becoming chaos.

Rocks. And I was heading straight for them.

THIRTY

Boone

SEAL. It stands for *Sea, Air and Land.* Cute acronym or not, there's a reason they put the *sea* part first. We're Navy, before we're anything else. Just because you'll find us in a desert these days doesn't mean we've forgotten that. Right from the very first day of training, we were in the water.

The old reflexes kicked in. I was leaping as soon as I saw her start to fall. I hit the water only a second or two after she did.

When I surfaced, I couldn't see anything. But I knew she was ahead of me. I felt for the current, controlled my spin so I'd be looking right at her. *Jesus* it was cold. If I didn't reach her fast, she was dead.

I still had a couple of the emergency flares left and—thank God—they were waterproof. I struck one and held it as high above my head as I could, but the sputtering red glow only went about ten feet out. And Kate was nowhere in sight. *Shit!*

I hurled the flare as hard as I could into the air ahead of me. The glow got fainter but wider...and there she was, being thrown around like a twig. "*KATE!*"

Oh God, she was heading for rocks. She'd be slammed against them and hit her head and that would be it. "*Left!*" I yelled. *"Go left!"*

She swam hard left, pushing against the current. She flashed past the rocks with less than a foot to spare. But there were more up ahead—

The flare went out.

The cold was unbelievable, soaking into every bone. But that wasn't what made it difficult to breathe, or what made my hand shake as I fished the last flare from my pocket. It was fear, fear for her. I struck the flare. Hurled it.

She was past the next set of rocks but...Oh Jesus, she was limp. She was floating like a ragdoll on the surface. She must have hit her head. I watched as her body was carried up against a fallen tree and pinned there by the current. The water pounded against her chest and neck, forcing her down and back. Forcing her under.

I swam. Harder than I ever swam in our most brutal training. Harder than on any op.

But I saw her slip beneath the surface.

And then the final flare went out.

THIRTY-ONE

Boone

ABSOLUTE. TOTAL. BLACKNESS. It was worse because the light from the flares had killed whatever night vision I'd had. I had to go by sound and by feel. I only had seconds to get her back above the surface. It might already be too late.

I had a mental image of where the fallen tree was and I kicked in that direction for all I was worth. But I had to try to figure out when I was going to hit it. The current was carrying me fast and I was swimming full speed on top of that. If I smacked into the tree and went under, we were both dead.

Three. Two. One. I put both hands out, feeling for it. Nothing....

I cried out as something sliced sideways across my palm. A root or a branch. The current had turned me around and I'd almost been carried right past the end of the tree. I grabbed hold of it with both hands and clung there for a second, getting my bearings. Then I started hauling myself along the trunk.

The water was pounding into my side, neck and head, doing its best to push me under. I could only catch every third or fourth breath. But I kept going until I figured I was where I'd seen her go under.

I filled my lungs...and dived.

As soon as I let go of the tree, the current slammed me forward. I felt my way down under the trunk, down into the web of branches that had trapped rocks, mud and anything else that had come down the river. The current pinned me against it—helping me, in a way. The hard part would be getting back out.

I swam further and further down. My hands felt like solid blocks of ice. There was barely any feeling in my fingers. If I felt her, would I even recognize her?

More bark. Twigs. Rocks. I felt my fingers touch a solid surface. I'd reached the river bed. Had I missed her? Dived in the wrong place?

My fingers felt something that might have been the fabric of her suit, flapping in the current. I felt for it, but I couldn't find it again. *Shit!* Had it just been a leafy branch?

Then I felt it. Soft and flexible. Knobbly. Silky smooth.

I'd know that braid anywhere.

I felt my way to her head, her shoulders. My chest closed up tight. She was as freezing cold as the rocks. Was she already gone?

Don't think like that.

I wound one arm under her arms and pulled her against me. Then I struck for the surface. But now I was trying to haul two of us out against the current, and I could only use one arm. My lungs were aching with the need to breathe. My legs felt like frozen, knotted rubber and every kick sent a new wave of jagged pain through them. *We aren't going to make it.* The current was too strong. My muscles were already too cold, too tired. I felt myself starting to slip backward.

And then her head bobbed back against my shoulder, as if she were looking up at me, that tight little braid tickling my collarbone. The whole of her body was pressed against mine, so small, so fragile, and yet so strong.

Goddamn it.

Goddamn it, you are not taking her. Not Kate. And I kicked against the pain, clawing at the water like I was tearing the Grim Reaper's eyes out. *Not her. Not Kate.*

My lungs were bursting. Every muscle in my legs was raw, burning agony.

Not Kate.

And I broke the surface. As soon as I stopped and gasped for air, the current slammed me back against the fallen tree, bruising my ribs. But I had her.

Holding onto her meant I only had one arm to try to haul us up out of the water. I grabbed hold of a branch, realizing too late that I'd used my injured hand. I gritted my teeth and kept going, my biceps straining as I pulled us up the side of the fallen tree and onto the top. Then I picked her up and carried her to the bank.

But she lay unmoving in my arms, a cold dead weight against my chest. I'd spent enough time in the blackness, now, that my eyes had adjusted again and my stomach lurched when I saw her skin was pure white. *No!*

I laid her down in the grass, pried open her mouth and started CPR. But when I pressed down on her chest, it was like practicing on a training dummy, cold and stiff. There was no life left in her. *This can't be her*. This couldn't be Kate, with her stubbornness and her bravery and her fire. With her voice like silk and her judo and her braid. *Come on, Kate!*

Her lips were normally a beautiful delicate blush-pink. They'd gone gray-blue.

I covered them with mine and breathed hot life into her. Saw her chest fill but there was no cough, no heartbeat. I went back to chest compressions, my teeth gritted. This time, I said it aloud. "Come on, Kate!"

Nothing.

I let out something like a growl and breathed into her again, all of my rage at the universe going into her. But her limp body just seemed to absorb the heat. The air slowly left her again, as if she couldn't accept it.

My eyes were wet. I pumped her chest again, pressing so hard I thought I was going to bust her ribs. "*Come on!*" I yelled. *"Come on!"*

But the darkened forest absorbed my cries and her frozen body absorbed my efforts and she just lay there, unmoving.

I'd lost her.

Silent, hot tears were running down my cheeks and falling onto her face.

I'd lost her.

I leaned over her and breathed one final time, pressing my lips to hers. I gave her everything I'd been feeling for her: the burning lust and the deep, instinctual need to protect her; the need I had to be with her, the deep yearning I felt whenever I looked at her.

And her body jerked. A tiny movement. A half-hiccup.

I pulled back, rubbing at her back, her chest, encouraging the water up. She jerked a second time and I rolled her onto her side and then the water burst from her mouth. She drew in a tortured breath and started coughing.

"Kate? *Kate?!*"

Another labored breath, as if she was inhaling razor blades. She was so cold, inside and out, that when she exhaled there was no cloud of vapor.

I picked her up and hugged her to my chest. She'd never felt smaller, frailer. But she was alive.

"Say something," I whispered. "Say anything."

She slowly opened her eyes and rasped. "*Hello.*"

I clutched her even tighter, relief flooding my body. But she didn't warm up, didn't wake more or become stronger. Her head lolled against me and her limbs were floppy.

She was too cold. She'd been in the water too long and now she was in soaking, freezing clothes. Her body was losing the battle to warm her.

I looked around. This close to the raging river, the wood would all be soaked. By the time I got a fire going, she'd be dead.

No.

When I got to my feet, my legs almost collapsed under me, the muscles agony from all the swimming. I was exhausted, soaked through and shaking with cold. But my old Navy instructor used to say, "When you think you're done, that's only about 40% of what you can do."

I wasn't going to let her die.

She protested weakly as I lifted her and put her in a fireman's carry. "Shh," I told her. "I'm taking you someplace safe."

My cabin was two miles away.

I gritted my teeth and started to run.

THIRTY-TWO

Boone

I COULD FEEL her chest moving against my back. That's the only way I knew she was alive. She wasn't warming up. She wasn't coming back to me.

I ran faster, lungs bursting, muscles screaming.

My cabin is high on one side of a valley with a view across to the other side. Getting her up the path that led there damn near killed me. But I finally staggered through the door and laid her gently down on the chair. Then I turned to the stove. I keep it filled with wood and primed, a match laid ready on top. I always knew there might be a time like this. I just figured it would be me who fell into a frozen lake or got caught in a storm.

I struck the match, slammed the stove door shut and looked down at Kate. Her eyes were closed. She was mumbling but it didn't make any sense. My chest closed up tight. She was close to slipping into a coma.

I picked her up and carried her across to the bed.

She wasn't shivering. That was bad. I had to get her clothes off. I sat her up and pulled the suit jacket off her, tossing it aside. Then I started down the remaining buttons of her blouse. The wet fabric parted and I stripped it back off her shoulders. Reached for her bra clasp–

I swallowed. I knew it was the right thing to do. I knew it was essential I get all the wet cloth off her to stop it soaking up her body heat. But...this was *Kate*.

I pushed it out of my mind and took off her bra. Then I lay her back on the bed and pulled off her shoes and pants.

Her panties.

I grabbed a towel and started drying her off. She was mumbling again, telling me to let her go to sleep. "No," I told her sharply. "You have to stay awake."

As soon as she was dry, I lay her on a blanket and then wrapped it around her like a cocoon. Then a second blanket. Then I brought the big caribou fur I'd bought from one of the guys in Koyuk and wrapped *that* around her until she was a thick, furry bundle with just her head sticking out. I picked her up and carried her over to the stove. By now, the logs had caught and it was roaring, sending out waves of heat that filled the tiny cabin. I put Kate down right in front of it. Then I quickly stripped off my clothes, toweled off and pulled on a dry pair of pants. I sat down behind Kate and pulled her back against me, sitting just as we had when we'd looked up at the stars. I hugged her to my chest, wrapped my arms around her and tried to let my warmth flow into her. "Come back to me, Kate," I whispered in her ear, over and over. "Come back to me."

And, slowly, she did.

Her head kept lolling but I wouldn't let her fall asleep. When it looked like she was going to drop off, I gently shook her and talked to her. I rubbed at her arms and legs to try to get the blood going. I hugged her tight, enfolding her in my arms and pressing my thighs either side of hers. I stacked the fire high and, as soon as she was opening her eyes and talking, I heated up some soup and fed it to her.

Her skin gradually turned from pure white back to its normal, healthy hue. She started to shiver as her body's own defenses came back, then stopped again as she got warm. Her breathing became easier.

"I—" She swallowed. "I think I'm okay."

I let out a long sigh and hugged her even tighter, pressing my head against hers and closing my eyes. "Goddamn you. Goddamn you, Kate. You scared me. I thought I'd lost you."

I felt her tense under the blankets. What I'd just said sank in. Not just the words but the way I'd said them.

I moved my head aside and she slowly twisted to look over her shoulder at me. We stared at each other. Those big mahogany eyes were alert, now, searching my face. Her color was back. I could see it in her cheeks. I could see it in her...lips.

Those lips. Back to their normal blush-pink. So warm. So soft.

I knew I had to push her away. I knew there was no way it could work. I opened my mouth to say something—

And then I leaned forward and kissed her. Because the hell with *that*.

THIRTY-THREE

Kate

I HAD TIME to see it in his eyes. To see that deep Alaskan blue finally lose its battle between fire and ice and blaze with raw, scorching heat. Then I was closing my eyes as his lips met mine.

And oh...my...*God.* It was a kiss the way a mountain is a lump of rock. It was as unlike a polite New York kiss as a dip in a freezing lake is unlike a bath.

This was the way people kissed a thousand years ago. This was man kissing woman. Claiming her. Owning her. His lips pressed mine, twisted and—*opened.* I felt the movement right down to my groin, going weak under him. He was moving, rough and savage and hot, his breath joining mine. I felt hands on my waist, twisting me around to face him, tipping me and my bundle of blankets back towards the floor.

Our lips parted. Met again, short but powerful little presses, fiercely hot. My back, cushioned by layers of blankets, hit the floor. He was hunched over me, kissing me quick and hard, his hot breath filling me, our teeth clacking together for a second in our haste. And then his tongue found the tip of mine.

Ever since he brought me into the cabin, I felt as if I'd been slowly coming back to life, rising upward through freezing blackness to a world of light and color. I sped through the final few feet and surfaced in a warm, gasping rush. I felt the power race through my body: it was like being switched on for the first time. Not the first time since the river. For the first time in years.

He was brutal and primal, his kiss hard and demanding. And for every ounce of hardness, I matched him with softness, opening under him, welcoming him in. I went heady. I was never normally so...*feminine.* I'd spent my whole life trying to prove myself and most of that meant showing everyone how male, how aggressive I could be. But under Mason's lips...all my layers of rock just collapsed inward to reveal melting pink marshmallow underneath. Every kiss, every breath, poured molten heat into me, turning me to liquid. And it really hit me for the first time that I was completely naked under the blankets.

I began to pant, pleasure radiating out from his kisses like little earthquakes and shuddering down through my entire body. Inside my bundle of blankets, I began to gently buck and twist, pressing my thighs together.

I opened my eyes for the first time as he started kissing his way down my cheek, then down the soft skin of my neck. Every touch of those hard lips sent a new burst of heat twisting down inside me. God, he was topless, every muscle hard, his huge body looming above me. I wanted to grab it, cling to it—but the blankets trapped my arms firmly against my sides. I was helpless. All I could do was *be kissed.*

His lips reached the base of my neck. My bare shoulder. They traced a scorching line of heat across my collarbone. And that's all of me he could reach, with me wrapped up. He stopped kissing me and we just looked at each other, both of us breathless. He was astride me, one knee on either side of the bundle, his arms either side of my head, bent so that our faces were only inches apart. His lower half was pressed tight against me and, even through three layers, I could feel the hardness of his cock.

He didn't say anything. He didn't need to.

He picked me up and carried me to the bed.

THIRTY-FOUR

Kate

HE LAID ME DOWN with my head on the pillow but with me still wrapped up in the bundle of blankets. He climbed onto the bed with me and I went weak inside as the mattress sank under the hard, muscled size of him. He swung a knee over me, towering above me. I gulped, delighted. He was so *big* and I suddenly felt so...small.

He leaned down like a beast about to devour its meal and took possession of my mouth again. This time, the kisses were open-mouthed and hungry, both of us addicted to the taste of the other, wanting more and more. His big hands came down and cupped my cheeks, thumbs stroking over my forehead and then my cheekbones, caressing me right down to my shoulders as if he wanted to know every curve. But while he could touch me, I couldn't touch him. I was still just a helpless bundle, my arms trapped by the blankets. It was frustrating and yet a part of me was thrilling at it. There's something about being unable to do more than buck and wiggle.

Boone looked down the length of the bed. He did something with his bare feet and then—

I gasped as he straightened his legs, his hard ass standing out through his pants. What he'd done was gather the bottom of the blankets around his feet. The whole bundle, animal fur and all, started to slide slowly down my body. I began to pant. Both of us looked down at the edge of the blankets as they crept over my upper chest, tightening as they stretched to get over my breasts.

I swallowed. This huge beast of a man was going to strip me naked. My eyes traced over the tan bulges of his biceps, the thick, flattened breadth of his forearms. I could feel my nipples hardening as the moving fabric rubbed against them and I started to grind my ass against the blankets beneath me.

The blankets slowly slid, revealing me inch by inch. They became the equivalent of a strapless evening gown. A *low cut* evening gown. A *traffic stopping* evening gown. And Boone's eyes ate up the soft, pale skin as it appeared, that deep blue scorching me until—

I drew in my breath as my nipples burst free. Boone's eyes clouded with lust and he descended on me, strong hands cupping a breast each as his mouth dipped down to lick at my hardened buds. My arms were still trapped, so there was nothing I could do except arch my back and cry out, pressing myself to him, digging my shoulders into the bed as he lashed my breasts with his tongue and then sucked a nipple into his mouth.

His legs kept moving. The blankets slid down, baring my stomach, stopping just above my groin. My arms were free down to my wrists, now. I knew I probably *could* free my hands—

But I didn't want to. Boone was squeezing and lifting my breasts in a slow rhythm, thumbs rubbing across my spit-wet nipples, while he kissed up and down my throat and between my breasts. I was drawing in quick, high little breaths, gazing up at him as he gazed down at me and—

My wrists made helpless little jerks against the blankets that held them, as if trying to get free...but not trying very hard. Being the passive one, for once, letting someone else take control, was really working for me.

His feet began moving again. The blanket slipped lower and my hands popped free. But at the same time, the soft, dark curls between my legs were uncovered and everything just...stopped. Boone froze, the blankets halting at my knees. He just knelt there, astride my legs, and he stared down at my sex with such intensity I was pinned. His gaze was so strong it was physical, a hot breeze that ran through the soft hairs and caressed my moist lips. I gasped.

"You're beautiful," he growled simply.

A warm swell of pride expanded out from that part of me. Then he was shoving the blankets the rest of the way off and I was naked under him. He slid a knee between my legs and parted my thighs and that made me finally abandon being passive and grab him, my hands finding his shoulders as I pulled him down for a kiss. God, he was like rock, like steel moving under heated skin.

He lowered himself between my legs and then the whole of that hard body was rubbing against me. The warm, solid weight of his chest stroked back and forth against my breasts. The hardness of his pelvis ground against my heated sex. The rhythm started to build, every part of me on fire, the pleasure circling and tightening inside. My hands roamed over his back, exploring the contours of him, delighting in the sheer size of him. I could feel his cock, hot even through his pants, against my inner thigh and...God, all the way up the crease of my *hip*—

I swallowed. And then forgot everything as he slid two fingers up inside me just as he kissed me again, our tongues dancing. Everything turned to hot, buttery pleasure and there was only the tightness and smooth friction of it and the hardness of his back under my hands and—

The pleasure reached a peak and my fingers clutched at his muscles. I squeezed my legs around his hand, rocking and moaning as I went over the edge, eyes screwed shut, panting up into his mouth.

I came back down to earth in time to see him kick off his pants and resettle himself between my legs. His cock was the same smooth tan as the rest of him, hard and primed and....

I swallowed again, butterflies in my stomach but heady with excitement. He started to lower himself and then paused. Shuffled forward on the bed.

I frowned. "What?"

"Shh," he said. "Just wait a—"

He lifted my head and shoulders off the bed. Fiddled. And my hair unraveled from its braid and spilled down my naked back. Boone smoothed it, then moved back between my legs, his eyes filled with lust. "I've been wanting to do that since I first met you," he said thickly.

"You don't like my braid?" I felt different,

somehow. Softer.

"I *love* your braid. It drives me crazy." He nudged my legs further apart. "But I want to see you like this. *Undone.*"

He lowered himself and I gasped as the tip of him brushed against me. He bent to kiss me again, paying service to my lips and breasts again as he rocked there and I got wetter and wetter. Then, in one long, slow push, he slid up inside me.

I drew in my breath, head craning back against the pillows, sliding on my newly-freed hair. My hands ran down his shoulders and the smooth curves of his biceps, then clutched at his wrists.

He went slow, laying kisses down my body as he pulled back. Then he went *deep,* our fingers knitting as he filled me, filled me, *Oh God* stretched me. My knees drew up, my toes dancing on the bedclothes and....

We were face to face and he was entirely buried in me, the root of him hard against me. I panted up at him. Just him being there, so hard and hot, was sending constant little flutters of pleasure out from where we met. But when he moved...my eyes closed and my hands clawed at his back, drawing him close as the friction turned to liquid silver inside me.

He began to move faster, faster, driving hard into me, his body pressing mine down into the bed. I was out of control. Every silken stroke lifted me towards my peak. Every brush of his hard chest against my nipples making me gasp and arch until I had to run my fingers down his body and over the smooth muscles of his hips, then over his ass. I couldn't get enough of the size of him, the solidness of him, the raw, endless strength of him. I wanted to touch every inch of him. My hands slid between us, fingers skimming the base of his cock, and he growled.

Both of us were covered in a thin sheen of sweat now, every trace of cold forgotten. This wasn't just sex. It was more raw, more wild, without all the *thinking* there would be in New York. And I loved it. It was simple and primal and I loved it. My hands locked around his waist. My ankles came up and hooked around his legs, pulling him to me. Undone? I *was* undone!

He looked down at me and grinned: a big, honest smile that made me light up inside...and flush a little. He'd released something inside me that I hadn't even known needed to get out.

He leaned down and kissed me hard as his hips rose and fell in merciless rhythm, pumping me, *pounding* me, my pleasure building and building until I was a helpless, shuddering, damp-haired mess beneath him. I only broke the kiss when my climax hit, arching under him, my chin against his shoulder as I screamed his name.

***

We must have fallen asleep because I woke cuddled up to his sleeping body, my head on his chest, one arm and one leg hooked possessively across him. I flushed, remembering. I'd never been like that before. I'd never been so out of control. And yet instead of worrying me, it painted a big smile on my face.

Boone was flat out on his back, fast asleep. I laid my head down on him again, loving the warmth of him. I was just dropping off to sleep again when he twitched.

I slowly raised my head. I could see it starting again. Maybe that's what had first woken me, the first flicker of pain and fear. I watched as it took control of him. This time, I could see more than just his face. I could see how every muscle tensed, his shoulders rising and his hands closing into fists. Whatever he was seeing, in his nightmare, he was getting ready to fight it: fight it for his life.

A chill went through me. I was lucky to have survived waking him, when we'd been out in the forest.

I slipped from the bed. The stove was still giving out a warm glow and, with a blanket wrapped around my shoulders, it was comfortably warm. I couldn't lie there next to him and watch him in pain and I didn't want to risk waking him, either. So I explored.

I hadn't really seen the cabin, the night before. In my semi-conscious state, the whole thing had been a blur. It was made of huge, thick logs, every crack sealed with what might have been mud or clay. The huge bed, its wood polished smooth with age, looked as if it had come straight from the Old West and must have been at least a hundred years old. Most of the other furniture—the chair, the small counter where he prepared his food—was handmade. There was no sign of running water or electricity. I turned in a slow circle. *That's it?!* There was only one room and it couldn't be more than fifteen feet on a side. I could see every inch of the cabin from where I was standing. Sure, that probably made it cozy and easy to heat, but how did he not go crazy, being shut up in here?

It was very...*him*. Everything was military-neat and things were sized big: the homemade chair, hewn from wood and then padded with animal skins, could have seated a rhino. But it was also brutal. Except for the huge, warm animal skin he'd wrapped around me when he was warming me, there was very little in the way of comforts. No TV? No books? What did he *do,* all day?

I eventually found a few personal items. Hanging next to the mirror was a pair of dog tags with his name on them. And beside those were a few faded photos showing guys in military fatigues. I barely recognized Boone, with short hair. He was grinning, his outstretched arms around a group of other Navy SEALs.

My stomach twisted. From what he'd said, everyone else in that photo was dead.

The mirror was tiny, a hand mirror he'd secured to the wall with a few nails. I stared at my long, loose hair. I never normally saw it like that: I took it down to wash it and to brush my hair each morning and then immediately braided it again. With it down, I looked like a different woman.

Dawn was breaking outside. I carefully cracked open the door, trying not to make a noise, and slipped out. The morning air was crisp and cold, my breath making dense little white clouds of vapor, but I was still warm from being cuddled up to Boone and there wasn't much breeze. I could stand the cold for a few minutes. I made my way across the porch, pulling the blanket tighter around me. I was aware that I was naked underneath and the blanket only just came down low enough to be decent, but there was no one to see me. It actually felt very freeing, being sort-of nude, outdoors.

I sat down at the edge of the porch, gasping at the cold wood and pushing some of the blanket under me so I didn't freeze my butt off. And then, as the sunlight started to break across the valley, I gasped.

It was beautiful. For the first time since I arrived in Alaska, I really saw that. Until now, I'd been so focused on how different it was to New York, how dangerous it was, that I hadn't had a chance to appreciate it. But as the light flooded down the sides of the mountains and washed through the forests on the valley floor, the sheer scale of the place hit me. It was beautiful *because* it was so big, so wild. Not seeing roads and telegraph poles, knowing we were all alone out here, still freaked me out. But it also made it clean and unspoiled. And while it was the worst place in the world to be lost, it was the perfect place to lose yourself.

I started to see why he'd come here.

Footsteps behind me. I whipped around and saw Boone standing there, gazing down at me. He'd pulled on a pair of pants but his chest was bare. *How is he not freezing?*

Without words, he sat down beside me. I unwrapped the blanket and whipped it around both of us, wrapping us into a warm little cocoon. He put one massive arm around me and snugged me close and I gasped as my naked side pressed up against him.

For a few minutes we just sat there, watching the dawn. It should have been awkward. I barely knew him and, last night, we'd not only had sex but he'd unleashed something inside me I'd never experienced before. I should have been red-faced and mumbling about how *that wasn't me.*

And yet...it wasn't like that at all. When I'd dated guys from the bureau, the sex had always changed things. The next morning, I'd become a trophy, something to brag to their friends about: *hey, I bagged myself a female agent!* Or for the more competitive ones, it had been a way to put me down, to reduce me from a colleague to *just a woman I've fucked.* It was one of the reasons I hadn't dated in almost a year.

But with Boone, there was none of that. There was no guilt, no shame, no games. His hand, as it roamed up and down my naked waist, told me that he still felt exactly the same about me as he had the night before. And the little smile on his lips when I caught his eye told me he wasn't shocked by how, um...enthusiastic I'd been. He liked it.

I leaned my head on his shoulder. His other hand came up and stroked my hair back off my cheek and then smoothed it down over my naked back, under the blanket. Strange how different it felt, loose. He really seemed to like playing with it.

"Did you make the call yet?" I asked, gazing at the valley.

"Call?"

"The call for help." When he didn't respond, I turned to him. "That is why we came here, right?"

He stared at me sadly and shook his head. "There's no phone here."

I blinked at him. "But you have a *radio,* right?"

He shook his head again.

For a moment, our own situation was forgotten. "You live all the way out here without *any form of communication?!* Are you *crazy?* What happens if you get ill? What if you get injured and need help?"

He looked at me sadly and then snugged me closer to him. His big, warm hand cupped my cheek, his thumb stroking across it. "Kate," he rumbled softly, "who would I call?"

Of all the things I'd seen of his life, of everything he'd told me, that was the one that hit the hardest. Of course. There wasn't a damn person he could call for help, not if he wanted to stay off the authorities' radar. He wasn't just isolated physically, he'd cut himself off from every living soul.

I couldn't help it. I threw myself against his chest and just hugged him under the blankets. He wrapped his arms around my naked back, pressing me to him, my breasts pillowing against him, and kissed the top of my head.

"Then what was the plan for us?" I asked at last. "Why even come here?"

He sighed and shook his head. "Sorry. Should have explained. When we were back at the plane, I was in a hurry. I just wanted to get you down off the mountain. I brought you here so we could rest up and get supplies, and get you into some proper clothes." He pointed off into the distance. "There's a town about three days' walk from here."

I pushed back from his chest and just stared at him. *Three days?* Three more days in the wilderness? I'd thought that this was *it*.

"It won't be how it was before," he said. "We'll have warm clothes. Food. Supplies. It'll be an easy hike."

I gaped at him for another few seconds. But as I wrapped my head around the idea of more walking, I realized he was right. Just a few days ago, walking further than the nearest Starbucks would have seemed crazy. But now, after the plane crash and the cliffs and the river...just plain hiking, in proper clothes, *didn't* sound so bad.

And it would be with him. I pressed myself to him

again. Three days of getting to know him better, sleeping under the stars with him...I could live with that.

Then it hit me, a cold blow right to the chest. *And then what?*

"Mason," I asked, my voice tight. "What happens when we get to a town?"

I was hoping I was wrong. But the way he went quiet told me I wasn't.

"They'll have a radio," he said. "You can call for help. The rescue services will pick you up within a few hours."

"And you?" I asked, my voice cracking.

He said nothing.

"No!"

He shook his head. "Kate, I'm a fugitive. For all we know, they've already found the plane and realized they have two prisoners on the loose. They could have sent pictures of me and Weiss to every town. A cop could pull a gun on me as soon as I show up there."

"So you just come back here?" I asked hollowly. "That's it? You just come back to your cabin and live as a—a—*hermit?* For how long, *forever?*"

Those Alaskan-blue eyes stared back at me, freezing over with ice. "What choice do I have?"

I grabbed his biceps and squeezed. "Come back with me! I'm FBI, I can bring you in, make sure you're not hurt. I can fight to get your case reopened—"

He was shaking his head.

My eyes narrowed. "Mason, goddamnit, don't give up on the system!"

He fixed me with a look. "Gave up on it a long time ago."

I glared at him. Maybe it was stupid, but I was part

of the system. It felt like he distrusted *me.*

He sighed. Under the blanket, his hands dropped to my waist. He picked me up, then set me down again on his lap, straddling him. He spoke slowly and each word was like a warm bomb going off in my chest. "Kate," he said, "You are the bravest, smartest woman I've ever met. If there was some way I could come back with you, I would."

My eyes were suddenly hot. "Your whole life is waiting for you," I told him. "It's just waiting for you to take it back. Surely that's worth the risk."

"Not just a risk," he said, his voice going hard. "Even if we got a retrial, I'd have to go to jail until then."

"A few months, maybe—"

"I can't take a day!" It was the first time he'd ever yelled. And it didn't feel as if he was yelling at me: if anything, he sounded mad at himself. But with his size and power, it still made me flinch. And when he saw that, he cursed under his breath and pulled me close. "See?" he muttered. "I'm a mess."

I looked up into that gorgeous, brooding face. When he eventually met my eyes, I said, as gently as I could, "Whatever it is..."—I glanced towards the cabin, to the bed where he'd had the nightmare—"there are people who can help with that."

He looked at me, then cast his gaze around the landscape. "Not out here," he said sourly.

And that's when I finally understood. Something had happened to him. Something that had stabbed right into the heart of him, through all his muscle and courage, and left something black and poisonous there. Something that left him in a cold sweat every night. Something that he had no choice but to live with because, immediately after it happened, he'd been court-martialled and then on the run.

His words from the cliff face came back to me. *I was MIA for a while.*

What the hell had happened to him?

He caught my eye...and shook his head. There was a part of him I couldn't know—maybe ever. Then his arms wrapped around my back and hauled me up his thighs and tight up against him. A hand on the back of my head tilted my head back and his lips came down on mine. This time, the kiss wasn't about sex. It was deeper, slower. It said *I need you.* And I pressed myself against him and returned it, my fingers running through his hair, because I needed him, too. Somehow, despite starting out thousands of miles apart, we'd found exactly the person we each needed.

And soon, we'd part again forever.

He reluctantly broke the kiss. I bit my lip, my eyes dangerously hot. For a few seconds, we just stared at each other as we both fought to hold it together.

Then he said gruffly, "I got something that'll make you feel better."

I gave him a disbelieving look.

"Seriously," he said. "I got you all figured out. Stay there."

He went inside. I gazed at the landscape for another few minutes, trying to compose myself. Then came a smell I recognized.

My head snapped around like it was on a spring. "*Coffee?!*" I scrambled to my feet and threw open the door. "You have *coffee?*"

"One of the things I bring back from Koyuk," he said. "Can only carry a couple of packs each trip so I have to make it last. Only let myself drink it on a

Saturday. But I'll make an exception for you."

I stared at the old-fashioned coffee pot in disbelief. I'd been *dreaming* about coffee. I hadn't had any since Seattle. All the pleasure receptors in my brain lit up green as they anticipated the taste.

I was still aching inside. My heart felt like a jagged crack was creeping across its surface and, when we reached the town and had to separate, I knew it was going to split wide open. But he was right: this *did* make me feel better. Both the coffee and the fact he was trying to make me happy.

"Let it brew for another few minutes," he told me, pushing me gently back outside. "Then we can drink it out here." He looked up at the sky and shook his head. "We should stay here for today. Looks like there's a storm blowing in. We don't want to be out there when it hits."

He turned to go back inside, then froze. He was staring at a point far off in the distance.

"What?" I asked. But he ignored me. He walked slowly to the edge of the porch, frowning at whatever it was he'd seen. Then he suddenly cursed and ran inside.

"What is it?" I asked. But he was gone. I stared where he'd been looking. I couldn't see-

Wait. *There.* A dot, barely visible, and another two behind it. All three were moving in a slow, up-and-down pattern as they came towards us.

Boone reappeared with an expensive-looking pair of binoculars. He stared at the dots, then passed the binoculars to me.

It took me a second to pan around and find them. When I did, I drew in my breath.

The dots were three 4x4s, bouncing up and down

as they worked their way over the rough terrain. The binoculars brought them close enough that I could see Weiss and another man I didn't recognize through the windshield of the lead one. Both had rifles cradled across their chests.

I lowered the binoculars and looked up at Boone.

"We have to go," he said.

THIRTY-FIVE

Boone

I HAD A PLAN, of course. I'd had a plan for four years. I always knew the military might find me and that I'd have to run. I knew what to take. I knew where to go.

Except in my plan, I'd never included a civilian. Especially one I was crazy about. I dressed for the outdoors every day but she was going to have to start from absolute scratch. And we'd need two of everything and...*shit!*

I was panicking because, for the first time, I had someone else to worry about.

I grabbed Kate and hauled her inside. "Get that blanket off!" I snapped. She shed it immediately. That left me looking at her naked body and, despite everything that was going on, I couldn't help but stare, unable to drag my eyes away. I didn't regret what we'd done the night before. Not for an instant. Not even knowing that, when we reached a town, I'd have to say goodbye.

If we live that long. And that thought got me moving again. "Get your underwear on," I told her. As she pulled on her bra, I started throwing things to her: a warm base layer, then waterproof pants. A tight, insulating long-sleeved t-shirt and then one of my thick shirts.

I looked at my spare pair of boots. There was no point even trying: my feet were twice the size of hers. "You'll have to go with your shoes," I told her. But she could at least wear some of my wool socks.

I glanced up to toss her the socks...and froze again. She'd just pulled the black thermal base layer up her legs and, as I watched, she struggled into the matching top half. Fortunately, they were stretchy enough that they were fairly tight even on her small form. She looked like some movie super heroine, all clad in skintight black Lycra. *Goddamn it, she makes even thermals look sexy.*

I threw her the socks and tore my eyes away. I kept a backpack packed for myself on a hook on the wall but I started packing one for her, throwing in an extra set of dry clothes, more socks and–just in case we got separated–a flint and steel for lighting fires. Hopefully, I'd get a chance to show her how to use it. I dug under the bed and pulled out a box, then started tossing plastic pouches into her pack.

"What are those?" She'd pulled on the waterproof pants, now, and was turning up the cuffs to shorten them.

"Military rations," I said. "We're not going to get a chance to hunt." My mind was spinning. I knew I had my pack ready, but I was trying to remember everything I had in it so I could give her one.

She started pulling on the shirt. "How long do you

think we've got?"

I glanced at the open door. "Depends how good their driving is. That's tough terrain even if you know what you're doing. They could get stuck. But...." I thought about the guy I'd seen driving, alongside Weiss. Big, with Slavic cheekbones and close-cropped hair. "I got a feeling they've got military guys helping them. They *will* know what they're doing." *Flashlight! How could I not think of that!* I grabbed my spare one, checked it worked and added it to her pack. Then I threw in a spare hunting knife. "What I don't get is why they're here. We're no threat to them."

By now, Kate was sitting on the edge of the bed. She had the shirt buttoned and was stretching her shoes over the top of the thick wool socks. "I think I know," she said, her voice grim.

I stopped what I was doing and looked at her. She was staring intently at me.

"We had it all wrong," she said. "I couldn't figure out why Weiss went to all that trouble, parachuting out of a plane. He had the marshals paid off...why not just escape in Nome? But now I get it. It's not enough to get away. He stole *billions.* He'll be hunted his whole life...unless no one knows he's alive."

"They'll find the plane eventually," I said, frowning. "They'll figure out he wasn't on board."

"Right, unless, after they bailed out, they went to the plane and put someone else's body on board. Maybe even three bodies: Weiss and the two marshals. If they burned the whole thing, there wouldn't be much left to identify. No one's going to ask too many questions: it's the right number of bodies, they knew who was on board...they're going to declare Weiss and the marshals dead and they walk away scot-free. *That* was Weiss's plan."

I caught up with her. "Except...when they went to the plane, they found out we survived. If we get to a town, we'll tell people what really happened. We'll blow the whole thing." We stared at each other and I watched as Kate turned pale. She'd come to the same conclusion I had: Weiss needed both of us dead for his plan to work.

I shook my head. "We've got to get out of here. *Now.*" I added a waterproof jacket to her pack and tossed it to her. Then I scrambled into my own clothes. I was still trying to figure out how the hell they'd found us. I *knew* I'd felt someone watching us...but why hadn't I seen anyone?

Kate met me by the door. By now, the 4x4s were close enough that I could see the figures inside without binoculars. We had minutes before they were on us. I looked frantically around the cabin, trying to figure out if there was anything I'd forgotten. I wished I had more time. Our whole situation had changed in a heartbeat. When I'd reached the cabin, I'd thought we were safe but this was going to be way more dangerous than anything we'd faced so far.

Then I saw that Kate was looking up at me, eyes wide with fear. My stomach knotted: she must be terrified.

I took a deep breath and tried not to think about Afghanistan. About what happened the last time I was tasked with getting a civilian out. I put my hands on Kate's shoulders. "Listen," I said. "We're going to go fast. We're going to try to get into terrain where they'll have to follow on foot. Then we can disappear."

She nodded but she still looked as if she wanted to throw up. I cupped her chin and forced steel into my voice. "They think this is going to be easy but they don't know me and they don't know you. I've seen what you can do. You and me, we're going to pull this off. You hear me?"

She swallowed. Nodded. Then she reached back behind her head, gathered up her hair and secured it in a ponytail. "Okay," she said. "Let's go."

My heart damn near melted. God, I loved this woman. I leaned down, grabbed her cheeks between my hands and kissed her hard, reveling in her softness, her sweetness, fueling myself for what was ahead. Then I led her outside and slammed the cabin door.

A distant rumble of thunder made me look up. *Shit.* I'd forgotten about the storm. But we had no choice: we had to go.

I pointed the way...and we ran.

THIRTY-SIX

Kate

BACK IN NEW YORK, I ran every morning. I'd lace up my running shoes and run a five mile circuit through the streets before work. On Sundays I'd push it to nearly seven miles, pounding the paths through Central Park. I'd finish right at the spot where the string quartet played and I'd reward myself with a coffee. I knew I could run.

I knew nothing. I found that out within the first mile.

This wasn't nice, smooth sidewalk. This was dirt and rock that slipped and gave under our feet and made every step exhausting. We had to cut uphill because the steeper slope would be tough for the 4x4s. It was like running up a flight of stairs that never ended, knowing that one careless step could end with me tumbling back down the slope, all the way to our pursuers' feet. We couldn't slow down. We had to keep going full pelt. And I was doing it all carrying a pack and wearing my goddamn work shoes.

After ten minutes, I was panting. Twenty and I was

exhausted. Thirty and I was soaked in sweat, my lungs screaming. And we hadn't even reached the top of the slope.

Beside me, Boone was plowing steadily on, matching my speed. I knew I was slowing him down. That was the worst part, knowing that, at any second, I might hear the sound of a shot and a bullet would rip through one of us. We knew they had rifles...

"You're doing great," Boone told me. *Jesus, he's not even breathing hard.* "Just keep going. Focus on the top."

I craned my head up to the top of the peak. If we could just reach it, once we were going down the other side we'd be hidden from view. Then we could disappear into the forest and they wouldn't know which way we'd gone.

But first, we had to reach it. And the way Boone kept checking behind us, I knew it wasn't looking good. I didn't want to look myself because the drop beneath us must be terrifying by now.

"How–bad–is it?" I panted the next time he looked round.

He shook his head. "Focus on the peak," he ordered.

But less than a minute later, I saw him take another look. He caught my eye. "We're fine."

"Don't–bullshit me," I panted. My leg muscles felt as if someone was rubbing them on a cheese grater.

Boone said nothing but I could see it in his eyes: they were close.

I gritted my teeth and tried to move faster but it was useless. The slope had gotten even steeper and we were almost on all fours, using our hands as much as our feet. The pack on my back, so light when we'd left the cabin, now weighed about a million tons, threatening to tip me back down the slope. The wind was getting up, too, blowing right into my face, and the temperature was dropping. It wasn't even noon yet and yet the sky was almost twilight-dark. The storm Boone had warned about was coming fast.

A big, warm hand grabbed mine. I looked up into Boone's eyes. "You can do it," he growled.

I panted and just shook my head.

He nodded and his hand gripped mine a little tighter. "Then I'll climb for both of us," he told me. And he started to haul me up the slope. That made it easier for me: all I had to do was scrabble with my feet to keep up with him. But it meant that he had to do everything one-handed, plus cope with my drag. There was no doubt that I was slowing him down. My eyes met his again, pleading. *I'm going to get you killed! Leave me!*

His grip on my hand became like iron. He stared right into my eyes and simply shook his head. A warm glow expanded to fill my chest. Whatever happened, he wouldn't leave me behind.

His big hand sunk into the dirt, his feet pounded at the grass and he *powered* us up the slope, with me pushing as hard as I could beside him. After what felt like hours, I put my hand up to grab the next handful of grass...and there was only air. We'd done it.

He pulled me upright—the first time I'd been able to properly stand in hours. We were on the very top of the ridge, a path only a dozen feet wide. Bracing myself, I finally turned and looked around.

Shit! My heart leapt into my mouth. Three men were charging up the slope behind us as if it was a running track. All of them were stocky with muscle and all were wearing military fatigues. *Soldiers?!* Who the hell did Weiss have working for him?

I didn't see the marshals or Weiss. And I didn't see the 4x4s: maybe Weiss and the marshals were staying in the cars, taking the long way around to cut us off, and these guys had been sent to run us down on foot. I looked again. Already, they'd made up another fifty yards.

"Come on!" yelled Boone. He pulled me towards the far edge of the ridge. The drop on the other side came into view and—

It was horrifically steep, more like a cliff than a hill, and so high I felt my stomach churn. I could see a river, far below, just a snaking blue line no thicker than a vein on my wrist. I saw whole clumps of trees that could have grown on my thumbnail without filling all the space.

I threw myself back, breaking his grip and falling on my ass. My fear of heights slammed into me full force and locked me there, pinning me to the ground like I had a truck parked on me. "You're crazy!" I panted as the world tilted and spun. "It's too steep!" My heart was going so fast, so hard, that I thought I might actually be about to have a heart attack. "We can't walk down that!"

"It's steep, but we can make it if we do it right." He held out his hand. "C'mon."

Is he insane?! I shook my head and snatched my hand away. I knew they were coming, behind me, but animal fear had taken over. "I can't," I rasped. "I just can't."

He glanced over my shoulder, then sank to a crouch in front of me. One big, warm hand cupped my cheek. "Kate, I know you're scared. But you can do this."

I stared up at him, a hot glow spreading through my chest.

"I'll be right there with you," he said. And he held out his hand again.

I stared at his hand. *I can't.*

But if I didn't, I was going to get him killed.

Feeling as if I was going to throw up, I took his hand. He walked me to the very edge of the cli—*don't think of it as a cliff. It's just a really, really steep, rocky hill.*

"Don't try to go slow," Boone told me. "*Run.* We have to go fast enough that our feet stay under us. But don't let it get away from you. You don't want to slip and roll."

I nodded. One trip, one stumble and we wouldn't hit the ground again until we hit the bottom. I was sure I was going to throw up.

"I'm going to hold your hand the whole way, okay?" He squeezed my hand for reassurance.

I nodded silently. I didn't trust myself to speak.

And together, we stepped over the edge.

Welcome to the single most terrifying three minutes of my life. It was like every nightmare I'd ever had about heights...only worse. It didn't feel like running. It fell like falling. I *plunged* face-first towards that distant river and the trees below, my clothes and hair billowing out behind me. Somewhere beneath me, I was aware of my legs pumping madly, not just running but sprinting, trying to keep my feet under my body. The rocky slope was so steep, I could feel my heels lifting off the ground as I tipped forward, a hair's breadth from going into a tumble that wouldn't end until I was a broken, bloody mess at the bottom. And the only solution was to run suicidally faster and faster.

The wind whistled past my ears and slammed its way down my throat. I'd forgotten all about the men chasing us. All I had room for was the sight of the ground, so very far away. My normal strategy with heights was *don't look down* but how can you not look when you're running towards it?

My lungs strained and threatened to burst. My legs, already exhausted from the climb, screamed in agony. Several times, I thought I was dead: I'd catch my foot on a rock or tilt forward too much and there'd be a sickening lurch as my feet left the ground and I started to full-on *fall.* But there was always a huge, warm hand tight around mine to haul me back upright. And then, just as my legs started to fail, I felt it.

The ground was under my heels again.

At first, I didn't want to get my hopes up. But...*yes!* The slope was leveling out. It felt more like running, less like falling. And then, as it leveled out more, we could finally slow down. A jog, then a walk, then a blessed, blessed *stop.*

I slumped over, bent almost double, as Boone finally released my hand. It was some seconds before I could even lift myself enough to look behind us.

The slope rose so high behind us it blocked out the morning sun. I craned my head back and back to try to see the top. *We came down* that?! I was still terrified, my whole body shaking with adrenaline. But there was a tiny rush of pride, too.

Boone put his arm around my waist and pulled me close, wrapping me in his arms. "We did it," he said, kissing the top of my head. "Look."

I followed his pointing finger. Right at the top of the cliff, silhouetted against the sky, the three men who'd been chasing us were just starting a careful, slow descent. It would be a while before they caught up with us. And by that point, we could be long gone.

Boone slowly released me and put his finger under my chin, tilting my head back to look up at him. "You got big brass balls, Lydecker."

I flushed and weakly grinned. Then we were jogging towards the forest.

Thirty minutes later, we were deep inside. Boone slowed to a stop, then just stood and listened. I stood next to him, listening too, digging my fingernails into palms, desperate to know....

"Okay," said Boone at last. "We lost them."

I took off my pack, put my back against a tree and slowly sank to my ass. My legs were just one big mass of throbbing, aching tiredness. "I don't think I can move again," I mumbled. "Ever."

Boone threw me an energy bar and a bottle of water from his pack. I glugged the water and wolfed down the bar. It had been hours since we'd woken. Then I let out a low groan and closed my eyes.

"What?" asked Boone.

"I just remembered the coffee you made." I hadn't had a chance to drink it before we left.

"You really like your coffee, huh?" He grinned. "You really are a New Yorker. You drink those big mocha caramel frappuccino things with whipped cream and stuff?"

I shuddered. I'm a purist, when it comes to coffee. "Americano. With *just* the right amount of mil—"

Crack.

I thought Boone had stepped on a dry branch. But

he was falling, sprawling on his ass on the forest floor. It was only when I saw the blood soaking his shirt that I realized he'd been shot.

THIRTY-SEVEN

Boone

ONE SECOND, I was kidding around with Kate. The next I was on my back in the dirt, trying to draw air while I shuddered from the pain.

My training saved me. I had my hand clamped to the wound and was scrambling to my feet before I'd even really registered what had happened. Kate was already running towards me but I shook my head, pointing to the trees, instead. *"Run!"*

We sprinted deeper into the forest but I wasn't sure we were heading the right way. They'd snuck up on us. I'd thought we were safe because I couldn't hear them crashing through the forest, searching. I hadn't figured that they might be slowly creeping closer, like a hunter stalking a deer. I hadn't figured on that because it was impossible....

Unless they knew exactly where we were.

I glanced across at Kate. She was staring at me, white-faced. "You're *shot!"*

For the first time, I let myself think about the wound. Immediately, the pain got worse, spreading up my arm and lancing through my body. The bullet had hit about midway between my left shoulder and my elbow. I loosened my grip a little and blood ran down my forearm. *Ran,* not *gushed.* It hadn't hit an artery, thank God. "I'll live," I grunted.

We splashed across a stream. I had barely any strength in the arm that had been hit and Kate had to help me haul myself up the far bank. "Goddammit," I muttered.

"How did they find us?" panted Kate as we started to run again. She was keeping up but she was already getting tired. She'd barely had a break.

I shook my head, trying to figure it out. "They didn't even have to search. They came right to us." I looked around. I had that itchy feeling between my shoulder blades from being watched. It didn't make any sense. There were thick trees all around us. *It should be a piece of cake to lose them in this.* And yet I could feel them closing in. *How? How are they doing it?*

The forest ended and we burst out into the open. Ahead was fairly flat, rocky terrain. There was a flicker of lightning and almost immediately a crash of thunder: the storm was almost right overhead. I looked up into slate-gray clouds....

And caught a glimpse of something white.

"Oh *goddamn it!*" I said with feeling as everything became clear. "Weiss, you son of a bitch."

"*What?*" asked Kate from beside me, her voice strained. I pointed. "What is it? A plane?"

"A drone," I said bitterly. "They've been watching us this whole time. Probably got a thermal camera on there." I imagined how we must look. Even under the cover of the trees in the forest, we would have stood out as two bright, white hot spots. The drone operator, probably sitting in one of the 4x4s with a laptop, could lead the others to us no matter where we went. Now I thought about it, it made sense. Weiss had billions in the bank: of course he'd hire the best mercenaries he could to help with his escape, and of course they'd have all the toys.

We were in big trouble.

The first fat drop of rain hit my scalp, followed by another and another. Then it was crashing down all around us, the rocks running with it, becoming slick and treacherous. In seconds, it was heavy enough that we could only see ten feet in front of us. The light dimmed even more as the sun was blocked out. We ran on but soon, we couldn't see the difference between the shadows and the cracks between rocks that would snap our ankles if we stepped in them.

Kate was doing her best but I could see she was flagging. It was tough going: as well as keeping up the punishing pace, every few minutes we'd have to climb down the side of a gully or haul ourselves up over some rocks. We were in waterproof clothes but that didn't make it pleasant: the rain was so heavy it ran down our faces, getting in our eyes and making it difficult to breathe. And we were both exhausted already—we'd been going non-stop since we left the cabin. We jogged on for close to another hour and I watched her stride slowly breaking down, her steps getting smaller and smaller. I yelled encouragement, grabbed her with my good arm and pulled her on, but each person only has so much to give. Eventually, her legs buckled and she fell.

I caught her before she hit the rocks and pulled her to me. She was a dead weight in my arms, her legs unable to support her. "We have to keep going!" I yelled over the rain.

She shook her head. "It's useless! Wherever we go, they'll find us!"

I frowned, wanting to argue with her...but she was right. With the drone, they'd inevitably catch us. We couldn't always take a straight line, because we sometimes had to double back to get around an obstacle. But, guided by the drone pilot, the men chasing us could go straight to us every time, eating away at our lead. I scowled. "Come on!" I said stubbornly. I didn't care if she was right. I wasn't going to let them get her.

But she looked up at me, utterly broken. "I *can't,"* she said. "I'm not strong like you." Water was pouring down her face but I could hear in her voice that she was crying.

One half of my heart just melted. The other tightened into white hot fury. I wanted to kill Weiss and his men for doing this to her, for turning her into prey to be hunted.

She had the hood of her waterproof jacket pulled up so all I could see of her was her pale, gorgeous face, shining with water. I pushed a strand of soaking hair back off her cheek. "You *are* strong. You're the strongest woman I've ever met. And you're stubborn." I shook my head. "*Jesus*, you're stubborn! You came all the way to Alaska to get justice for those women. You made sure you got on that plane. You made it through all this. But right now, if you don't run, *Weiss is going to win.* You want to let that happen?"

She sniffed. Shook her head. I saw a little of the fire

I knew return to her eyes.

I took her cheeks between my hands, letting my warmth soak into her, and kissed her hard on the lips. She returned it: slowly at first, her breathing shaky, but with gradually growing strength. I broke the kiss...and she heaved herself upright, her legs wobbly but holding.

We set off again. We were still exhausted but Kate ran with grim determination, her jaw set. Another mile and the terrain started to slope gently down. Now we were in an area I recognized. I'd scouted this way a few times but there weren't many animal trails so I'd abandoned it.

I heard boots again in the distance. Then a shot rang out and Kate and I both flinched. It went wide, splintering a rock next to us, but it showed they were in range.

We tried to move faster, Kate stumbling with fatigue and me wincing at the pain in my arm. But a half mile further on we heard another shot, this one from a different direction. They were starting to surround us.

We aren't going to make it. However hard I tried to shut it out, I could feel the cold, hard reality closing in. We'd pushed ourselves to the limits but it just wasn't enough. We were outnumbered and outmaneuvered.

I slowed to a stop and Kate stumbled to a halt beside me. "It's no good," I told her. "We can't just keep running. Not with that drone up there."

She kicked at a rock in frustration. Now *she* was the one determined to go on. "There's got to be some way to beat it. What do you do in the military?"

"In the military, it's our side who have them," I

said savagely. I'd benefitted from having a drone overhead plenty of times, in Afghanistan and Iraq. I'd never felt the deep, animal panic that comes with being the one being watched. No matter where we ran, there was nowhere to hide. I actually felt a pang of sympathy for the insurgents.

Kate was frowning. "We use helicopters, sometimes, on big busts to make sure none of the bad guys escape." She thought for a second. "You know what they do to get away? Find a building. A big parking garage or a shopping mall. Somewhere they can go into and come out a different side."

I stared at her, thinking hard. It was a pretty good plan...the only problem was, there wasn't a building close by. The only place that couldn't be seen from the air was—

I screwed my eyes shut. *No. Jesus, no. Not there.*

"What?" asked Kate. "Is there somewhere like that?"

I shook my head angrily. But I knew I couldn't fight it for long. The idea was too good not to pursue.

"*What?*" Kate demanded. "You thought of somewhere! Where?"

I shook my head again, wracking my brains. *There must be somewhere else. Anywhere else....*

"Mason, *where?*"

I sighed in defeat. It was our only chance. "The caves."

THIRTY-EIGHT

Boone

LESS THAN TEN MINUTES LATER, we were running down a gully. "Are you sure?" yelled Kate. "It looks like a dead end."

"Trust me," I said grimly. I'd never been in but I'd bought a map of the cave system and studied it. I'd figured that, if I did that, it was a good excuse for leaving this one part of my surroundings unexplored.

The gully narrowed until it was a squeeze for me, then until it was a squeeze for Kate. She had to turn sideways to fit. "Are you serious?" she asked.

"It opens up," I said. I had to fight to keep my voice level. As I slid sideways through the crack, there was less than an inch between me and the rock in front of my face. I could feel my breathing starting to go, slipping out of control like a train running away down a hill. The back of my neck prickled into sweat. The world flickered in front of my eyes....

And then we were inside, in a room as big as my cabin.

"Wow," said Kate. She gazed around at the stalactites hanging from the ceiling, at the natural pool of water in the center of the room.. "It's beautiful," she said quietly. She turned around to grin at me. "Do you think they saw us come in?" Then she frowned. "You okay?"

I was still standing there, trying to get my breathing under control, one hand braced against the damp rocks overhead. *Why does the damn ceiling have to be so low?* I thought irrationally. "I'm fine," I said and looked down at my arm. "Went light-headed. Must have lost some blood."

She ran over to look. Unlike me, she could run around in here and not worry about hitting her head. She pulled out her flashlight and shone it on my arm, then sucked in her breath.

It was the first time I felt like we could stop to look at it. And I was in no hurry to go deeper into the caves. I twisted my arm around so I could see what Kate had seen.

"It's not that bad," I muttered when I saw it.

"Not that bad?" She was staring at my blood-soaked shirt. At the ragged, blood-filled wound beneath it.

I twisted my arm the other way, cursing under my breath as that caused a fresh spike of pain. Kate groaned as she saw the even bigger hole on the other side. "No," I said. "That's good. Means the bullet went straight through."

"Great," she said, sounding unconvinced.

I took a first aid kit from my pack and cleaned the wound as best I could, then dressed it. Focusing on the wound calmed me a little and, for some reason, talking to Kate was helping control my fear, too. "No,"

I said as I finished up.

"No?"

"No, I don't think they saw us come in here." I tested my arm: it hurt, but less than it had. "And the rock's way too thick for them to see us on thermal. So until they come down the gully and find the entrance, they won't know we're in here. And by then, we can be coming out one of the other ways."

"Great!" said Kate. She looked around. "So which way do we go?" She shone her flashlight at the far side of the room where a dark hole the size of a car door led downward. "Through there?"

And immediately, just looking at that black tightness, the fear came back. "Yeah," I said. "Through there."

Kate stepped forward to lead the way, eager to be off. She actually seemed *happy* down here. For once, everything–the low ceilings, the small openings–was perfectly sized for her. But I shook my head and gently pulled her back. "I should go first," I said tightly. "In case I can't fit. Then we don't get separated."

I hunkered down in front of the opening, clicking on my own flashlight. The nearer I got to it, the smaller the damn thing looked. I was going to have to twist like an eel to get through. I hesitated, my spine prickling, sweat breaking out on my back. *Goddammit, why did we have to come down here?*

"You sure you're okay?" asked Kate quietly.

I whipped my head around. "I'm fine!" I snapped. Then immediately felt guilty. *It's not her fault I'm a fuck up.* I glared at the opening instead, trying to will it bigger, but it just sat there, a gaping maw laughing at my weakness.

Goddammit.

I crawled into the hole.

***

One mile in, my heart was hammering in my chest and I was sucking air in through gritted teeth. I had to keep shining my flashlight around each chamber to reassure myself there was space around me, and that the darkness didn't hide walls that were just inches away. *Hold it together, Boone!*

There was another problem, too. I could still hear the hiss of the rain coming down outside, echoing through the chambers. The floor was running with water - only an inch deep, but getting higher. And all that water was going in the same direction as us: down.

We had to hurry.

But a half mile further on, the tunnel narrowed. My shoulders started to brush the sides and I felt the panic start. The ceiling dipped until I had to duck and then hunch and then crouch. Ahead, the only way through was a crawlspace: wide, but less than a foot high.

There suddenly seemed to be not enough air in the cave—

"Mason?" Kate's voice. I realized I'd stopped and was just crouching there, staring at the crawlspace. I shook my head and pressed on. I had to do it. The water was definitely flowing faster as more and more rain filtered down through the rocks above. Another fifteen minutes, maybe, and the crawlspace would be underwater.

The ceiling got even lower. It widened a little but we'd have to crawl on our bellies. I dropped to my knees, fear making my movements slow. I started to lie down on my stomach, but realized that would put my face in the running water. *Dammit.* I'd have to go face-up, just like—

"Mason?"

Just go fast. Get through it fast and you'll be fine. I rolled onto my back and started to slide myself along the ground, waterproof jacket scraping along the rock. I watched the ceiling descend towards my face with each inch. I could hear my breathing speeding up, each gasp echoing around the cave—

"Mason?"

I angrily rammed myself forward. I was right in the crawlspace, now, rock under my back and more rock no more than an inch from my eyes. I had to tilt my head a little to the side to fit.

Go fast! Get through it before—

I hauled myself further in but I only had one working arm and I moved painfully slowly. I could feel the ceiling pressing down on my chest, tight enough that I couldn't take a full inhalation. *Quick, quick!* I tried kicking with my legs but that did nothing except remind me of how little space I had. *Oh Jesus.* I couldn't get a full breath so I breathed faster and faster, huffing like a goddamn steam train—

The panic uncoiled inside my chest, a sleeping monster I'd stupidly awakened. It spread, sinking its claws into me, and every place it touched went numb. My neck. My face. My arms.

No! Not here! Not now!

I heard Kate's voice again but she was far, far away...out of reach. The rock was turning to wood under my fingertips, the smell of it in my nose. I stopped moving because I couldn't even wriggle my shoulders, anymore. The coffin was too tight, too tight—

And then the horror of it forced my mind into the only safe place it had.

Inside.

THIRTY-NINE

Kate

Oh Jesus. Oh God no.

I'd pushed myself into the crawlspace next to him. I was lying on my back, head twisted to the side so that I was looking right into his eyes. And there was nothing there at all. He stared right through me.

Is he dead? His breathing had gotten faster and faster but now I couldn't hear it at all. Had he had a heart attack?

I put my face as close to his as I could, grunting and straining my neck. I still couldn't hear anything but I could feel a faint breath of life on my cheek. I shook his arm. "Mason?"

Nothing. He was still alive. He just wasn't *there* anymore.

Post-Traumatic Stress Disorder. Or something very like it. He'd had an attack and locked up completely. *You idiot, Kate!* I was meant to be good at reading people! How had I missed every single sign? He'd been scared just coming into the cave, more when we first had to crawl. This crawlspace must have been an unimaginable hell. I stared into his unseeing eyes. *Why didn't you say something?*

Because he'd had no choice. My guts twisted. *Not if he wanted to keep me safe.*

And there was another problem. The water that had been washing across the cave floor was getting deeper and the crawlspace was low. Already, it was already only a few inches from Boone's face. Soon, he'd drown in there.

I inched back out of the crawlspace and took hold of his feet. *I'll just pull him out. Then, when he's got some space around him, I can help him.* I braced myself and heaved.

Nothing happened.

I heaved again. Nothing.

A third time, panicking, now. He was just too heavy, the rock he lay on was too rough and, crouched as I was, I had no leverage. If it had been *him* pulling *me,* no problem. But I just wasn't big enough.

Tears in my eyes, I called myself every name under the sun. I've never hated being five foot two so much.

And then I crawled back into the crawlspace beside him. The water was still climbing.

If I couldn't pull him out, I'd find some other way.

I wasn't giving up on him. Not ever.

FORTY

Boone

THERE'S A PLACE you can go to, right down inside yourself, where nothing can hurt you. It's where you go when an IED takes your leg off or when you're being raped.

It's where you go when you're being tortured.

And the more times you go there, the easier it becomes to visit. And the harder it becomes to leave.

You can't hear anything. You can't see anything. Stuff's going on around you but you're not part of it, anymore. You don't even think. You just...are.

Sounds peaceful? It isn't. Because the one emotion you have left is fear. Simple, animal fear. You're cowering and you know that *it*—the pain, the rapist, the torture—is right outside that mental door, waiting for you to come out. You haven't escaped. You've hidden.

You only come out when the need to live, to carry on, outweighs the terror of facing your fear. And if it doesn't? If your fear is so strong it keeps winning out?

Then you just stay in there forever.

I lay there for what felt like hours before I became aware of something. Out on the edges of my perception, I could still feel the ceiling and floor. Sometimes they were rock. Sometimes they were planks of wood. But they were always hard.

Now there was something else. Something soft that slipped between those hard walls, reached inside me and caressed my mind. A voice.

Her voice.

It was barely a whisper and I had to strain to hear. I couldn't leave my hiding place but I could climb up inside and listen. I had to know what she was saying. I was addicted to that voice.

"—and I know that you're scared. I don't know what happened to you. I don't know what those bastards did to you over there but you're not there now. You're here with me. And I'm going to get you through this because you've got me through so much."

The voice died away and there was another noise, one that sent a stab of pain through me. Then she started speaking again.

"I get it," she said. "I get it now. I've figured it out. I get why you can't risk going to jail, not even for a month. And I am so, so sorry I pressed you."

That noise again, the one that hurt me. I pulled myself a little higher so I could figure out what it was.

Crying. My woman was crying. A big, hot wave of emotion rose up inside me, lifting me up towards the exit of my hiding place. I wanted—*needed*—to stop her crying.

"And I swear, Mason," said Kate. "I swear, if you come back to me I will not press you again. You can stay in Alaska. You can live out your whole life here, with *space.*"

My stomach flipped over. The tears were still in her voice. She was talking about giving something up. She'd let me stay here. But she *wanted* me with her. And I wanted to be with her.

"But Mason, right now, *right now,* I need you to come back to me. I need you to come back because we have to get out of here. The cave is filling up with water and I can't move you and *I'm not leaving you behind!*" She was crying again. "You hear me, Mason? I am *not leaving you behind* so you come back to me *right now!*"

And my hiding place started to fill with thick, red anger. Anger at how the fear had controlled me. Anger at how it had made me isolate myself for so long. Anger at having a shot with a life with her, with this amazing woman, and being too scared to take it. Anger at myself because Kate was going to die down here in a dark cave if I didn't—If I didn't—

The anger filled every corner of my hiding place, crushing me, but I didn't fight the rage: I fed it. I thought of how Kate had looked when she drowned, her skin cold and her lips blue. I thought of her dying like that, down here, because she was too damn stubborn to leave me and I was too damn scared to—

The pressure built and built until my hiding place was too small to contain it. And then it exploded, launching me past the fear and *up*—

Back to her.

My eyes focused and she was there, as close as if we were lying in bed. Had she been there the whole time? Her soft skin was streaked with cave slime and her mahogany hair was soaked and dripping on one side from the water. That need to protect her swelled up inside me: this was no place for her. But it was her eyes that hit me the most: wide and scared. I'd scared her.

I looked into those eyes and grabbed her hand. "*Sorry*," I managed at last. The water was lapping against my cheeks. "Let's get the fuck out of here."

And I began to haul myself on through the crawlspace. The fear wasn't gone but it had been forced down deep enough that it felt like it wouldn't return for a little while.

I made it through and went to help Kate, but with her size she slithered through just fine on her own. In the next chamber, the water was up to my knees which meant it was halfway up her thighs. But the floor was starting to angle upward.

Another half hour and we caught our first glimpse of daylight. Ten minutes after that, we hauled ourselves up into a small cave that led out into a forest. By my rough guesswork, we'd come out over a mile from where we went in.

I stared back at the dark hole we'd emerged from. I couldn't believe I'd made it through. How the hell had she done that? Somehow, she'd triggered something in me even more powerful than the fear. I'd been way down inside myself and she'd guided me out.

I shook my head. I'd made it back...*this time.* But now that the adrenaline was wearing off, just the idea of being in a small space made my chest tighten up. I'd gotten lucky. I'd very nearly gotten her killed down there.

I caught Kate's eye and suddenly my face was burning. I felt like I wanted to crawl right back down into the darkness again. This whole time, I'd been hiding my problems from her. Now the guy she'd come to rely on had suddenly turned out to be a mess.

I stomped over to the cave mouth, where she was standing looking out at the rain. "Thank you," I said. It came out as a low growl.

She bit her lip and just nodded. Her eyes were liquid and that made my face heat even more. *I don't need your sympathy!*

"We should move," I grunted. "In case they send someone in and follow us, or trace the caves on a map."

I headed out into the rain, leaving her to follow. I felt shitty for doing it but I couldn't face talking about what had happened. She'd seen a part of me I hid from everyone...hell, even from myself. That's why I was living all the way out here, so I wouldn't have to face it.

That was why I couldn't go with her, if we made it to a town. Once she was safe, we needed to part ways.

"Where are we headed?" Kate's voice, behind me. Asking much more than just our destination.

I paused, getting my bearings. Both of us were exhausted and we'd barely eaten since we left the cabin. We needed a place to rest and regain our strength.

"I know a place," I told her. And led the way.

FORTY-ONE

Kate

THE RAIN SLOWED and finally stopped. The storm clouds gradually broke up and the mid-afternoon sun started to filter through.

After another hour of walking, the sky was almost clear and the sun was warm enough that I stripped off my waterproof jacket. We were in a sheltered valley so there was almost no breeze and that helped, too. The forest had opened up, with large clearings filled with soft ferns and mossy banks, and it was easy going. The storm hadn't reached this far and it was a relief just to be somewhere dry. It would have been a pleasant walk except...Boone was silent. Totally and utterly silent. He strode on ahead, his huge body carving a path for me through the foliage.

I knew we needed to talk but I had no idea how to start. Every time I tried to catch up to him, his shoulders hunched and his head dipped, closing me out. And with every minute we didn't talk, I felt the tension building.

I was just about to try again when he suddenly stopped, unslung his pack and tossed it down on the ground. "We're here," he grunted.

I'd been watching him so hard, I hadn't looked up at our surroundings for a while. I stopped...and gasped.

We were in a circular clearing, the ground underfoot soft, springy turf thick with wildflowers. In the center of the clearing was a spot that had been cleared of grass, the ground scorched and blackened. *He's been here before.* Through the trees I could glimpse the sun reflecting off water and there was a noise in the background I couldn't identify, a low roar.

It was beautiful. But all my attention was on Boone. He turned and caught my eye for a moment and I opened my mouth to speak–

"I'll get a fire going," he muttered and stalked off towards the nearest tree. He stripped off his jacket, pulled a lethal-looking folding axe from his pack and swung it at the trunk without breaking his stride, burying it deep in the trunk. I flinched.

He turned his back fully to me, then pulled the axe out and swung it again, stubbornly ignoring his injured arm. Wood chips arced over his shoulder. Again. Again, tearing through the tree like it was his enemy. Yet he didn't curse or yell, just glared down at the destruction, grimly silent.

"Mason," I said timidly.

The tree creaked and then crashed to the ground. He started splitting off logs with brutal efficiency, the axe rising and falling, the muscles of his arms gleaming and hard.

"Mason?"

He gathered the logs in his arms and stalked past

me on his way to the scorched ground.

"*Mason!*" I grabbed hold of his arm as he passed. His body throbbed with heat under my fingers, the muscles like rock. He could have easily pulled out of my grip but he froze there as if he'd rather suffer anything than risk hurting me.

I swallowed, searching for words. "We should talk."

He shook his head.

I opened my hand and he slipped past, out of reach. He crouched in the center of the clearing and began slamming the logs into place, his hands so big that he held each one-handed.

"It might help—"

"No it *wouldn't!*" His voice shook the trees. His back rose and fell as he panted in anger, eyes fixed on the fire, body taut with barely-contained violence. It would have been terrifying if I hadn't spent so much time with him over the last few days. The one thing I knew for certain was that he wouldn't hurt me.

Three cautious steps took me to his side. I squatted down next to him but he wouldn't even look at me. "I get now why you're out here. I get why you can't risk being put in a cell. I want to help."

"You can't," he said flatly. "No one can. I went out there; I came back...changed." But his voice didn't say *changed*. It said *broken*.

It said *weak*.

Oh God. Is *that* how he sees it? I fell silent and he went back to building the fire.

"Mason," I said softly.

He kept going.

"*Mason*."

He raised his hand, still with a log in it, but he

didn't lay it down. He was so mad with himself he was panting, nostrils flaring like a bull.

"Listen to me," I said, "because I need to say something. What you went through out there: I can't even imagine. I don't know what you were like before that. But I know you *now.*" My voice dropped and, as I spoke again, I saw his shoulders drop just a little, as if the sound of it soothed him. "I've seen your nightmares. I've seen you at your worst. And I *don't care.* I still...I—" My throat closed up. "I *think I'm falling in love with you.*"

He finally turned to look at me. Glared at me. Demanded that I be lying.

I sucked in a long, low breath, my eyes never leaving his. And nodded.

When he spoke, each word came as if he was hauling it up from enormous depths. "You saw what I was like down there. It's not just about small spaces. It's about being *trapped.* Imprisoned. And that's what they're going to do to me. They're going to lock me up. Maybe you'll get me an appeal and maybe it'll work but it'll take months. As soon as they chain me up, I'll be like I was down there. And this time, *I might never make it back.*" He shook his head. "I can't go back with you, Kate."

I'd thought I understood, but I hadn't. The real prison he was afraid of was inside him. He carried it around with him, even out here in Alaska, knowing that it could suck him down into himself and seal him there at any time. He hadn't been healing, these four long years. He'd just been avoiding his triggers. If he stayed up here on his own, sooner or later he *would* wind up in that catatonic state, and with no one to talk him out of it...*Jesus, he'll die up here.* "I know," I said, my voice catching. "But it doesn't change how I feel about you. And if you can't come back with me...." The words were on my lips before I even knew I was going to say them. "Then maybe I can stay here with you."

I saw his hands tighten on the log he was holding. The muscles flexed all the way up his arms until I thought the wood was going to crush in his grip—

And then he hurled down the log and grabbed *me*.

Suddenly his weight was bearing me down to the ground, my shoulders slamming into the soft grass, his big body straddling mine. "Goddammit, Kate!" he snarled. "This is no place for you!"

"It's no place for a woman?" I said defensively.

"It's no place for *anyone!* Do you know how long it is since I read a newspaper? Saw a football game? Do you know how long it was, before you showed up, since I'd talked to another person?" He shook his head. "Don't say what you don't mean."

I stared up at him. I was still reeling from what I'd just said: I was at least as surprised as he was. My head was full of New York: the FBI and shopping with my friend Erin and that little rooftop bar I knew where you could sip a glass of wine while you watched the sun go down and really *freakin'* good coffee—

But if I went back, I'd never see him again.

"I do mean it," I whispered. It scared the hell out of me. But in my heart, it felt *right*.

He drew in a deep, shaky breath, glaring down at me. I reached for him but he shook his head savagely, grabbed my wrists and pinned them to the ground. "Why do you have to be so goddamn stubborn?" he snapped.

I stared right up into his eyes, unrepentant. "Because it's what you need."

He growled and turned his head, staring off into the distance. I could see him fighting to control himself. He was teetering on the edge....

He turned back to me, eyes blazing...and then he shook his head as if in disbelief at what he was doing. "*You're* what I need."

And with my wrists still pinned to the ground, he leaned down and kissed me.

FORTY-TWO

Kate

THE KISS took my breath away. His lips spread mine, demanding that I make way for him. All his strength and raw animal power blazed down into me through those hard lips and, just like at the cabin, I went *weak*. His tongue found mine and swirled around the tip and I felt all the layers of steel and rock I put up just disintegrate, crumbling from the inside out. They melted, vaporized, and I became soft as cloud, wrapping around him.

His hands slid down my arms. He cupped my cheek with one hand, controlling my head as his mouth took possession of me. His fingertips slid through the tight strands of my hair while his other hand moved down and—

I gasped as his warm palm slipped under all my layers of clothes and slid up to my breast. He pushed the cup aside and cupped my soft flesh, his thumb working across my nipple. I arched my back up off the ground, feeling the heat of him pressing against me.

But then his lips left mine and I opened my eyes, panting up at him.

He was staring down at me, eyes narrowed with need. "You've been driving me crazy since the first time I saw you." His hand ran down my side, smoothing over my skin. I could hear the frustration in his voice, like it almost angered him to be so attracted to me. "You're just so..." One hand ran over my tightly-bound hair, then fingered my ponytail. "But so..." The hand under my clothes rose and found my breast, squeezing it.

What? I wondered. *What does that mean?*

He shook his head ruefully. Helplessly. "God *damn* you, Kate."

I swallowed, heat blossoming inside me and sinking straight down to my groin. I'd never made anyone helpless before.

He growled, leaned down and kissed me again: a kiss that had rhythm, that rose and fell. One big hand scooped under my head and cradled it as he kissed me, his thumb toying with the band that held my ponytail in place. My lips pressed up against his, needing him. My hands grabbed the front of his shirt.

He rolled us over so I was on top. I sat up, my palms exploring his chest and—

"*Whoah!*" He caught me as I toppled sideways. "You okay?"

I blinked. I'd gone suddenly light-headed. "Yeah," I said breathlessly. "I just went spinny for a second." I leaned down to kiss him.

He put a hand on my shoulder, peering intently at me. Then he shook his head. "Dammit. I'm a moron." He picked me up by the waist and gently set me down on my ass.

"What?" I was bemused...and still ready to go.

"How long is it since you ate something?" he asked.

I thought back. I'd had an energy bar when we stopped that morning and.... I frowned. Come to think of it, that was all I'd had, all day. "A while," I admitted. I started to get up. "But back in New York, I skip meals all the time."

He grabbed my shoulders and pushed me firmly back down to the ground. "Back in New York you're sitting at a desk. You've been running and climbing all day. You're running on empty."

I wanted to tell him he was wrong. Every time I looked at him, I couldn't stop my gaze from going down to that huge, broad chest and those big shoulders. I wanted him pressed against me, wanted that feeling of being soft and vulnerable under him. I wanted it so bad it was almost frightening.

But...now that I thought about it, I *did* feel weird. I'd been running on adrenaline so long, I'd gotten used to it. Now that we'd stopped I just felt utterly wiped out and I was so hungry my stomach was cramping.

I met his eyes and he gave me a look. *See?*

I nodded grudgingly. "But—"

He put one huge finger to my lips, silencing me. He put his face close to mine, his stubble grazing my cheek, and said, "Stop arguing. I'm going to get some food inside you and then I'm going to do every damn thing to you I've been wanting to." I felt him smile. "So just be patient, you damn hussy."

I flushed. "I'm a New Yorker," I mumbled. "We're not good at patient."

He slid an arm around my waist and guided me over to where he'd laid the fire. "Then get over here and help me get this lit. We need to keep you warm."

He got the flint and steel out of my pack and showed me how to scrape a little dry wood from inside the log to use as kindling. Then he took my hands in his and guided me, showing me how to strike flint against steel to make a spark. I couldn't get it at first. I looked up at him in frustration.

"Keep going," he said firmly. "I want you to know how to do it. Just in case."

I focused...and after three more tries, I got it. The kindling caught, we blew on it until it flared and I saw a flame lick up against the logs. A little surge of pride hit me. *I made fire!*

Boone dug in his pack and pulled out some brown plastic pouches. He tossed them to me. "Choose."

I blinked down at them. "What are these?"

"MREs. Military rations."

There was no logo, no colorful branding or shots of the prepared meal, just some plain black text. *Meal. Ready-to-Eat.* I had a choice of *Chili with Beans, Beef Stew* or *Chicken Chunks*. I handed him the *Beef Stew*. "This is what you lived on?"

"When we were out in the field, pretty much."

He opened the pouch and tipped the contents into my lap, then showed me how to put the entree bag into the flameless heater bag and top it up with water to trigger the chemical reaction. Meanwhile, I sorted through the rest of the ration: there was a candy bar, peanut butter and crackers, fruit drink powder, a spork, seasonings and– "Wait, there's a *matchbook?*" I looked at him accusingly. "Why did you make me use the flint and steel?"

"Because it won't run out. It's good as a last resort. Put it in your pocket."

I stuffed it in my jacket pocket and kept looking through the ration pack contents. *Instant coffee!* I fingered the little packet lovingly. I'd save that for the next morning.

By now, the food was heating up. I sniffed the pouch experimentally. It smelled *sort* of like beef stew.

"Don't expect too much," Mason warned. "It's meant to keep you alive. It's not gourmet cooking."

I dug in. Maybe it was just because I was so hungry but it actually wasn't too bad: salty and very processed, but I'd eaten worse things back in college. I couldn't imagine eating food like that for weeks on end, though. I devoured the stew, then the crackers and candy bar. I was so busy eating, I didn't realize until the end that he was watching me. "What?" I asked self-conscious.

He shrugged those massive shoulders. "I just like looking at you."

"You like watching me *eat?*"

"I like watching you do anything."

I flushed and stared at him. *Could this really work?* Once we'd made it to a town and raised the alarm about Weiss's escape, could I really stay here with him? Part of me was still reeling from what I'd done. I'd never come out with something so impulsive in my entire life. And staying with him was a half-solution, at best. He'd still be a fugitive, unable to have any contact with anyone. He'd still be denied justice and the man who'd actually killed that family in Afghanistan would still be free. He'd still relive the horror he'd been through every single night. And I'd never see my friends, my family...I'd never see *anyone* again.

But a half solution is better than no solution. *We'll make it work.* Because every time I looked at him, every time I felt his touch, I just felt...protected. In a way I'd never felt my whole life.

He was still gazing at me. "Stop it," I mumbled, embarrassed. "I'm all—" I lifted my arms, indicating my outsize, borrowed clothes, my bedraggled hair.

"You look great." And I could hear in his voice that he meant it. Somehow, that made me feel better about myself than any number of compliments during a fancy date.

"I feel like I haven't washed in a week," I muttered, looking down at myself.

A smile slowly spread across his face.

"What?" I asked. Part of me was just drinking in that smile: big and honest and just a little bit dirty, a smile that went right to where I lived. When I'd first met him, he'd *never* smiled.

He stood up. "You feeling okay, now?"

I nodded cautiously. The light-headedness had gone.

He reached out his hand. "Then come with me."

I took his hand and he hauled me up, then led me through the trees. Every few steps, he'd squeeze my hand as if he was excited to show me something. We emerged into another clearing and—

Now I knew what the roaring I'd heard was. A stream was fed by a waterfall which crashed down from a towering cliff. A white mist rose up from where the water hit, soaking the rocks around it.

"It's beautiful," I said. Then I looked at him questioningly because I couldn't figure out why he'd brought me there, in the middle of talking about—

I froze. "Oh no. Oh, *hell* no!"

He grinned. And unbuttoned his shirt.

"No. *No*. Are you kidding? Tell me you're kidding."

He undid his pants. "You said you needed a wash."

I glanced at the waterfall. "Do you know how *cold* that'll be?" My voice was shrill. "You *cannot* be serious."

"This is where I wash, when I come through here." He took off his pants and boots.

"I'll *freeze!*"

"You'll warm up. That's what the fire's for." He pushed his jockey shorts down his legs and just stood there, grinning at me and—

I couldn't take my eyes off his groin. His cock was swelling and hardening, rising up...just from looking at me.

"Come join me," he said, eyes eating me up. And he turned and strode towards the stream.

I stood there, flushed and uncertain. The water would be freezing but the thought of the two of us in, it, naked....

If I'm going to live in Alaska....

I cursed and took off my clothes. The sun was just beginning to set and it was still warm where it hit my body. I picked my way carefully over to the stream.

As I watched, Boone plunged in. The water was knee-high, for him, and he didn't wince or even grunt, just strode in as if it was a heated pool. He turned and looked at me over his shoulder and the look he gave me sent such a deep, hot *throb* down to my groin that I crushed my thighs together.

I saw his cock jerk in response. Then he was under the waterfall, the water half-hiding him as it cascaded down his muscled back.

It can't be that bad, I reasoned. *It's probably like*

swimming in the sea, where it's sometimes warmer than the air. I took a deep breath and stepped down into the stream.

The cold rushed in from every millimeter of skin. My leg felt as if it had been flash-frozen to a lump of hard, blue ice. It was so cold it *hurt.* The feeling rocketed up inside me and came out of my mouth as a long, agonized moan of horror.

The foot which was still on the bank pressed down instinctively to lift me out...but then I looked at Boone under the waterfall. The water sluiced down the muscles of his shoulders and back, making them shine, before flowing down over the taut cheeks of his ass. I wanted to be in there with him.

He turned around and looked at me again and, this time, he gave me a grin. Gentle and just slightly mocking: *if it's too cold for you....*

That did it. Gritting my teeth, I put the other leg in the water. *Ahhh!* The second leg wasn't any better than the first. Before I could change my mind, I began wading towards Boone, every movement sending fresh waves of cold up my body, my eyes going wider and wider. As I reached him, he stepped aside a little to make space for me under the waterfall.

I looked up at it. At the moment, only my legs were freezing. Did I really want to?

Maybe that's the trick. Maybe it's better when you're fully under. I steeled myself. *It'll be bracing and fresh and—*

I stepped forward and the water hit me. My jaw dropped open and I attempted to suck every molecule of air out of Alaska in one huge inhalation of horror. Then I exhaled every curse word I'd ever heard.

"God*damn,* Lydecker." Boone sounded impressed.

"You kiss your mother with that mouth?"

I punched him on the arm and tried to speak but I was shaking too hard to form words. "You *b—b—b—bastard!* How are you not cold?"

"I *am* cold. I was just hiding it. I wanted to see you come in."

I punched his arm again and turned to get out. But suddenly he gathered me up, one arm under my naked ass and one under my arms, and lifted me up out of the water. An instant later, his lips were on mine and our bodies were pressed together.

I panted in shock and then opened up to the kiss, drawing warmth and strength from him. My nipples had gone as hard as pebbles and were scraping across his chest. He had one leg slightly bent and his thigh was pressed up between my legs, grinding in just the right place. The whole back of my body was freezing, the fast-moving water sucking the warmth from me. But the whole front of my body was tight against Boone and his hard body throbbed with heat. His kisses were hungry, now, urgent and primal. Full-on *wild.*

I suddenly remembered what he'd said, before he made me stop to eat: *I'm going to do every damn thing to you I've been wanting to.*

He hefted me a little higher on his body and my legs wrapped around his waist. The cold was still making me breathless, but with every kiss I filled up with fire. I felt him pull off the hair band that held my ponytail and then my hair was hanging long and loose and being drenched by the waterfall.

He clutched me tight to him and started walking us out, still kissing me. As soon as the water stopped hitting my body, I became aware of every millimeter of my exposed skin. Everything was tingling and new, as if the cold had washed away not just the dirt but years of stress and grind. I was still shivering and gasping but I felt *amazing*.

And very, very turned on. My groin was hard up against his and, with every step, his cock ground against me. By the time we'd waded to the bank I was a hot mess. Then he stepped up onto the bank, carrying my weight effortlessly, and strode towards the fire.

FORTY-THREE

Kate

I finally broke the kiss and pulled back a little so that I could look at him.

The last light of the day was hitting him from one side, making his wet body gleam like burnished copper. Every muscle stood out, highlighted by warm, golden light and deep black shadow. I couldn't stop myself. I covered his lips and cheeks with kisses, feeling his stubble scrape against me. My hands ran over his shoulders, his biceps, his chest. Just as at the cabin, I could feel something unlocking, deep inside me. This man made me *frantic.* I couldn't get enough of him, wanted his whole hard form against me *now.*

He crouched and lowered me to the ground. The grass beside the fire was warm and the flames bathed my chilled body in glorious heat. I lay there panting, looking up at him as he knelt between my legs and gazed at me. I still couldn't get used to the way he just *watched* me. Like I was the most amazing thing he'd ever seen.

"I'm nothing special," I thought, embarrassed. And then, as I saw his expression change, I realized I'd said it out loud.

His brow knitted. "What stupid son of a bitch made you think *that?"* he growled.

I just stared up at him, flushing. He planted his hands either side of my head and slowly lowered himself down on arms that were so solid, so deliciously *thick,* that they made me shiver the last of the cold out of me. He kissed my forehead. "I love your brain," he told me. "You're smart and you can talk to people—a lot better than I can. You can make anyone do any damn thing." He kissed my eyelids. "I love your eyes. I love the way you look at Alaska, seeing everything for the first time. I love it when I see you getting turned on and those eyes go all big and wide and you start panting—like right now."

I opened my eyes and—yes—I was panting. I looked down at my body. "I'm too *small."*

He made a scoffing sound, deep in his throat. "Too small? What's *too small?* I've met Special Forces guys who don't have half the guts you got." He leaned down and punctuated his words with kisses. "You are *exactly. The right. Size."*

A warm glow joined the deeper, darker heat that was building inside me.

"I love your breasts." He leaned down and kissed one hardened nipple, making me gasp. "Firm and lush and just goddamn beautiful. I love 'em even more because you hide them under that damn suit. I wanted to strip it off you from the first second I saw you."

He kissed his way down my stomach. I realized where he was heading and drew my breath in, instinctively closing my thighs.

He glanced up at me, pinned me with a look and shook his head.

I melted...and let my legs part.

He slid down my body and his elbows spread my knees. *Wide.* I gasped. No one had ever looked at me down there in the way he was: like he was soaking up something that was beautiful, as well as making him hard. "You're gorgeous," he said, his voice going growly with lust. "Goddamn gorgeous."

And then he lowered his head to my groin and I realized *this* was one of the things he'd been wanting to do. I began to pant, anticipating...I could feel the tiny drops of water still rolling down my sensitive flesh. I could feel the heat from the fire gently warming me. And then—

I'd been half-sitting up, watching him, but suddenly my head pressed back against the ground. The very tip of his tongue was drawing a scorching line down the length of one lip. It blazed down me with agonizing slowness, sending twisting, lashing streamers of silver pleasures up inside me. He reached the bottom and started up the other side and I groaned and rocked my head back, closing my eyes.

His tongue glided around my clit, teasing it, never quite touching it directly. The pleasure grew stronger, harder, the streamers coiling in my center and contracting into a growing ball of heat. "*M—Mason!*" I gasped. I couldn't believe how gentle he was being, wouldn't have dreamed his huge body was capable of it. I could feel the heat turning to slick moisture, my ass beginning to grind against the ground.

He started to lap at me, then open me, and I clutched fistfuls of grass. Two fingers slid inside me, exquisitely thick and *ohgodyesknuckles*. My eyes flew open and I stared up at the sky. As the sun sank, a million pinpricks of light were just starting to glow in the dark blue. I was tiny: barely a speck in this vast land, and so naked, lying there exposed on my back....

And yet, for the first time, Alaska didn't feel huge and terrifying because I had *him* right there, anchoring me. And now his lips were closing around my clit, his fingers twisting and pushing deep, pumping in an insistent rhythm as I tossed my head against the grass.

The pleasure was rippling through me, soaking into the tight, hot ball I knew was going to explode. I sucked in air through my nose, biting my lip. His free hand slid up my body and found my breast and I arched up, pressing it into his palm. The pleasure swelled and shuddered, about to burst. My thighs tried to press together—

And found the thickness of his shoulders bracing them apart, solid and immovable, and that sent me over the edge. I cried out, my voice rising to the treetops, and shuddered against him. Then I collapsed back onto the grass, panting, and he slid up and held me close. It was long minutes before I was capable of speech. "For a guy who hasn't seen a woman in four years," I managed, "You're suspiciously talented."

"I've had a lot of time to think about what I'd do," he growled. "About *all* the things I'd do." He shifted his body against mine and I felt his cock press against my thigh: still damp from the waterfall, scorching hot and very, very hard.

I looked up at him, seeing the lust in his eyes. I swallowed, feeling myself getting even wetter.

His thighs nudged mine further apart. There was something about feeling his muscled hips sinking between my legs that made me giddy. The head of him brushed up against my moist folds and I caught my breath. He hooked his forearms under mine and then—

My eyes went wide as he sank into me, buttery smooth, steel wrapped in silk. I gasped at his size, his thickness, my toes dancing. "M—*Mason!*"

He slowed but didn't stop, filling me millimeter by tight, hot millimeter until all I could feel was me wrapped around him, until there didn't seem to be any air left in my lungs. And then I felt the damp curls of his hair press against me and I knew he was rooted in me.

He leaned down and kissed me, owning my mouth, taking me hard and deep as he showed me what he was about to do to my body. My head lifted off the ground, meeting him, showing him I wanted it at least as badly as he did. My fingers slid through his hair, stroked up his stubbled cheeks—

And then he was moving. First slow, gentle thrusts like the tide. Then, as the smooth friction overtook us both, he started driving into me, making me close my eyes and gasp in pleasure, my chin pointed to the stars. I grabbed for him but his hands caught mine in mid-air and pressed them to the ground either side of my head, our fingers intertwining. I panted up at him, feeling the cool grass against my knuckles.

Our breathing become one: quick little pants of air as his body slammed into mine, faster and faster. Something about the size of him, about the way he hulked over me, about the way I looked up and saw only him, his wide shoulders blocking out everything else, turned my insides soft as water. It was utterly different to sex with the men I'd dated in New York:

this was simple and primal and wild. I could feel the soft grass under my ass, the cool breeze on one side of me and the warmth of the fire on the other but part of me still couldn't believe it: *I'm outside. I'm doing this outside!*

He sped up again, his breathing quickening, staring down at me with those Alaska-blue eyes. I realized he was watching for something, hungry for it.

He wanted to see me *undone*. And he was going to.

As he lowered himself more, bracing his muscled forearms on the ground, his chest started to stroke against my breasts. The touch of his hard body against my nipples sent ripples of pleasure spreading outward, colliding and combining, twisting down into a white-hot, throbbing center. God, he was so gorgeous, his naked body painted gold and orange by the firelight, every muscle standing out. My hair tossed on the grass, my breathing growing ragged. I couldn't take it any more: I had to touch him.

I wrestled my hands out from under his and ran them over his back, feeling every muscle, clinging to him. I saw his mouth curl up at the corners as he saw my desperation...and it felt good. I'd spent my whole life being strong, never for a second letting anyone see me lose it: not even in bed. *Especially* not in bed, with some guy who might use it against me. With Boone, I had no choice. I couldn't hide what was going on inside me and I didn't need to. Boone relished my pleasure.

I was arching and straining, now, flexing my groin up to meet his every thrust, my hips circling in a way that made him growl. I could tell he was getting close, too. He leaned on one elbow and cradled my head, staring down into my eyes. His lips sank closer and closer to mine, until there were only a few inches between our faces. We were connected completely, like I'd never been with anyone. The pleasure built and tightened, my hands hooked around the small of his back and dragged him desperately in—

He suddenly leaned down and kissed me, lips spreading mine, tongue driving deep, and the sudden touch of him there sent me over the edge. I came with a scream that echoed far out into the forest, bucking and shuddering against him, hooking my legs around his. And then he was growling deep in his throat and lunging into me and I felt the hot explosion of him deep inside.

***

Afterwards, we clung to each other, kissing softly. The fire kept our naked bodies warm but, eventually, the heat started to seep from us and we needed to wrap up in something. Boone pulled a sleeping bag from his pack, got in it and crushed himself right back against the far side, then scooped me in in front of him, my back to his chest, and I zipped up the zipper to seal us in. He wrapped his arms around me: one muscled forearm around my waist and one across my breasts so he could gently cup one in his hand. Mason's big body stretched the sleeping bag tight: we only just fit. If I'd been a regular-sized woman, I'm not sure it would have worked. But him and me together: that was perfect.

We were so closely pressed that I could feel every rise and fall of his chest, every beat of his heart. It was the coziest I could ever remember being. Then he gently rolled us over so that we were lying on our backs, me on his chest. I yelped in surprise.

"That okay?" he rumbled.

"Yeah," I said, because it was fantastic, like lying on a heated bed. "But am I crushing you?"

He didn't answer but I felt him smirk, as if he could happily stand three of me on top of him. He squeezed me a little tighter.

I looked up at the stars. The sky had darkened to black and the storm had blown away to leave a clear night. A million stars gleamed above us. Funny how, in New York, I'd always thought of the night sky as *dark*.

Our breathing slowed but sleep didn't come. I could feel something building in the silence between us. Something that hadn't been able to come out, before. But now that I'd said I'd stay in Alaska with him, something that had to.

He took a slow, deep breath...and told me what happened to him.

FORTY-FOUR

Boone

I STARED up at the stars. The huge, open sky was exactly what I needed to get me through this. But it wasn't the most important thing. That was lying stretched out on top of me. The smell of her hair, the soft press of her against my chest, the smoothness of her breast under my palm. That was what convinced my brain I was safe in Alaska. That was what kept me distant enough from the memories that I could bear to revisit them.

"The insurgents found me standing over the bodies of a family," I said. "All of them had guns pointed at me and I figured I was dead...but they took me prisoner instead. At first, I thought maybe they'd trade me or execute me....but no. They wanted me to suffer."

She didn't say anything, maybe didn't want to stop my flow. But she pushed her body down against mine in sympathy, our nakedness meaning that I could feel her warmth all the way from her toes to the top of her head.

"They took me to this basement: a house right in the center of the city. They put duct tape over my mouth so I couldn't make a noise. I could hear US troops in the street outside, searching for me, but they had no clue I was there. The insurgents couldn't figure out what to do with me, at first. So they blindfolded me and chained my wrists and ankles, and then chained me to a radiator. No food or water, just darkness."

I felt her body stiffen against mine. "How long?" she asked.

"Three days." I felt her shudder and squeezed her tight. I knew she was thinking of my arrest, in Koyuk, and the time I'd spent overnight in chains. Of the plane and the way I'd sat chained there, halfway to slipping back into the nightmare, until she'd brought me the water.

"Then, on the fourth day, some guy pulled off my blindfold and stared down at me. I recognized the face: not one of their leaders but he was high up. He spoke a little English. Told me I was going to enter hell. I thought he was going to kill me..."—my breath caught—"but that wasn't what he meant at all."

"The basement had a dirt floor." I said. "They started digging a pit." I was surprised by how calm my voice was, so far. "About six feet long, four feet wide. Like a single bed." I let that sink in for a moment. Heard Kate's scared intake of breath: praying that this wasn't going where she thought it was going.

"Then they brought in a coffin," I said. "And I figured it out. We'd been trained on how to survive things: interrogation, torture. But this wasn't that. Even if I'd wanted to give up my country, they weren't interested. There was nothing I could do to stop it. It was going to happen."

Kate was taking tiny little panic breaths, now, just the thought of it getting to her. She reached back and felt for my hand and I squeezed hers tight.

"They left the chains on when they lifted me in. When they put the lid on the coffin, I figured that was it. An hour of air, maybe, and then I'll suffocate. But no." I could hear my voice going tight. "The guy was serious, when he talked about me entering hell."

It took me a few seconds before I could continue. I had to stare very hard up at the night sky. I had to feel the wind against my face and smell the wood smoke from the fire to really ground myself in Alaska.

"There was a rubber tube," I said at last. "Leading up out of the coffin. For air and water."

Kate's whole body went rigid as the image hit her. "Oh Jesus," she breathed. "Oh, Jesus, *no!*" She tried to turn over to face me but there wasn't space in the sleeping bag. In a way, I was glad. There was nothing I wanted more than to see that gorgeous face...but if I saw her eyes, I wasn't sure I'd be able to continue. And I needed to get this out. I'd been waiting four years.

"The lid was maybe an inch from my face," I told her. "Even without the chains, there was no space to move around, but the chains meant I couldn't stretch, couldn't even try to move. "I felt the coffin lift and then lower—they had to use ropes, like at a funeral. And then I bumped down at the bottom and I heard the first shovel full of earth hit the top. It was already nearly pitch black but there'd been some tiny cracks of light: gaps between the lid and the coffin. Now, it went totally dark. Dark like you've never—"

Unexpectedly, my voice went: just dropped away to nothing and I couldn't talk. I could smell the wood and feel the splinters against my knuckles. I could feel the icy-cold metal of the chains against my wrists and hear the fading *whump, whump, whump* of dirt hitting the coffin lid. The stars disappeared. The fire disappeared. I'd gone too close to the memories and now they were taking me, the thing that lived inside me rising up to swallow me whole....

But then *she* was there, stretching the sleeping bag almost to breaking point as she twisted over and lay flat on my chest, arms wrapping around me, hugging me tight. Her lips pressed to the line between my pecs and she clung on for dear life—

I pulled myself out of the darkness towards her warmth and softness and slowly, slowly, I came back.

"And then there was just quiet," I said. "But not *total* quiet. They hadn't buried me that deep. I could still hear stuff, muffled but *there*. Traffic going past outside. Helicopters overhead. Troops—*our* troops—on the street outside, patrolling. By now, they'd stopped looking for me. They figured I'd been captured and taken off into the mountains and executed. They had no idea I was right there."

I sucked in a long breath, trying to slow my heart rate. "I couldn't move. I could hardly breathe. There was no day, no night, just *dark*. I didn't suffocate, so I guessed they'd wedged the tube somewhere where air could get in. And now and again they'd pour some water down the tube and I learned to catch some of it in my mouth, so I didn't die of thirst. After the first few times that happened, it sank in: *this isn't going to end. I'm trapped.*"

"I lost all track of time: there was no way to gauge

it, no day and no night, just dark. After a while, I wasn't even sure if I was asleep or awake. I saw buddies I knew were dead. I saw Alaska. I saw all sorts of shit, never sure if I was dreaming or hallucinating. And when the dream ended, I was always still in the coffin, still trapped...."

Kate inched up my body and pressed her cheek to mine. Hers was wet with tears. "How long?" she whispered.

I swallowed. "Thirteen days."

She raised herself up on her arms, stretching the sleeping bag. Her face had gone snow white and her eyes *commanded* me to make it not so. Then she fell against me, burying her head in the crook of my shoulder, her hot tears soaking my cheek.

"How were you rescued?" she asked at last.

I stared up at the stars. "I wasn't."

I felt her turn her head to look at me. Just knowing she was there gave me the strength to get through the next part. In some ways, it was the toughest part of all.

"They dug me up," I said. "Lifted out the coffin, pried off the lid. I hadn't seen light in almost two weeks so at first, my eyes couldn't even focus. And my mind was cracking—or maybe it *had* cracked. I wasn't sure if it was real or just a dream. It had taken three of them to lift me in but now it only took two to haul me out: I was a bag of bones. I figured they were going to kill me, finally, maybe behead me and put it on YouTube. But no." I swallowed. "They had food."

I couldn't look at Kate. I had to keep staring up at the stars to make sure the thing inside me didn't claw its way up and suffocate me. But I squeezed her hand so tight I was worried I'd hurt her. "The plan," I said tightly, "was to feed me up. Get me strong enough that I'd survive another two weeks. And then do it again and again and again. For as long as they could keep me alive."

"*Oh Jesus,*" I heard Kate whisper faintly.

"They thought they'd broken me. They were right, in a way. They'd put this...*thing* inside me, this fear, that's still there today. But they'd misjudged what makes a SEAL a SEAL. The training makes us...." For the first time, I turned my head and looked right into Kate's eyes. "It makes us almost as stubborn as you," I told her. "And when I figured out I was going back in the box...that was enough to make me grab the guy, weak or not, and smash his head into that damn radiator. They'd gotten sloppy, left me with only one guy to guard me while I ate because they thought I was too weak to fight. And hell, they were almost right. Took me about ten minutes just to get up the strength to get the keys off his body and drag myself up the stairs. But I managed to sneak out of there to the street and then stumble along until I found a US patrol."

My voice grew cold as I reached the worst part. "They took me back to the base. No one even recognized me, at first, I was so thin and weak. But I thought that, once they did, it would be...*happy*. I mean, I thought I was safe. I thought I was home." I shook my head. "Then they told me I was under arrest for slaughtering civilians. They let me heal up in the infirmary for a little while and then they shipped me home and court martialled me. Hopkins—the guy who actually shot that family—he'd already told his story and it had had weeks to set in stone. No one wanted to mess with that, especially with Hopkins' dad pulling strings behind the scenes. Easier to throw me in a cell for twenty years. Except, as soon as the handcuffs went on...."

"You were back in the coffin," said Kate in a choked whisper.

I nodded and slowly exhaled. The worst part was over now, my story pretty much done. Somehow, her being close had let me get through it. "I knew that if they put me in a cell, I'd last a couple of hours at best and then I'd be *gone*. This thing inside me would take me over and I'd be back in the coffin again, for good. I couldn't take that. So the first chance I got, I ran. Hitchhiked to the only place I knew where I could disappear, where I could breathe."

"Alaska," said Kate.

I looked up at the stars. "Alaska. Out here, I can control it. At least while I'm awake. But it's still there. That's what the guy in Afghanistan meant, when he said I was going to enter hell." I touched the side of my head. "The hell is in here. And it's always one step away from taking me back."

"Bastard," Kate said under her breath.

I took long, slow breaths of cool night air. "You know why he did it?" I asked. "You know why that guy did all that, told them to bury me alive?" I was still staring up at the stars but I felt her shake her head. "The family Hopkins killed were related to him. His sister, his brother-in-law, his nieces and nephews."

"Jesus."

"Someone did that to my sister's family, I'd want to do just as bad to them. I don't hate that guy. I hate Hopkins, for letting me take the rap."

Kate nodded, her silken hair brushing against the roughness of my stubble, and I turned to look at her.

I'd gone four years without ever speaking to anyone about what happened when I was captured. In the military debrief, I'd just said I was held prisoner: I hadn't been able to face the details. But with Kate there to keep me grounded, I'd finally done it. I sure as hell wasn't *healed* but, just like in the caves, I'd found I had a new weapon against the thing inside me.

She looked so different, with her hair down. Softer, more vulnerable. But also wilder, more sexual. I wanted her again immediately. But even stronger than the urge to fuck her was the need to wrap my arms around her tight and never let her go. That feeling I'd had ever since the plane, that need to protect her...it had developed into something else, something much deeper.

She was way smaller than me. She was nothing like me: she was as *city* as I was *country* and we were on opposite sides of the law. And yet...the way her body fitted against mine was just perfect, like we'd been built for each other. She was the softness I needed...but she had the stubborn streak she needed to break through to me when any sane woman would have given up.

Kate was blinking at me, searching my face for what I was thinking. "What?" she whispered.

We were face-to-face, only inches apart, our bodies pressed together tight by the sleeping bag. I've never felt so goddamn close to someone my whole life. "You said something, before," I mumbled, stumbling over the words. "Before we ate. Before we kissed."

I felt her breath catch as she remembered. "Yeah?" she asked cautiously.

"Yeah," I said. My voice had sunk to a low mutter.

Goddammit, I wasn't good at this stuff. "I wanted to tell you..."*—this is insane!*

But it felt *right*.

"I wanted to tell you I feel the same way." I said.

She swallowed. "You think you're falling—"

"No," I said, cutting her off. "Not *think*."

We stared into each other's eyes. And then I was kissing her, deep and hard but slow, like we were joining together. I closed my eyes and, even with the stars gone and the breeze having died, I still stayed right where I was instead of slipping off into the blackness. I could feel Kate's silken hair tickling my cheeks and her soft lips on mine, could hear her breath and smell the warm, feminine scent of her...and that was all I needed in the world.

FORTY-FIVE

Kate

AT SOME POINT, we drifted off to sleep. We were on our sides, face-to-face, with his arms locked tight around my waist and my head cradled on his shoulder. I could have happily slept like that for a week, after everything we'd been through that day, but I woke up after only a few hours. The fire was dying down but it was still cozy inside the sleeping bag. At first, I couldn't figure out why I'd woken.

Then I felt Boone twitch. He was dreaming again, his eyes tight shut. And now, for the first time, I really had some sense of what he was going through. *Dear God.* Trapped in a coffin, the wood an inch from his face, knowing there were hundreds of pounds of dirt on top of him...it was a testament to the strength of his mind that the nightmares only came at night. He still thought he was weak for being damaged; the truth was, any other man would have broken completely.

I knew not to wake him, now, but I couldn't leave him, either. I pressed myself closer to him, letting him feel my warmth right along his body. But his face was still twisted up with fear and I could feel his heart hammering in his chest. I stroked his back, crushed myself to his chest, but none of it worked. I've never felt so utterly useless.

And then, not knowing what else to do, I put my lips to his ear and started to whisper to him. I told him it was okay. I told him he was safe. I told him I was there.

I told him I loved him.

And gradually, gradually, his face started to relax and his heart slowed. I felt his arms and legs soften and it was only then that I realized they'd been locked solid...as if chained. My heart twisted. *He goes through this every night. Every. Night.* Maybe he would forever. And I was all he had to help him.

I knew there were professionals who could help much more: psychologists, counselors. But those people were in cities. I understood why he could never risk going back to civilization: even in some tiny place like Nome, they'd be searching for him. And as soon as some cop put cuffs on him, or locked him in a cell...I imagined Boone disappearing into himself, becoming a hunched, glazed-eyed shell of the man I knew. By the time they let me visit him, he'd be beyond help, his mind locked in the blackness forever. My arms tightened around him. *No way. Not my man.* I was all he had? Well, so be it. I'd stay in Alaska with him. I'd hold him every damn night.

But when he'd dropped back into a deep, restful sleep, I had trouble joining him. I was having doubts: not about how I felt about Boone, but about myself.

Could I really give up everything I'd ever known? And there was something else: a sense that this wasn't right. When we got to a town, Boone could stay on the outskirts and I could raise the alarm about Weiss's escape and maybe Weiss would be brought to justice...but what about getting justice for Boone? He was going to be on the run for the rest of his life, while Hopkins went free.

It went round and round in my head until I had no hope of getting back to sleep. Also, I had to pee. So I slipped out of the sleeping bag, inching my way out like a worm so as not to wake Boone, and pulled on my clothes–it was chilly enough, out of the sleeping bag, that I even pulled on my jacket. I snuck away through the trees: fortunately, there was enough moonlight to see by. Once I was far enough from our camp that I felt modest, I ducked behind a tree.

I was halfway back when I stopped and frowned. My eyes had adjusted to the dark now and I could see Boone standing by the fire. *Dammit!* He must have woken up. He'd be wondering where the hell I was. I opened my mouth to call to him...and then froze.

The sleeping bag was still full. Boone was still asleep.

The man by the fire turned, peering into the darkness.

Weiss!

FORTY-SIX

Kate

HE WAS STARING right at me...but with the bright light of the fire right next to him, the forest must have just looked like inky blackness. We stared at each other for another three beats of my pounding heart...and then he turned back to Boone.

I went to shout a warning...but I realized Weiss wouldn't have come alone. His mercenaries or whoever the hell they were could be all around me. I was more use if I kept the element of surprise. So I forced myself to keep quiet and ducked behind the nearest tree. I peeked out just as Weiss booted Boone in the stomach. "Wake up!"

I winced as Boone groaned and cursed. He came to fast, though, and started to scramble to his feet...only to find Weiss's rifle in his face.

"Where's Lydecker?" asked Weiss coldly.

Boone let out a growl and sprang to his feet. Weiss swung his rifle and knocked him back to the ground, then cocked it and put the muzzle an inch from Boone's eye. "Where's *Kate?*" he demanded. The way he said my name, sickly-sweet, made my stomach turn.

"Halfway to the next town," Boone growled. "We split up: I led you one way, she went the other, asshole."

Weiss smiled. "Cute. Except we found you with the drone hours ago. I've been watching you on thermal while we drove. I particularly enjoyed watching you go down on her. Pity there's no sound. Looked like she really screamed."

Boone suddenly grabbed the muzzle of the rifle and ripped it from Weiss's hands. My heart leapt...but just as he got it turned around and pointing at Weiss, the three mercenaries stepped out of the trees, guns leveled at him. Behind them, the two marshals, also holding guns. Boone froze, hate-filled eyes still locked on Weiss, and Weiss grabbed his weapon back.

"Be careful," muttered one of the mercenaries to Weiss. He sounded a little disparaging, as if he didn't think Weiss should be in charge...and there was something about his voice, a heavy accent that I'd heard but couldn't place.

"He just surprised me," spat Weiss. He drew back his rifle and slammed the butt of it into Boone's stomach, doubling him over. "Now *where's the bitch?*"

I had to bite my lip to keep from crying out in sympathy. The pain was as intense as if it was me who'd been hit.

"I can get him to talk," said the lead mercenary. That accent again. What was it?

Weiss shook his head. "I owe this son of a bitch," he said. "We should be out of this godforsaken place by now."

As they argued, Boone lifted himself...and looked right at me. He must have glimpsed me earlier and had been avoiding looking at me until now. He stared into my eyes...and mouthed *go*.

It felt like the ground had dropped out from under me. *What?* Was he seriously suggesting that I.... I glanced around at the dark forest. Imagined myself out there, alone. Imagined Boone as Weiss's prisoner. *No!*

But Boone stared at me, his face like stone. *Now,* he mouthed.

I shook my head.

And then Weiss looked down and saw Boone's gaze. Followed it to me. Peered into the darkness and raised his rifle—

I saw Boone launch himself at Weiss's legs and the shot went wide. But then the mercenaries were opening up, bullets ripping into the trees all around me.

I had no choice.

I ran.

FORTY-SEVEN

Kate

WITHOUT BOONE slowing them down, I would never have made it. But I could hear his growls of fury and the sounds of his punches slamming into their bodies. The one time I dared to glance over my shoulder, he was tearing into all of them, using his size and brute strength to beat their numbers. I remembered what Marshal Phillips had said about his arrest: *brawling*. Mason brawled like no one else.

I sprinted through the darkened forest with no direction in mind other than *away*. I stumbled over the uneven ground and almost fell flat on my face a couple of times, but my panic lent me speed. After a half hour of headlong running I slowed to a stop, my lungs bursting and my legs aching. I strained my ears but there was nothing. I'd lost them.

I slumped over and just stood there bent at the waist for a few minutes, getting my breath back. It was only when I straightened up that my situation sank in.

I was alone.

That sensation I'd had ever since I first landed in Nome came back: I was an insignificant little speck in the middle of an unthinkable vastness. Only now, for the first time, I was on my own.

And I had *no idea* where I was. The forest looked the same in every direction. I had to keep moving, to try to get to the town Boone had been taking me to. But where was *that?*

Nausea started to churn in my belly, that same slow, sickening panic you get when you're a kid in the department store and you turn around and your mom *isn't there. I'm on my own. Completely. On. My. Own.* The sky was starting to lighten: dawn was coming. But I was still days away from reaching a town. I was going to have to spend the night out here, alone.

I can't do this! I hadn't realized how much Boone had made me feel protected. Ever since the plane crash, he'd been no more than six feet from me. Now, I'd never see him again.

I dug my nails into my palms to stop that thought. If I went down that road I'd break down completely.

Think! What would Boone do? I took a deep breath. *Eat.* I should get some breakfast and get my strength back, then take a bearing from the sun like he showed me and head north—that's the direction we'd been going in. I'd have one of the rations. I went to unsling my pack—

MY PACK!

I froze, staring at the empty place on my back, willing it not to be true. I looked at the ground around my feet in case I'd absent-mindedly unslung it when I stopped. But my pack was still sitting beside the campfire, where I'd slept.

The chill seeped right into my bones. I had *nothing*. No food or water, no flashlight, no bedding, no changes of clothes. I was in the wild by myself with nothing but the clothes on my back. Even *Boone* wouldn't be out here with so little. *Oh, shit....*

I could feel my legs weakening. I just wanted to sink to the ground and I knew that, if I did, I wouldn't want to get up again. So I did the only thing I could do: I looked at the dawning sun, figured out which way north was and set off into the forest.

It was utterly quiet. The sound of my shoes in the undergrowth was swallowed up by the vast wilderness on every side of me. I tried to focus on walking, to not think about my situation, but the panic was rising inside me. *I am so completely screwed. I have nothing to drink, nothing to eat.* And back there somewhere, Weiss had Boone. Tears welled up in my eyes. Was he still alive? Weiss seemed to take great pains not to kill him: why hadn't he just shot Boone in his sleep and been done with it?

Boone had told me to go. I knew I'd done the right thing: I'd had no chance against six armed men. But the thought of never seeing him again....

Distracted, I snagged my foot on a fallen branch and stumbled, arms windmilling. I managed to get my balance again but my ankle ached. I gingerly put weight on it and found it was okay but the experience left me shaking. What if I'd sprained it, or even broken it? Out here, there was no one to help. I could have wound up dragging myself through the forest with my arms until the wolves found me....

After that, I walked more carefully.

By midday, the first hunger pangs were really hitting. By mid-afternoon, my stomach was trying to eat itself and my mouth was painfully dry. I'd been walking all day but there was no sign of progress: the forest looking the same in every direction. *How does Boone do this? How can he be out here alone, for weeks at a time?*

There were only a few hours of sunlight left when I saw the rabbit. It had its back to me as it nibbled at some grass.

Oh God. No, I can't.

I looked down at my hands. I had no knife. I'd have to break its neck. Nausea rose inside me at the thought. But *that's what Boone would do. I have to eat.*

I crept up behind it, hands flexing, barely daring to breathe. *Move like Boone moves. Slow and then quick.* I leapt—

And suddenly it was in my hands. A flurry of paws but I held on.

The rabbit bent its head around and looked at me with big, black eyes....

I sighed and opened my hands. The rabbit hopped away into the trees. *I'll go hungry.*

I knew I needed to make some sort of shelter. The temperature would plummet at night and I had no sleeping bag to keep me warm. I had no knife so I had to twist branches off trees and then lay them together to make a sort of lean-to against the trunk of a tree: it might keep a little of the wind off me but I'd still be freezing.

That's when I felt the hard, awkward shape of something in my jacket. When I realized what it was, I wanted to punch the air. The flint and steel Boone had given me. I could make a fire!

It took me a half hour of collecting twigs and

hunting around for dry leaves to use as kindling, but I finally got it going. The first crackle and spit as a twig caught, the first glow of warmth against my hands...it was like heaven. I threw on branches, building it up, and sat down beside it. I hadn't realized how cold I'd already gotten.

The elation didn't last, though. As I sat there in my pathetic little lean-to, holding out my hands to the fire, night fell. The forest went black, beyond the tiny circle of firelight. Somewhere close, a wolf howled.

I'm not going to make it.

Boone had said the nearest town was three days' walk from his cabin. But when we fled, we hadn't necessarily been going in the right direction. We'd gotten back on track but it could still be almost three days away and that assumed I could even find it. And somehow hunt enough food to stay alive. And find water. And avoid getting injured.

I lay down on the cold ground. I was exhausted but I was too hungry and too scared to sleep. And the longer I lay there awake, the more the thought of Boone as Weiss's prisoner ate at me. I'd had no choice, I'd had to leave him. But by the time I reached the town raised the alarm about Weiss's escape, Weiss would likely be long gone and Boone would be dead. *How did it come to this?* Hopkins—the real killer in Afghanistan—, Weiss, the two marshals...all the bad guys were going to get away. And Boone, the man who'd saved my life, would die still branded as a murderer and a disgrace to the military. *This isn't right!*

My whole career—my whole *life*—I'd believed in what I was doing. I'd believed the legal system and the FBI was just the formal version of something bigger, something that was written right into our world. I'd believed in justice.

But Boone had been right: there was none.

My cheeks wet with tears, I slept.

FORTY-EIGHT

Boone

FOR A FEW MINUTES, I thought I might have a chance. There were more of them but I was bigger and I attacked them like a grizzly defending his mate. I wasn't going to let them chase after Kate.

I picked one guy up and hurled him into the others, scattering them like bowling pins. I got in a good punch to Marshal Hennessey's side and a really satisfying right hook to Weiss's face.

But then the mercenaries surrounded me and they were trained. One of them grappled me from behind and forced me to the ground and another pressed his gun to my head. I closed my eyes and waited for the shot. At least I'd delayed them enough to give Kate a head start.

"No!" snapped Weiss, knocking the gun barrel away from my temple. "We might need him. If we corner Lydecker, I want to have leverage.

The mercenary cursed under his breath and then

muttered something disparaging to his buddy. The hairs on the back of my neck stood up. I didn't understand the words but I recognized the language: *Russian.*

That changed everything. I'd presumed that Weiss had hired some local mercenaries to help him escape the country. There are plenty of former military guys who don't give a shit who they work for. But these guys must be former *Russian* military, maybe even former *Spetsnaz,* Russian special forces. Russian Mafia bosses often used people like that for bodyguards. Had Weiss done a deal with the Russian mob?

Another Russian ran up, panting, and reported: they'd lost Kate in the forest. Weiss cursed but my heart soared: there was still hope for her. Then I noticed her pack, still sitting on the ground. *Shit.*

They kept me on my knees while the marshals cuffed my wrists. Immediately, I could feel the sleeping beast inside me uncoil. Sharing everything with Kate had helped but it hadn't cured me. The march through the forest wasn't so bad because at least I could feel the air moving against my skin. But when we reached the edge of the trees and they put me in the back of an SUV, it got *bad.* They chained my ankles, too, and that pushed me dangerously close to the edge. My chest grew tight. I was almost back inside the coffin.

Marshal Phillips climbed into the back seat next to me and sat listening to the short, quick breaths I was taking. "What the fuck's the matter with you?"

Weiss was in the passenger seat. He turned and glared at me. "He's crazy." He leaned back and slapped me hard across the face. "That's right, isn't it,

Boone? Christ knows how you persuaded Lydecker to bang you. Does she realize you're a basket case?"

I said nothing, just glared back at him. The anger helped to hold back the fear, a little.

The Russian in the driver's seat muttered something.

"What did you say?" snapped Weiss.

"I said: for a crazy guy, he give you good run-around," the Russian said in broken English.

Weiss glowered at me. "Not anymore," he said. And slapped me again, hard enough to snap my head to one side. He seemed to really like hitting people who couldn't fight back. "That's for setting back my plans," he told me. "Head for the camp. We'll track that bitch down tomorrow, when the drone's refueled."

The Russian shook his head. "We should go back to Nome. Get on boat. We're days behind schedule already."

Weiss whirled around and jabbed his finger in the mercenary's face. "I am *not* having the government looking for me for the rest of my life! It has to look like I died in that crash and that won't work if that little bitch tells the authorities I'm still breathing. You want more money? I'll pay you fifty thousand, *each,* per day we're here. But we are *not leaving* without her. Tomorrow, we'll hunt her down with the drone." He looked over his shoulder at me. "And you better believe: all the extra money this is costing me? I'm going to take it out of that cute little ass of hers."

I growled low in my throat.

Weiss grinned. "Oh, you don't like that?" He leaned back between the seats and spoke slowly, making sure I heard every word. "I'm going to have *fun* with Kate." He touched his eye, which was already turning purple where I'd slugged him. "I might even make you watch."

My stomach turned. Not just from what he was threatening but from what I could see in his eyes. This guy had had power all his life: power over people, brought by having millions and then billions of dollars. But now he'd discovered a new, addictive sort of power: the power that came from being the one holding a gun. He could *kill*...or do even worse, especially to Kate. Out here, there was no one to stop him. And he loved it.

My hands formed fists. I had to stop this maniac getting his hands on her, no matter what. But I was chained, useless...and I was slipping fast into the black depths of my memories.

Weiss pointed forward...and we drove off into the night.

***

I had to spend the whole journey focusing on the star-filled sky and the silhouettes of the mountains outside the windows: they were the only things that convinced my broken mind that I was in Alaska and not buried. By the time we arrived and they took off my ankle cuffs and hauled me out, I was so numb with fear, I stumbled and fell. Weiss thought that was hilarious.

I knelt there beside the 4x4 and took a deep lungful of mountain air. The thing inside me grudgingly retreated a little. Another few minutes and I would have been gone for good.

As they pulled me to my feet, I looked around.

Their camp was well-organized: there were three tents, spare fuel for the 4x4s, even some food cooking on a campfire that made my stomach growl. It was just about dawn and I wondered where Kate was and what she was doing. Would she be able to find anything to eat? I hadn't had a chance to teach her to hunt. My chest tightened as I thought of her out there alone. I could feel a cold ache on my front where she should be nestled up against me.

They pushed me down on a log next to Marshal Hennessey. He was rubbing his side where I'd punched him. "Think you busted a rib, you son of a bitch," he muttered.

"Good," I spat viciously. My injured arm was still throbbing from hitting him, but I'd gladly do it again. I reserved a special hatred for the two marshals. I didn't expect much from mercenaries but for a man of the law to take a bribe...that was low.

He shook his head at me as if I didn't understand, but he didn't say anything more. Only when Weiss walked past, clutching a flask of what smelled like vodka, did he speak up. "You said I could see Megan when we got back."

Who the hell was Megan?

"I said you could see her when we caught them," said Weiss savagely.

"I can hear her!" said Hennessey, his voice pleading.

Weiss ignored him and walked off. I strained my ears. And now that I was listening for it, I could hear it, too. Weeping. Too high to be a man's but not a woman's, either.

My stomach twisted. A child's.

I looked at Hennessey...and suddenly his role in all

this twisted a hundred and eighty degrees in my head. "They have your kid?"

He glared at me. As far as he knew I was still a wanted fugitive, his natural enemy. He'd probably read my file and knew what I'd supposedly done. But eventually, he nodded towards one of the tents. "My grandkid."

I could see it all unfold in my head. Weiss's people had found out which two marshals were flying him from Nome to Fairbanks. Phillips, they'd simply bribed. But Hennessey must have had a reputation for being a straight arrow...so they'd had to use blackmail, instead.

"They grabbed her outside her school," said Hennessey, never taking his eyes off the tent.

Shit. All this time, I'd hated him for helping a criminal escape. He'd had no choice. That's why Phillips could order him around despite Hennessey being his superior.

We both sat there listening to the weeping. It was getting louder and louder, turning into full-on crying.

"For fuck's sake," I heard Weiss say. He stormed over to the tent and hauled back the flap. "*SHUT UP!*" he yelled.

A terrified pause...and then the crying resumed, louder than before. Next to me, Hennessey tensed. "Let me go see her!" he said. "I can calm her down!"

Weiss stalked over to us and then pointed at me. "If you'd done your job and kept control of this asshole on the plane, we wouldn't be in this mess! You can see her when we've caught both of them, not before." There was a cruel gleam in his eye and it made a deep, scalding rage boil in my chest. He wanted the kid to be quiet...but he didn't want to give up even an inch of his leverage over Hennessey. And I could see what was going to happen now: Hennessey would snap and attack Weiss. Weiss would shoot him.

And then the kid would be expendable.

I suddenly knew what I had to do. I was still shaky, the cuffs on my wrists still keeping the memories dangerously close. But I forced the fear down inside me as hard as I could and—

"Let me go," I grunted.

Hennessey and Weiss both stared at me.

Luckily, Hennessey reacted exactly the way I'd hoped. "*No!*" he said. "Jesus, he killed a family. *Children!*"

Weiss narrowed his eyes, trying to work out if I was playing him. But I just looked back at him steadily. "I can get her to be quiet," I said.

Weiss looked at me, looked at Hennessey's pale, terrified face and laughed. "Fuck it," he said. "Go ahead. You got two minutes. Then I'll go in there myself and give her something to cry *about.*"

He backed off a few paces, still wary of me. I slowly got to my feet and turned around to face Hennessey.

"You so much as *touch* her," said Hennessey, panting with fear and anger, "And I'll—"

"I'm just going to talk to her," I told him in a low voice. "Would you rather Weiss go in there?"

He blinked at me, gaping, and went quiet.

I walked off towards the kid's tent. I could feel Weiss's eyes on my back and the Russians were keeping a careful eye on me, too. "Have fun!" Weiss called after me, just to needle Hennessey. The fact he'd send me, a supposed murderer, in there spoke volumes. I had no doubt that, if I couldn't shut the kid up, he really would beat her into silence. *Jesus. If this is a white-collar criminal, give me blue-collar ones anytime.*

I reached the tent, then realized I had no way of pushing the canvas door aside with my hands cuffed behind my back. I had to go in blind, ducking down and pushing my way in head-first. So she saw me before I saw her: I heard a scared little intake of breath.

And then I managed to twist around, still bent almost double, and got my first look at her.

Megan looked to be about eight. A tiny little thing: she wouldn't have come up any higher than my waist, even standing up. And right now she looked even smaller because she was crushed into one corner of the tent, a blanket tugged tight around her, looking up at me through long blonde curls. Her eyes were red from crying.

That's when I realized I had no idea what to do. My plan hadn't extended any further than stopping her and her grandfather being killed. *How the hell do you stop a kid crying?*

"There, there," I mumbled, still looming over her.

She started crying even louder. Outside, I thought I heard Weiss laugh. *Shit!* I was the world's worst person for this. I'd barely talked to another person in four years. I'd thought talking to Kate was hard, but a *kid?* A scared one?

But I had no choice. I had to figure this out, or Weiss would come in here and—my stomach knotted at the thought of him beating her.

Megan was still howling, fresh tears streaming down her cheeks. I looked down at myself. *I guess I do look pretty scary.* I practically filled the tent, I had thick black stubble on my cheeks and wild hair. And I was sort of looming over her.

I sat down on my ass. That put my eyes almost at her height but the crying didn't stop. And anytime now, Weiss would storm in and–

"I'm Boone," I told her. "Or...*Mason.*" Saying that made me think of Kate. "Let me tell you about someone," I said. "Her name is Kate. She cried too, when she first got here. Just wanted to go home. I guess that's how you feel?"

Megan kept sobbing, but I got a nod.

"But she's been really brave. She's been kicking ass, these last few days. She even stood her ground when we ran into a bear."

Megan's tear-filled eyes widened. "A–A real one?" she choked out.

"A real one. Close as you are to me. Kate works for the FBI. You know who the FBI are?"

Another nod. The sobs had slowed down a little. I had no idea what I was doing, but it seemed like the more I kept her talking, the less she remembered to cry.

"She catches bad guys." I lowered my voice. "Like those guys out there."

Megan sniffed. Her sobbing had slowed some more but she was smart enough to see where this was going. "I'm not a g–grown up like Agent Kate," she said, shaking her head.

"Agent Kate's not all that much bigger than you," I said. "She's only a little thing, with this cute little ponytail that makes her all–" I broke off, because I couldn't figure out a way to make that part kid-friendly.

"But they let her be in the FBI?" asked Megan.

I felt myself smile. "I don't think they had a choice.

She's stubborn. But that's a good thing. She doesn't let the bad guys get away." I was working up to *so maybe you could be like Agent Kate and try to be brave—*

"It sounds like you like her," said Megan.

I blinked. I hadn't expected that. But if it stopped her crying.... "Yeah," I said with feeling. "I really do."

Megan nodded, sniffed...and the tears stopped. I let out a long silent sigh of relief.

"Are you going to get married?" asked Megan.

I could feel my heart breaking. Kate was out there somewhere, lost and alone. And I was dead: either they'd catch her and kill us both or she'd slip away and I'd no longer be needed. But....

"Yeah," I said, because it was in my heart and *fuck* reality. "Yeah. I'd really like that."

I thought of Kate, looking amazing in a big white dress, walking down the aisle to meet me. *Right now, I'd settle for just having her make it out of this alive, even if I don't.* Could she find her way to the town? Could she survive?

Kate, I thought. *Where are you?*

FORTY-NINE

Kate

I WOKE, shifted my legs...and immediately cried out in pain.

I was curled up on my side in my little lean-to. It was dawn and the fire had long since died, the charred remains providing no warmth. The cold had soaked into my body right down to the bones. Every muscle had gone tight and stiff as tire rubber and every one screamed when I tried to uncurl.

It took a few minutes of cursing and rubbing circulation back into my legs before I could even stand and even then I was hunched and aching. I was exhausted, too: I'd slept but my dreams had been full of Weiss, grinning as he beat Boone...and then did worse to me. I remembered that comment about watching Boone and me having sex and my skin crawled.

I found north again and headed out. I was still half asleep, every step made me wince at the pain in my tight hamstrings, and I was so hungry my stomach was cramping. But there was nothing I could do about it, so I pushed on.

An hour later, I came to the edge of the forest. The ground had been steadily rising and I emerged at the edge of a cliff. Less than a week ago, the height would have made me want to throw up. Now, it still bothered me...but I could actually look at the view. And the view took my breath away.

I was gazing down into a valley with tall, snow-capped mountains on either side. A river wound its way lazily along the grassy valley floor and the morning sun was making the water gleam like liquid gold.

I saw what Boone saw. I felt what he felt. This *was* a beautiful place. Terrifying, huge...but beautiful. You just had to be stubborn enough to want to live there.

And right on the horizon, I could see smoke. Just a tiny wisp but, when I shaded my eyes from the sun and squinted, I could make out buildings. I wasn't ready for how good that felt. The town looked tiny, much smaller than Nome. Just days ago, even Nome had seemed like the end of the world but now I got a deep, warm glow in that part of me that had been cold and dark ever since I left civilization. The town was a day's walk away, maybe two. But maybe, if I could find food along the way, I could do it.

There was a rough trail that led down the edge of the cliff. I put one foot on it....

...and stopped.

It felt wrong.

That's crazy. I'd had no choice. Boone had told me to go. What other choice was there? If I'd stayed and fought, they'd have killed me.

But I have a choice now. I turned and looked over

my shoulder, towards the forest.

That's ridiculous. What choice? What other choice is there? I was an FBI agent. My job was to get to the town, warn them that Weiss had escaped and get the FBI, the state police and everybody else searching for him. After being days in the wilderness, cut off from everything I understood, I was within sight of getting back to it.

But...it felt wrong.

Why did they keep Boone alive? I'd seen them fighting with him. Why not just shoot him? It had been bothering me since I fled but now I saw it: they wanted *me*. They could track me down using the drone but I could still take cover somewhere, like we had in the caves. They might waste days actually getting hold of me. They wanted a way to lure me out, once they got close. They'd put a gun to his head, or torture him. If that happened, I knew I'd crack. I'd come out of hiding. And once they had both of us, they'd kill us.

So stick with the plan, said my FBI-mind. *Go to the town.* I took a step towards it.

*Except...*I stopped again. Even if by some chance I made it, they'd still kill Boone. They knew how far away the town was. Once there was a reasonable chance I'd got there—tomorrow morning, at the latest—they'd give up, put a bullet in Boone's head and flee.

Either way, Boone was dead. I couldn't let that happen. But there was no third way.

Unless....

No. That was just stupid. That was beyond stubborn, beyond dumb. Just thinking about it made a sick, cold fear creep through me.

The third option was to get Boone back. To go up against a criminal, two corrupt marshals and three trained mercenaries, all of them armed.

It was near suicidal. I was hungry and exhausted, I had no equipment or military training. I was just one FBI agent. I sat at a desk most of the time!

I looked at the town again. That way was the system: the one Boone feared so much. Cops and jails and military police and the FBI. The reassuring network that I surrounded myself back in New York, that I'd missed so much when I arrived. The system I'd always believed in. The same one that had let Boone down so badly.

That same system was about to fail again. By the time I reached the town, Boone would be dead. If I wanted to save him, I couldn't rely on the system anymore. *I* had to do this. *Me.*

This is insane.

And yet every other option felt wrong. This felt right.

I turned around to face the forest. I knew where they must be: they'd be to the south, as close to the forest as they could get in their 4x4s. I figured I had just one advantage: surprise. They were looking for me but they'd never expect me to do something as monumentally stupid as come after them.

Bending, I plucked a stalk of the knee high grass, scooped my hair back into a ponytail and bound it tight with the grass.

I'm going to get my man back.

***

I set out through the forest towards the south side.

I knew they'd be looking for me but hopefully they'd sent the drone towards the town, expecting me to head there.

By noon, my hunger cramps had settled into a dull, permanent ache that was impossible to ignore. It had been almost two days since I'd eaten and I was fantasizing about crispy French fries, loaded with salt and ketchup, or ice cream drizzled with caramel syrup. I tried to work out how much money I'd give for just a juicy, fresh apple.

In the middle of the afternoon, I found a stream. I knew I should boil the water but I didn't have anything to boil water *in*. It looked clear enough and I'd die without water so eventually I just crouched down beside it, cupped my hands and drank. It was icy cold and the best thing I'd ever tasted.

Just as the sun was setting, I emerged from the trees, light-headed from hunger and exhausted from the walk. I saw their camp immediately: the 4x4s and tents, in the middle of all this vast emptiness, stood out a mile. Unlike us, they didn't have any need to hide.

I wished I had binoculars. I crept closer, closer than felt safe, and peeked out from behind a tree. My heart lifted as I saw Boone sitting on a log, his hands cuffed behind his back. He was still alive! I could see one of the mercenaries and the two marshals but no one else. And there were only two 4x4s: where was the other one? As I watched, the mercenary listened to his radio and then shook his head at Marshal Phillips, who cursed.

It took me a moment to figure out what was going on: Weiss and the other two mercenaries must be off searching for me, probably in that valley that led to the town...but they couldn't find me because I was here. They'd left the mercenary and Phillips there to guard Boone and–I frowned. Why was the older marshal, Hennessey, sitting beside Boone as if he was a prisoner, too?

I'd figure it out later. Right now, I had an opportunity to get Boone out. The others could come back from their search at any time. They might already be on the way back. I had to plan my attack....

I caught myself. *What the hell am I doing?* I had absolutely zero training for anything like this. I wasn't some military badass like Boone! And I was completely cut off from the agency, from everything I knew. I'd never felt so utterly alone.

But if I didn't pull this off, Boone was going to die.

I studied the camp, trying to contain the rising panic in my chest. What *did* I know? I'd raided houses a few times with the FBI. Our tactic was always to go through the front and back doors simultaneously, to put the bad guys off balance and give them two things to worry about. Except there was only one of me.

I needed a distraction.

The two 4x4s were parked at one end of the camp, together with what looked like fuel cans. The tents and the log where Boone sat were at the other end.

Very slowly, I picked my way through the trees. I got as close to the 4x4s as I could but actually reaching them would mean crossing a hundred yards of open ground with nothing but long grass to hide me. One of the mercenaries and Marshal Phillips were standing guard not far away, rifles in hand. The sun was going down but there was still just about enough light to see by. If they so much as glimpsed me....

At least I'm small. I got down on my belly and

started to crawl, as slowly and quietly as I could. The grass was barely long enough to hide me. I didn't even dare stick my head up to check my position so I had to just hope I was following a straight line. My heart was slamming against my ribs so hard I was sure they'd be able to hear it. I expected to hear a shot to ring out at any second and feel the bullet rip into me. *How does Boone do this stuff?*

My hands bumped against something hard. I had to choke back a scream. I was sure I'd crawled right into one of their legs.

I looked up. My fingers were scraping the tire of one of the 4x4s. I let out a long sigh of relief and huddled behind it, out of sight. But then I heard boots tramping through the grass. *Shit!*

Not knowing what else to do, I ducked down and crawled under the 4x4, then lay flat, grass scratching at my face and neck. I watched two sets of boots come closer, closer...*can they see me?*

The boots stopped, so close to my face that I could smell the leather.

Marshal Phillips' voice came first. "I don't get where she is. She can't have made it to the town already. Maybe she's dead. Maybe she slipped and fell in a gully and her body's already cold—that's why they can't find her on thermal."

Then the mercenary, his English rough and fractured. "They will be back soon. You must get Weiss to leave the woman and go. We can't stay any longer. This was not deal we made."

This time I recognized the heavy accent. *Russian.* Weiss had brought Russians over to help him escape?!

Phillips snorted. "That psycho doesn't listen to me. He was ready to leave me on the fucking plane. He'd have killed me *and* Hennessey by now if he didn't need us. He's only keeping us in case we run into the police in Nome and need to talk our way out of it."

I heard the mercenary's clothes rustle as he shrugged. "Then *we* will make him listen. We leave. Tonight."

They walked off and I was left lying there, debating. I was going spacey from hunger and fatigue and it sounded so tempting. *They were ready to give up and go to Nome!* All I had to do was crawl back into the grass and wait. In another hour, they'd be gone. I'd be safe and I could take my time getting to the town.

But as soon as the mercenaries convinced Weiss to leave, Boone would no longer be needed. They'd shoot him. My mind hardened, pushing the tiredness away. *No. No way.*

I slid out from under the 4x4 and crept around to the fuel cans. It was fully dark, now, and I could barely see to unscrew one of the lids. The stink of gasoline rose up to meet me. Now I needed something to use as a fuse. The waterproof jacket Boone had given me had a drawstring to tighten the waist and I pulled that out and soaked it in gasoline, then left one end dangling in the can and ran the other down the side.

Lighting it was an exercise in terror: I only had the flint and steel, which threw out sparks in all directions. If one of them flew into the can, I'd be in the center of a ball of burning gas.

After a few heart-stopping moments, the end of my makeshift fuse caught light. But I had no idea how long it would take for the flame to reach the gas. Crawling back through the grass to the trees seemed to take forever. Then I had to skirt the camp again to get back to where Boone was. The whole way, my shoulder blades were hunched up, braced for the explosion. *I should have used a longer fuse!*

But I arrived back at the other end of the camp, panting and drained, without seeing a fireball. Phillips and the mercenary were standing right by the log where Boone and Hennessey sat. I crouched in the shadows, every muscle tensed, ready to run. As soon as the explosion went off and the guards left, I'd go in, grab Boone's arm and lead him into the trees. Then we could disappear into the night.

I waited, holding my breath...but nothing happened. *Did the fuse go out?*

And then it got worse. I heard the roar of an approaching engine. Headlights lit up the camp.

Weiss and the others were back.

FIFTY

Kate

I FELT the last reserves of energy drain out of me as despair set in. *No! I was so close!*

A 4x4 pulled up. Doors slammed. I heard Weiss snapping out orders in that sullen, sneering tone of his. Then the three mercenaries were rounding on him—they'd obviously all agreed it was time to make a stand.

"Fuck that!" I heard Weiss yell. "We leave when all the loose ends are tied up. I'm paying you enough!"

"No use for money if we're all in American jail," said one of the mercenaries, who seemed to be their leader. "They find plane, soon. We go. *Now*. You come with us... or make own way back to Nome."

I saw Weiss take a step towards him but the other two mercenaries subtly raised their rifles in warning. Clearly, even they were getting tired of Weiss's attitude.

"Fine," Weiss grated. He pulled out a gun. "Get the camp packed up. I'll deal with Boone."

They split up. Weiss started walking towards Boone. *No. No!*

At that second, the gas can exploded. A fireball boiled up into the sky, lighting up the night like an early sunrise. Flaming gas rained down, starting a hundred little fires in the dry grass. Weiss was close enough for some to hit him on the back and he cursed and tore off his jacket, stamping on it. The mercenaries scrambled to move the 4x4s so that they wouldn't catch fire. Both marshals ran over and started trying to put out the blaze.

I was so shocked, it took me a few seconds to remember to move. Then I was sprinting, hunched low, over to the log where Boone sat. He heard me when I was just a step away and twisted around to meet me. "*Kate?!*"

I knew we needed to move fast. I had it all ready in my head: grab his shoulder and pull him towards the trees. But as soon as I was close, all the fear, the two days and a night on my own, the thinking I'd never see him again...it all welled up inside me and I slammed into his chest, arms hooking around him to pull me in tight. The solid warmth of him was the best thing I'd ever felt, like coming home. I just clung there for a few seconds, panting in relief, and then tilted my head up just in time to meet his lips as they came down.

He allowed himself one quick, hard kiss and then drew back. "*How did–*"

I shook my head. "Later. Let's go." I grabbed his shoulder and pulled–

But he resisted. I could see the battle going on in his eyes as he debated something.

"*What?!*" I begged. What could there possibly be to think about? We had to go!

Boone gave me a long, sorrowful look. “We can’t leave.”

FIFTY-ONE

Boone

I've never felt anything like it. Everything was pulling me towards Kate, towards the safety of the darkened forest. We could disappear in seconds. By the time they were done with the fire, we'd have slipped away. And I'd heard the argument Weiss had had with the mercenaries: they wouldn't tolerate any more delays. They'd go and we'd be free.

I drew in a long, shuddering breath. All I wanted was to be with her. *Christ,* she was gorgeous. Even now, even exhausted and bedraggled, she looked perfect to me. Her hair was back up in a ponytail, all tight and efficient. Her jaw was stubbornly set in that way that just made me want to kiss her. *Just go!*

But I couldn't.

"There's a kid," I told her. And I explained about Marshal Hennessey and Megan. Kate's eyes grew wide. I could see her putting it all together: why Hennessey had been so reluctant to let her on the flight; why he'd told her *it's not like that* when she'd accused him of taking a bribe; why Phillips, his subordinate, was able to order him around.

"As soon as they get on their boat to Russia, the kid's useless to them," I told Kate. "Hennessey, too." Both of us looked towards the fire. Hennessey was helping put it out—I guess he thought that it might spread to the tents and put Megan at risk. There was no way I could get him away from the others...but we could try to save Megan.

Kate nodded. "Okay." She dashed around behind me and started untying my wrists. Thank God the marshals had gotten tired of searching for the handcuff key every time I needed to piss, and switched to rope. A few seconds and Kate's quick fingers coaxed the knot loose.

I stood up, stretching out my shoulders, and we started towards Megan's tent. But we were less than halfway there when a shout went up. I looked over my shoulder. One of the 4x4's headlights was pointing right at the empty log where I'd been sitting. They knew I was gone.

I pushed Kate towards the tent. "Go! Get the kid! I'll slow them down and meet you in the trees, *there*." I pointed at a spot in the tree line. Kate opened her mouth to argue. "*Go!*" And I turned and ran the opposite way, leaving her no choice.

FIFTY-TWO

Kate

I STUMBLED A LITTLE as I ran, my chest tight with fear. *We were so close!*

I rushed through the door of the tent. A blanket-wrapped bundle in the corner squeaked in fear and shied away from me. But then, before I could explain, the kid perked up. "*Agent Kate?!*"

I blinked. *How does she know my*—"Yeah."

She scurried across the room and dived at me, hugging me around the waist. "Are you rescuing me?"

I stroked her blond curls. "*Yes.*" I scooped her up into my arms, carried her to the door of the tent and peeked out. I was just in time to see Boone pick up a rock twice the size of my head and hurl it at one of the 4x4s, smashing one of its headlights. He ducked back into the darkness again as the mercenaries opened fire on him.

Seconds later, he emerged from the shadows again, grabbed one of the mercenaries and punched him to the ground. I held my breath, but he was gone again before they could shoot him. And it was working: everyone was looking in his direction. They had no idea I was even in the camp. "Be very quiet, okay?" I whispered to Megan.

But as soon as I got through the tent's door, Megan pulled at my sleeve and pointed. "What about granddaddy?" she whispered.

My heart sank as I followed her finger. Marshal Hennessey was still fighting the fire, way too close to the Weiss to try to grab him and lead him away. "He's going to get out later, honey," I whispered. I felt crappy for lying to her but I had no choice.

Megan turned big eyes to me. "Will he be okay?"

The truth was, Weiss would likely kill him as soon as they got on the boat. "Yeah, honey. He'll be just fine," I said, feeling sick.

Megan nodded and clutched me tight. I hurried to the trees, staying low and moving as fast as I dared. I kept expecting a shout to go up but all I heard was gunfire. Then the rising roar of an engine as one of the 4x4s shot forward...and a crunch of metal as it slammed into something solid.

I spun around, nausea rising, thinking I was going to see Boone crushed between bumper and tree...but he was sprinting away. One of the 4x4s was lodged against a rock, its front wing bent out of shape, and the driver was cursing. They must have tried to run him down and he'd dodged out of the way. As I watched, Boone ducked into the forest.

I ran with Megan into the trees, both Boone and us now heading for the point. When he arrived, he'd have the mercenaries and Weiss hot on his tail. We had to be there waiting for him, ready to go. Luckily, I stumbled onto an animal trail. I hugged Megan close and went as fast as I could. I started to feel the first faint stirrings of hope. It was just possible that we could pull this off.

"Are we going to see Mr. Mason?" asked Megan.

I nodded. "Yes. Yes we are."

"I like him," said Megan quietly. "He's nice."

I checked over my shoulder but no one was following. "Yeah," I said. "He really is."

Megan leaned in so she could whisper in my ear. "*He wants to marry you.*"

A big, unexpected swell of emotion hit me. I blushed and went quiet, then ruffled her curls. "Let's go see him," I eventually managed in a choked voice.

I put my foot down and there was a metallic *click* I'll remember for the rest of my life. A memory made me freeze, all of my weight on that foot.

"What is it?" whispered Megan.

I looked down, barely daring to breathe.

My foot was on a bear trap.

FIFTY-THREE

Kate

I WILLED IT to be something, *anything* else. But there was no mistaking the semi-circle of gleaming metal teeth. It wasn't even well covered with leaves. I'd have seen it no problem if I hadn't been rushing.

My foot was right in the middle, on the bar that pressed down to release the jaws. The mechanism was sticky with age: that was the only reason the jaws hadn't snapped shut yet. But they were right on the verge: I could actually see them tremble each time I inhaled.

I tried lifting my foot, shifting just an infinitesimal amount of weight to my back foot. Instantly there was a warning metal shriek as the mechanism shifted. I pressed down again, hard, my heart thumping, and the noise stopped.

I was trapped. If I tried to move...I squeezed my eyes shut as I remembered what the trap had done to the stick. What it was designed to do to the powerful leg of a bear. I tried not to think of the word *shattered.*

I opened my eyes. "Megan?" I said in a strangled voice. "It's really important you don't move. Okay honey?"

Megan gave a tiny nod and went rigid against me.

Boone came sprinting through the trees. His face lit up when he saw us. Then he saw my expression. He came closer. Saw the trap.

"I can fix this," he said quickly. "I can get you out. I just need tools."

"There's no time," I told him. Already, I could hear the men approaching behind him. "You have to get Megan out of here."

"No!" He glared at me, eyes fierce. "No way! I'm not losing you again!"

The footsteps were getting closer. "We don't have a choice," I said tightly. "Take her. Megan? Go to Mr. Mason, honey."

I gently pried her away from my chest and held her out. Every muscle in my body had gone tense: I knew that just the shift in weight of her leaving me might set the trap off. I was waiting for the metal *snap* and the agony that would follow a split-second later.

Boone knew it, too. He shook his head, his eyes never leaving mine.

"*Please,*" I begged.

He gritted his teeth...and put his hands on Megan's waist. Very gently, he took her weight.

The trap creaked. My heart stopped beating for a second...but the jaws held.

"Go," I told Boone. The men were very close, now, seconds away.

"What about you?" asked Megan, looking

distraught.

"I'll be fine, honey," I lied. "Mr. Mason will get you out of here."

Suddenly, a big, warm hand wrapped around mine and squeezed it tight. I looked up into Boone's eyes. That painfully bright Alaska blue, blazing with rage and need. His lips moved but nothing came out. Like me, he was struggling to find the words.

"I know," I whispered, squeezing his hand tight. "Me too."

He held my gaze for one more heartbeat, staring at me with a longing that hit me right down to my core. Then he was running into the trees. My heart felt like it was being torn in two. *I'm never going to see him again!*

I could hear the men getting closer and closer. My instinct was to hide, to make myself as small as possible. They might miss me, in the dark.

But I couldn't do that. My only way out of the trap was with their help. If they did miss me, I'd die out here. Which was worse: let them go past and then, when my legs got too tired and I collapsed, the trap would break my leg and I'd bleed to death in agony? Or alert them and likely be shot?

A bullet would be quick. Maybe even painless. And if they were occupied with me, they wouldn't be chasing Boone and Megan.

I took a deep breath. "Here!" I yelled. "Over here!"

FIFTY-FOUR

Kate

I WAS THE LAST THING they expected to see. One of the mercenaries burst through the trees and just stopped and stared. Then he thought to point his gun at me.

"There's no need," I whispered. And looked down at my feet.

In seconds, I was surrounded. It felt like a bad dream: the people I'd been running from for days were now my saviors. Marshal Phillips tried to be a hero and pull me out before I screamed at him not to. Everyone stood around staring at the trap. The mercenaries said they might be able to hold the jaws down but I shook my head. I'd seen how powerful the springs in these things were. A strong man could force them open, with enough leverage...but not even Boone could stop them snapping shut.

Then someone thought to call Marshal Hennessey, who was still back at the camp. A few minutes later, he ran up, carrying a jack from one of the 4x4s. As he crouched down beside the trap, he looked up at me. "Thank you," he muttered, low enough that only I'd hear.

He must have discovered Megan was gone, and figured out what we'd done. "She's safe," I whispered.

He nodded his thanks. Then I figured out something else: when he heard they'd caught me, he'd come here. But with Megan safe, they had no leverage over him. He could have just run off into the forest, found Boone and escaped with him and Megan. He'd given up his freedom to save me.

He spread the arms of the jack, making a wide V. Then he held it inside the open jaws, facing down. "Okay," he said in that whiskey-rough voice. "Take your foot off."

I gazed down at him. It would work, in theory. The jaws would snap shut and the jack would catch them before they reached my leg. But...it all relied on the jack staying exactly where it was. If Hennessey flinched or moved even a few inches....

"I got this," said Hennessey. "Take your foot off."

I took a long, shuddering breath. Another. Another.

And then I quickly lifted my foot.

There was a metal screech as the mechanism fired. I felt the rush of wind against my leg as the jaws snapped closed. There was a metal *clang*—

I kept staring straight ahead, afraid to look down in case the pain just hadn't hit yet.

"It's okay," said Hennessey.

I looked down. The jaws were straining against the sides of the jack, the teeth a few inches short of my leg. I gingerly lifted my foot out of the trap. Hennessey pulled the jack out and the teeth slammed all the way closed. I slumped in relief.

Then Weiss stepped out of the darkness. He'd been at the back of the group, watching the whole thing, letting it all unfold for his sick entertainment without doing a thing to help. And the slow grin he gave me made my insides turn to water.

I suddenly regretted shouting for help. He wasn't going to shoot me.

I'd just become his prisoner.

FIFTY-FIVE

Boone

I DIDN'T GO FAR. I took Megan a safe distance away and up a slight rise where I could look down on the scene, then we watched it all unfold from behind a bush.

Goddammit! We'd been so close! How had it all gone so wrong, so fast? I nearly had a heart attack, watching that moron Phillips try to pull Kate out of the trap...then I slumped in relief as Hennessey managed to free her.

"Granddaddy!" whispered Megan excitedly. I squeezed her hand.

I watched, sick fear churning in my stomach, as Weiss grabbed Kate's arm. *Keep your damn hands off her!* But I couldn't jump in there and start a fight: not with Megan right next to me.

This is all my fault. If I hadn't told Kate we needed to rescue Megan....

But then I looked down at the kid and I knew I'd done the right thing. We'd had to save her. Only now

Kate was in their hands...and I had Megan. *How the hell do I look after a kid?!*

"What do we do about Boone?" I heard Marshal Phillips ask. "Do we go after him?"

Weiss shook his head. "Fuck him. He was never the problem. He's a fucking fugitive: he's not going to the cops. *She* was the problem." He turned to the mercenaries. "We're going back to Nome."

The lead mercenary sighed. *"Finally.* And her?" He looked at Kate.

"We'll take her along," said Weiss. He cupped Kate's jaw and grinned.

Kate spat in his face. I pulled Megan to my chest before she could see Weiss slap Kate in response. The noise rang out across the forest. *Oh, you son of a bitch. You're going to pay for that.*

But there was nothing I could do: not with an eight year-old kid in my arms. They trooped off, pulling Kate along with them.

Maybe they'll head out tomorrow morning, I thought. I could get Megan to safety at my cabin, then come back and–

But as I watched from a hilltop, they started packing up the camp. They didn't even bother taking the tents, just grabbed the stuff they needed, piled into the two undamaged 4x4s and drove off. The last thing I saw was Weiss hauling Kate into the back seat alongside him.

And then they were gone.

FIFTY-SIX

Boone

FOR A SECOND, I just stood there, watching their tail lights disappear. I had one hand on the top of Megan's head as I cradled her to my chest. I had to get her to safety. That's what Kate wanted. I knew I was doing the right thing.

But it didn't feel like that. It felt like they'd ripped Kate right out of me. When we'd been apart before, at least I'd known she was free. Now *he* had her...and that left me so mad I could barely think.

"Is Agent Kate going to be okay?" asked Megan. She was clinging tight to my chest, her voice shaky.

I couldn't answer for a second.

"Mr. Mason?"

I drew in a deep breath and stroked the back of her head. "Yeah," I said. "Yeah, she is."

"But isn't she with the bad men?"

Oh Jesus, I am so the wrong person for this. I closed my eyes. "Yeah." I swallowed. "But she's... undercover. She's only pretending to be their prisoner."

"So she can save my granddaddy?"

I nodded, my chest tight. "Exactly that."

And then she went quiet and I looked up to the stars and wondered what the hell I was going to do. *What would Kate do? I don't know how to look after a kid!*

And the whole time all I could think about was Kate, in that 4x4, getting steadily farther and farther away.

What would Kate do?

She'd do whatever was necessary. Whether she was qualified for it or not. If she could climb a damn rock face, I could do this.

Megan had started to shiver. The temperature was dropping fast, now the sun had set. She was probably getting hungry, too. I gently peeled her off my chest and set her down on her feet. Then I took off my jacket and put it on her: it was big enough to wrap around her twice. "That warmer?"

She nodded.

"Okay." I scooped her up again. "C'mon." And I started walking.

"Where are we going?" she asked.

"Someplace safe."

It took a few hours to carry her to my cabin. When I opened the door and set her down, she looked around with wide eyes. "You live here?"

I nodded.

"All the *time?*"

That made me stop. And suddenly, I was looking at the cabin with fresh eyes. I've always been proud of my place. Cozy and functional and military-neat. But...now, looking at it how *she* saw it, it didn't look cozy...it looked small. It didn't look functional; it looked Spartan. And the neatness was because there was only one person to get it messy. It was...*sad.*

Was Kate shocked, too? Did she just hide it better?

And then I saw the suit Kate had stripped out of, lying on the bed. *Kate!*

"Mr. Mason? Could I please have something to drink?"

That brought me back to the present. I got a fire going in the stove and then searched around for something to give her. What the hell did kids drink? Coke? I didn't have anything like that. *Wait....* At the back of the cupboard, I had a bar of chocolate I'd brought back from Koyuk—a rare indulgence. I broke off a chunk and gave her the rest of the bar to eat. Then I mixed up some milk from water and milk powder, heated it and stirred in the chunk until I had a kind of hot chocolate. Megan wrapped her tiny hands around the mug to warm them and my heart damn near melted.

When she'd finished, I put her to bed. Sitting there watching her sleep in the light from the stove, I felt the same deep, protective urge I'd felt with Kate. In a way, Megan was all I had left of her.

Kate!

But it was useless. I had no phone, no way of raising the alarm. There was nothing I could do.

My chest tightened. Not from *there.*

The only chance Kate had was if I went to Nome. I'd have to drop Megan off someplace safe and then intercept them before they could get on a boat to Russia. There was no way I'd catch them on foot but they'd left the damaged SUV behind. If I could fix the wheel....

Except— I closed my eyes. Except I couldn't go to Nome. I was still a fucking fugitive. By now, the whole area would be aware that a plane had crashed and prisoners had escaped. If Weiss got stopped by the cops, he had the two marshals to smooth things over: they could pretend they were just transporting him to custody. But me? I'd be cuffed and thrown in a cell in seconds. And I'd be in that cell for the rest of my life. Confined like that, the thing that lived inside me would rise up and take possession and this time, I'd never come back. It would be everything I'd feared since I came back from Afghanistan.

I couldn't do it. I'd failed her again. I'd failed to get her to safety and now I was stuck here, useless, like—

Like a hermit. A crazy, embittered mountain man who doesn't speak to anyone. A fugitive.

That's when I got mad. I stalked over to the far side of the cabin, braced my hands either side of the window and ducked down so I could stare out into the night. I could feel the rage build inside me: in my arms, first, my fingers tensing against the wood as if they wanted to claw right through it, my biceps straining like I was going to rip the window out of the wall. I took a deep, shuddering breath. My boots pressed hard into the floor, soles sliding like I was a linebacker trying to block a quarterback. Every muscle in my back stood out.

They'd put something in me, over there. Something that had never let me go. That guy who'd told me I was going to enter hell: I'd thought I'd understood him but I hadn't. I'd thought the nightmares and the attacks were my hell but I'd been wrong.

This was hell. This life. Everyone thinking I was a murderer but being too scared to fight it. Living up here on my own, not realizing how lonely I was until someone came along and showed me. And *this, now,* this was a new circle of hell: being so paralyzed by my fear that I couldn't save the woman I love.

My muscles strained, the veins standing out on my arms. I was shaking with rage and the vibrations were moving through the whole cabin, making mugs and plates right over on the far side rattle. The floor creaked under my feet. The wall groaned under my hands.

The thing inside me rose up, eager to claim me. I'd gotten angry plenty of times before and fear always won out.

But as I stood there, hunched over and raging, the balance was finally tipped. Being imprisoned again, having the fear lock me down forever...that would be unimaginable agony.

But losing Kate forever...that would be worse.

I suddenly let go of the wall and stood up ramrod straight. The wall stopped groaning. The floor stopped creaking. The mugs and plates went quiet. The only sound was a rhythmic squeak of metal.

I turned around. My dog tags were still swinging on their nail by the mirror.

I grabbed them.

***

Under the bed, there was a box I hadn't opened since I'd come back from Afghanistan. I took out my old, black military fatigues and pulled them on. Added boots and streaked a little camo paint under my eyes so I could blend into the dark better. I threw some tools and gear in a bag and added food and water for

Megan. Then I gently woke her.

She blinked up at me. "You look like a soldier."

"Good." I scooped her up. "We're going for a ride. But it's cold out there, so—" I placed her down on the covers, then rolled her up in them with just her head sticking out. I got my biggest backpack, slotted the whole roll in, then lifted her onto my back. She giggled excitedly and put her chin on my shoulder. "Try to doze off," I told her. "It's a long walk."

"Are we going to save Agent Kate?" asked Megan.

I opened the cabin door and stepped out. "Yeah, kid. We are."

FIFTY-SEVEN

Kate

I STARED out of the window, watching the darkened landscape roll past. It was amazing how fast, how effortless it was, after all those hours spent walking. It was even warm in the SUV and the seats were soft leather.

I would have given anything to be cold and exhausted with Boone again.

Weiss was sitting next to me in the rear seat. I could feel his eyes on me but he hadn't said much, yet. I was doing everything I could to avoid looking at him.

Eventually we came to a stop. I could see dark forest ahead and I knew we must be up high because we'd been climbing for a while. The mercenary who was driving turned around. "We're here." He looked at me. "We put her on plane?"

I drew in my breath. *We must be back at the crash site.* And they were going to finally set the wreck on fire, together with the stand-in bodies for Weiss and the marshals.

And, maybe, me.

For the first time, I slowly turned to look at the man who would decide my fate. And the look I saw on his face pushed every ounce of warmth out of my body. He was *deciding*. But not in the way you decide to have a pet put to sleep, or decide whether to have a painful or necessary operation, or decide whether to tell your kids you're getting a divorce. There was no stress or guilt or sorrow in his eyes.

He was deciding my fate the way he'd decide whether to have the veal or the salmon. *Which will give me more pleasure?*

"No," he said at last.

"Killing her now is cleaner," said the mercenary. "No one will look for her."

Weiss smiled a slow smile. "No one will look for her anyway."

The mercenary sighed, shrugged and gave a string of orders in Russian over his radio.

"Why?" I asked, hating how tight my voice had gone. I didn't want him to know how scared I was.

"Because I owe you a little something for fucking up my plans."

There was something in his eyes, when he spoke to me. A dark lust, the opposite of the primal hunger that I loved so much in Boone. This was twisted and cruel: he was going to use me as a toy. Use me until he broke me.

There was only one way to avoid that. I had to convince him to kill me. "You should put me on the plane," I said. "If you keep me alive, you'll nev—"

Weiss threw back his head and laughed: an ugly, shrill sound. "Go on, say it!" he taunted. "*You'll never get away with it!*"

I went silent.

"I got away with stealing over *two billion,* you insignificant little bitch. Yeah, it would have been nice to keep it simple and have you *and* Boone be found in the plane. But this? This is even better."

"When they realize I survived, they'll look for me," I said. I wanted my body burned up and destroyed, however much it hurt, because then *he* couldn't hurt me.

But I'd underestimated him. He knew how to hurt me in ways I hadn't even imagined.

He shoved his face close to mine. "You haven't worked it out yet, have you? You haven't realized the gift you gave me, when you let yourself get captured with Boone still out there, free." He gave me that awful, thin-lipped grin. "See, they'll find the plane wreck, all burned up. They'll find what they think is my body. They'll find the pilot and what they think are the marshals' bodies. But you and Boone will be missing. A respected, heroic FBI agent and a wanted murderer."

Oh shit. Suddenly, I saw it. *Oh, God, no....*

"They'll search the area," said Weiss. "And if they don't find his cabin, I'll tip them off myself. I bet your DNA is *all over* that place, isn't it? In the bed? They'll think he raped you, killed you and buried the body."

No. NO!

That had been the one thing I'd been clinging onto: that at least Boone was still free. He'd just taken even that away from me, hurting both of us in the worst way possible. *They'll think he killed me!*

There was a sudden *wumf* from outside and I saw orange flames roar high into the sky. The light from the fire lit up Weiss's grinning face like the devil's.

"You're dead," he told me. "In every way that matters. No one's going to miss you. And that makes you mine."

FIFTY-EIGHT

Boone

I MADE GOOD TIME back to Weiss's camp. Once there, I started up the crashed 4x4 and got the heater on, then bundled the dozing Megan into the back seat. Only then did I look at the damage.

It was bad. The car had smashed into the tree hard enough that the right front fender was actually wrapped around it a little. One headlight was gone: I'd smashed it with a rock. The right wheel was pointing in a completely different direction to the left, as if the two were trying to meet in the middle. The fender was wedged against the tire and had shredded it. It was a wreck. Most garages would have told me to buy a new car.

But if I couldn't fix it, I wasn't going to be able to save Kate. *Okay, then....*

I didn't have the time or patience to try to reshape the bent fender. So I grabbed it in both hands and *heaved* until it came free, then turned and hurled the thing into the bushes. I could drive to Nome with one goddamn fender. I didn't care how the car looked.

Next, the wheel. I jacked it up and, with a hammer and a pry bar, started knocking it back into place. It was a precision job but I was anything but precise: I just wanted the damn thing to turn. I hunched over it for nearly an hour, heaving and hammering, straining with my back and arms to bend the metal. And, eventually, I had the wheel pointing in the right direction and steering okay. It sure as hell wasn't road legal but it would do. I changed the tire and I was done. We had a working car.

I climbed in and gunned the engine. We were hours behind them but I knew the area and they didn't. Plus, I figured they'd call at the site of the plane crash on the way, to burn it. My stomach churned at that thought. Would Weiss put Kate on the plane before he lit it? That's what he'd originally planned to do to both of us.

No. I'd seen the way he'd looked at her. The bastard would keep hold of her. And then, when he got her alone....

My knuckles went white on the steering wheel. *No.* Not if I had anything to do with it.

I put the car into gear and roared off.

FIFTY-NINE

Kate

NOME HAD SEEMED SMALL in the daytime. Now, at night, it seemed even smaller, just a few illuminated signs and some softly glowing windows, their drapes thick to keep out the cold. A tiny outpost of humanity next to...*that*.

The ocean took my breath away. The wind had gotten up and I could hear massive breakers crashing against the rocks. It was even scarier for not being able to see it, like a huge dark monster curled around the town. And I was going out there. I'd once thought of Alaska as a dark void but this was the real thing: fifty miles of black, freezing ocean. And then, when we reached Russia....

Weiss hadn't touched me, so far. Instead, he'd taken great pleasure in telling me his plans for me, lapping up my fear.

He was going to break me. Taking me by force: that was no challenge. Instead, he was going to gradually destroy my spirit, through pain and hunger and cold, until I *begged* to be used by him. He was prepared for it to take a long, long time. Even *wanted* it to. "I'm buying a big house in Moscow," he told me. "There's a basement we can use. I'll have it soundproofed."

I knew he was serious. He was rich, now, absurdly so. He'd had his fun separating people like my parents from their money. Now it was time for a new game. And I had no illusions that anyone would care what happened to me. I was going to be legally dead, a non-person even in America, and since they were smuggling us in, there wouldn't be any record of me arriving in Russia. If anyone *did* hear a scream coming from behind a door in a billionaire's cellar...well, money has a way of making people look the other way.

"Here." Weiss bent down by his feet and picked up an insulated flask. "We might as well get started." He unscrewed the top and then poured some of the dark liquid into a cup. Steam rose and the smell filled the car. I even saw the mercenary's nose twitch.

Coffee.

"I'll give you some," said Weiss. "All you have to do is say...."—he thought about it—"*Please, sir.*"

Coffee was all I'd been dreaming about for days but I wasn't about to give him the satisfaction. I reached out as if to take the cup and then suddenly upended it over him.

He sucked in air through his teeth as scalding coffee splashed across his legs, staining his suit. I was ready for the slap when it came but it still hurt: an explosion of pain across my cheek and the taste of blood in my mouth.

I could fight him. I *would* fight him. But I wouldn't be able to do it forever. I was going to experience what

Boone had: torture designed to break my mind, just in a different way. And when he won, I'd be his until the day I died. I couldn't think of anything worse.

The 4x4s left the road, drove down a ramp and came to a stop on a deserted beach. Our driver left the headlights on, pointing out into the roiling black waters like searchlights. Looking across at the other 4x4, I could see the marshals in the back seat. Phillips was grinning, no doubt looking forward to his reward and the start of his new life in Russia. But Hennessey looked as grim as I felt. He'd been a prisoner all along...but now that Weiss had lost his leverage over him, the others had been keeping an even closer eye on him. And now that we'd made it through Nome and away from any cops, he was expendable.

He knew he was never going to see Megan again.

The mercenary who was driving muttered into his radio, then turned around. "Five minutes."

Five minutes. And then I'd be Weiss's forever.

SIXTY

Boone

IT WAS A LONG TIME since I'd driven a car. My cabin was only accessible by foot: I'd had to haul everything I needed there on my back, or on a sled in the winter. And between the rough terrain and the rogue wheel, it wasn't a gentle re-introduction.

But he had Kate. So I used forest paths like they were highways and forged foot-deep streams like they were puddles. Twice, cutting across steep slopes, I felt the car tip sickeningly to one side and had to throw my weight the other way to prevent us rolling over.

But it worked. Dawn was still a way off when I saw the lights of Nome ahead of me.

Immediately, the thing inside me stirred. There were police there. They'd cuff me. Stuff me in the back of a car behind steel mesh. Then a tiny cell with a high, barred window. The fear fed on itself: I was scared of being imprisoned but I was more scared of what would happen next: losing myself in that darkness and locking down completely, becoming a prisoner in my own mind. My foot eased off the gas and we rolled to a halt....

He has Kate.

My foot slammed on the gas and we roared off again, entering the town.

A brutal wind was lashing the buildings: one of those real paint-stripping gales that you only get on the coast. When I pulled up in front of the church and opened my door, the wind almost pulled it out of my hand. I picked up Megan in her bundle of blankets, hugged her to my chest to shield her from the gusts and carried her to the door, then hammered on it.

It was a few minutes before the preacher answered, his white hair disheveled and a bathrobe wrapped around him. His eyes widened when he saw my military fatigues and my camo paint-streaked face.

I gently pushed Megan into his arms. "Take her to the police," I told him. "Her name is Megan. They're looking for her."

He blinked and then nodded. I knew I was probably putting the cops right on my tail, but what else could I do: leave her in a damn doorway? I had to make sure she was safe.

"Mr. Mason?" I was halfway back to the 4x4 but Megan's voice made me turn. She looked at me through tangled blonde curls. "Please save Agent Kate."

I nodded and ran for the 4x4.

The wind had shaped the ocean into a heaving, angry mass. Clouds were across the moon and you could barely see where the night ended and the water began: it was just a thundering black void that would smash anything crazy enough to enter it. The one advantage was that, between the early hour and the weather, the streets were empty. That would make finding them easier—

My stomach knotted. *Unless they'd already left.* I had no idea how fast they'd made it here. They could have got on their boat an hour ago for all I knew. If that was the case, I'd never see Kate again.

I stamped on the gas, making a fast circuit of the town. I checked the harbor first but couldn't see the 4x4s. But there were plenty of small bays where you could land a boat. I passed one after another, all of them empty—

There!

One of the 4x4s had its lights on, acting as beacons for the small launch that was being tossed about by the sea. The mercenaries, their black fatigues making them almost invisible, were just running out to help pull it ashore. *I'm in time!*

I stopped the car before they heard my engine, grabbed my bag and started to creep towards the beach. They were armed and I wasn't, but they weren't expecting trouble. If I was lucky, I could jump one of them and get his gun....

"Hold it!"

I was so surprised, I whirled around. Very nearly the last thing I did, because the gun pointing at my head twitched and nearly went off. "*Freeze!*"

Oh shit. Oh God, not now....

A cop car had pulled in right behind my 4x4, no siren and lights off. I hadn't heard their engine over the wind. They'd probably picked me up as I sped around town in a smashed-up car. Two cops were leaning over their open doors, guns pointed, one muttering into his radio.

I swallowed and tried to speak calmly. But I was a

big guy in black military gear, jacked up on adrenaline and my voice came out as a growl. "You don't understand. I gotta go."

Their guns twitched nervously. "You're not going anywhere."

I checked behind me. The launch was on the beach and—my heart lifted for a second as I saw Kate get out of the 4x4, Weiss pushing her from behind. *She's alive!* But in another few minutes, she'd be gone. "The boat. There's an FBI agent—"

The first cop had been listening to his radio. He suddenly cut me off. "Jesus, it *is* him! The one who escaped! *GET DOWN ON THE GROUND!*"

Oh no...the station must have been reading him a description of me. I checked over my shoulder. Kate was getting into the boat.

I sank to my knees because, if I didn't, they were liable to shoot me. Immediately, I was back in that basement, kneeling beside the radiator as they chained me to put me in the hole. I could feel the thing inside me uncoiling, rising up to claim me. I couldn't breathe. "Please," I groaned. "Take me in, but just stop that boat!"

The cops ignored me. "*FACE DOWN ON THE GROUND!*"

I lay down, hands behind my back, craning over my shoulder. The last thing I saw was the boat being pushed out into the surf and the mercs jumping aboard.

Then a knee was in my back and the cuffs were going on. Steel closed around my wrists and I felt the thing inside me rise to claim me.

SIXTY-ONE

Kate

"*Jesus!*" yelled Weiss over the wind.

For a second, we were airborne. Then we slammed down into the trough of the next wave and the shock went up through the hard bench seat, compressed every disc of my spine and slammed my teeth together so hard I heard it.

"Can't the yacht come any closer?!" yelled Weiss. "I'm getting fucking bruised!"

The lead mercenary turned around and glared at him. "Three nights ago, when we *should* have crossed? Smooth as glass. Boat has to stay far out or coast guard interfere."

Weiss grumbled but went quiet. His arm was around my waist and that chilled me even more than the fierce wind and spray. But I didn't dare try to push him away. It would only take one shove from Weiss and I'd be overboard...and in the freezing waters, I'd be dead long before I could swim to shore.

Already, the lights of Nome were almost out of

sight behind us. It was just black in every direction. I couldn't understand how the pilot could see: then he turned and I glimpsed the night vision goggles on his face.

At last, the boat slowed. I still couldn't see anything ahead. Then, looming out of the darkness, the prow of a yacht, all its lights off. It would be invisible from the shore.

A rope was thrown and the launch tied up. Then, one by one, they helped us aboard. The two marshals were led off down a companionway but I was pushed forward by Weiss, onto the bridge. A man in a suit stood there, his heavy body stretching the fabric. He turned to us—

I recognized the face and the carefully-coiffed blond hair immediately. *Dmitri Ralavich.* He'd taken over the running of half of St. Petersburg's underworld from his father. I knew him because he'd been trying to expand his network of brothels and dealers into the US. He'd been ugly even before some rival Mafioso had beat him half to death. Now, his fat face was a wreck.

"Mr. Weiss," he grinned, and embraced him. "Three days late," he said, mock-sternly.

Weiss scowled at the mercenaries. "Your men will be compensated."

Ralavich waved it away as if it wasn't even a thing. The fact that he'd come out here personally spoke volumes about how much Weiss must be paying him to help him disappear. Ten million? Twenty? That was nothing to Weiss, but it would fund a big, aggressive push into the US by Ralavich. I felt sick. I'd heard what went on in Ralavich's brothels.

"And you come to us considerably richer," said

Ralavich. I realized he was pointing at me. He grinned: it was as if he was trying to be charming, but he'd learned it from a book. There was absolutely no warmth in his piggy eyes, just ugly, twisted lust. "Is she a girlfriend? Someone you couldn't leave behind?"

"Kate is an FBI agent," said Weiss.

Immediately, Ralavich's expression changed. The lust didn't diminish: it doubled. "I may need a little extra money, when we dock. You understand: two people, instead of one."

Two? Not four?

Weiss looked at me and grinned, reading my expression. "We don't need the marshals anymore."

My stomach twisted. I'd suspected as much but I'd been praying I was wrong. I had no love for Phillips but Hennessey was innocent: he'd been dragged into this against his will. Everyone was disposable, to Weiss. I would be, too, once he'd extracted all the pleasure he could from me.

Ralavich stepped closer to me and I took an automatic step back. He wasn't as big as Boone and unlike Boone he ran to fat, but he was still intimidatingly tall and wide, especially next to me. "I could be persuaded to absorb the extra cost," he said to Weiss. "If I could spend the crossing with her. I would love to make the acquaintance of an American federal agent." He spat out the final three words as if they were sweet-tasting poison.

Oh Jesus, no. Ralavich was almost Weiss's opposite: a big, thuggish criminal who'd risen to the top through luck and inheritance, not cunning. Both were evil but the idea of Ralavich's fat hands gripping my throat, holding me down...that scared me just as much as Weiss's planned torture.

I thought I was safe, though. Weiss was convinced I belonged to him. He wouldn't let some other man touch me.

But as Weiss turned and grinned at me, my spine prickled. He wasn't jealous, like a lover. He saw me as a possession. He'd loan me out just to prove his ownership.

I couldn't help myself. I shook my head, begging him. Then I realized that my show of fear had sealed my fate. He'd do this *because* it terrified me.

"Why don't you take her to a stateroom?" Weiss told Ralavich.

I turned and bolted from the room.

But we were way out to sea, in the middle of a storm. I knew there was nowhere to run.

SIXTY-TWO

Boone

THEY WERE TRYING to stuff me into the back seat of the patrol car. With my size and my hands cuffed behind my back, it was awkward, especially because my body had gone rigid with fear. Eventually, they shoved me in and I fell sideways onto the seat, landing right on my injured arm. My legs were folded in and they slammed the door.

I lay there panting. It wasn't like when I was in the back of the 4x4, on the way to Weiss's camp. The storm clouds had blocked out the stars and it was utterly black in the back of the patrol car. My face was inches from the seat back in front of me: I could feel my breath being reflected back onto my lips—

Don't let it—

I tried to sit up, to get my head up where there was space and air, but I had no leverage.

Don't let it—

My hands jerked desperately at the cuffs but the chain held.

Don't—

Too late.

The thing that lived inside me rose, victorious. It had waited four long years for this and now it finally had me. It expanded through my mind, stole the air from my lungs—

"What the hell's the matter with him?" I heard one cop say, listening to my ragged breathing.

"He's a fucking basket case," said the other. "Went psycho in Iraq, or Afghanistan, or wherever, and shot a whole family. Military's after him."

The terror built and built and built...and then, as it peaked, everything went calm, like the eye of a hurricane.

I'd been running from this moment for so long, there was a hint of relief that I'd been right all along.

Because part of me knew the truth. The *real* truth. The one I hadn't shared even with Kate.

I knew all this—escaping the coffin, the trial, Alaska, Kate—I knew it was all just another hallucination. I'd always known that, at the back of my mind. That's what made it *hell.* I always knew that, at any time, I could wake up in that suffocating blackness and know I'd never left. Time can stretch out, in dreams...I had no idea how long might have passed. How many times had they dug me up, fed me, and put me back in the ground? A hundred times? Two hundred? I could have been buried for years.

That was what was at the heart of the fear, what gave it its strength. The best defense against a nightmare is to switch the lights on and reassure yourself it's not real. But how can you do that when you know that your own mind can play tricks on you?

Of course I'd dreamed of freedom: the biggest sky,

the freshest air. *Alaska.* Who wouldn't? I'd done my best to limit my dream. I'd hidden away in the mountains, avoiding all human contact. Even when I dreamed up a gorgeous woman like Kate, I'd done my best to avoid the temptation, terrified that she'd be ripped away from me when I woke. But at last, I'd given in....

I'd been in the coffin the whole time and now I was waking up. Fighting it would only prolong the pain. The best thing was to give myself up to it, to let my mind lock down.

The cops and the patrol car faded away and I fell down, down through the earth, all that weight pressing down on top of me. It was so black, I didn't know if my eyes were open or closed. And then I was back there, my face almost touching the wood, the cold chains around my wrists, the damp stink of the coffin making my nose crinkle.

My mind *locked.* I was back. I was buried.

Forever.

SIXTY-THREE

Boone

THERE WAS NO AIR. There was no light. There was nothing but darkness and fear. Tiny sensations were shocking: a drip of water on my lips from the tube or the patter of dirt across my cheek as a truck went past outside and the soil sifted through the tiny cracks in the coffin lid.

And then, after an endless time, there was something else. A sound. A voice. Not muttered words in Dari or Pashto like my captors: *English.* A woman's voice. A voice like silk.

It said, *I need you to come back to me.*

Lies. She's just a dream.

It said, *I think I'm falling in love with you.*

I made her up. Women like her don't exist.

It said, *I'm not leaving you behind.*

And suddenly, impossibly, she was right there in the darkness next to me, so close I could feel the softness of her cheek on mine, so close I could feel the satin stroke of her braid on my collar bone and—

And I knew my imagination wasn't that good. I couldn't have come up with Kate, stubborn and determined and gorgeous, with that tight little braid and the nipples I loved to rub my thumb across, all wrapped up in an FBI suit. So small, so perfect.

Kate was real.

And if Kate was real, then Alaska was real. All of it: escaping, coming home, the plane crash, Weiss...all of it was real. And I wasn't buried in Afghanistan. I was in the back seat of a cop car, on my way to a cell.

And she needed me.

I tipped back my head and gave a silent scream of rage. The anger rippled out of me, shattering the coffin's wood, melting the soil around me.

I felt myself rising through the earth, slowly at first but getting faster and faster. Maybe I'd needed this. Maybe I'd had to come to this moment and face what I'd dreaded for years in order to give me the power to escape.

I burst through the surface of my fear and opened my eyes just as the cop car came to a stop. I lay there panting for a second, disoriented. I could see a lit-up police station through the side window. The cops got out and one sauntered around to the rear door to let me out.

I only just managed to get myself moving in time. I drew back my legs and, as he opened the door, I kicked it with both feet as hard as I could.

The door flew open and knocked the cop back on his ass. He landed hard and was still sprawling when I inch-wormed my way along the seat and slithered out, then got to my feet. My hands were still cuffed behind my back so, as the other cop ran around the rear of the car, I drew back and then met his charge with a headbutt. He crumpled to the ground.

I bent, reaching awkwardly with my cuffed hands, and searched through his belt and pockets until I found the handcuff keys. I released myself and then stood and just breathed for a moment, taking in the fresh Alaska air.

I was free. *Actually* free. For the first time since they'd put me in that coffin. Everything seemed brighter, clearer. Kate had made that possible.

I stalked around the cop car and got into the driver's seat. Both cops were still on the ground, groaning, but they both looked like they'd be okay. Of course, I was going to have every cop in town on my tail in a couple of minutes.

Fine. Let them come. Let them lock me up. My paralyzing fear of it had gone. *Just let me save Kate, first.*

I slammed the car into gear and roared away.

I didn't bother trying to find my way back to the beach where they'd left. I knew they were long gone. What I had to do now was catch the boat that Weiss must be meeting up with. I raced down to the harbor and straight onto the pier, tires screeching. Even this early, there were a few people around, mostly securing their boats against the storm.

The cop car had a shotgun holstered in the driver's door and I drew it. The cops had thrown my bag in the back seat when they'd arrested me and I dug in it until I found my night vision goggles. Then I stepped out into the wind. It was even stronger, here, the roar and the crash of the waves deafening. There were two guys trying desperately to lash down a small inflatable boat so that the wind didn't take it and they didn't notice me coming until I was close enough to tap one of them on the shoulder with the shotgun. He turned around and saw me, shotgun, camo paint and all, and fell over the boat in his hurry to escape.

"I'm taking your boat," I told them. Neither of them argued.

I undid the ropes and hauled the thing down to the shore. There was nothing visible to the naked eye, just churning blackness, the water impossible to separate from the night. But when I put on my night vision goggles I could see waves ten feet high...and a yacht on the horizon that had to be them.

I waded out, pushing the boat in front of me, grunting as the freezing water soaked through my pants. Almost immediately, a wave smacked into the front of the boat and tried to flip it right over my head. I clung on and wound up underneath it for a second, ass grating along the rocky beach as the wind pushed me back.

When I got to my feet and went to try again, the two guys I'd stolen the boat from shook their heads. "You can't go out there!" yelled one.

I gritted my teeth and this time ran at the waves, smashing through them and hurling the boat down on top of the heaving water. I hauled on the starter cord and the outboard motor roared into life. "Try and fucking stop me," I muttered. And headed out into the storm.

SIXTY-FOUR

Kate

I RAN. Down the stairs, along the companionway, searching for a way out. The mercenaries standing guard didn't bother to stop me. They knew there was no escape. If I went outside, the wind and pitching deck would probably send me overboard. If I stayed inside, Ralavich would hunt me down.

I checked over my shoulder and moaned in fear. He was advancing down the companionway, each heavy footstep shaking the floor under my feet. He was so big that his body filled the narrow space, his shoulders brushing the walls. His size triggered the exact opposite response in me to Boone's: it didn't make me feel protected, it made me afraid. And it didn't make me feel small and feminine, it made me feel fragile and vulnerable.

I was trying to push everything I'd heard about Ralavich's "brothels" out of my mind. Places where trafficked women provided sport for rich businessmen who wanted to indulge their darkest fantasies. *Brothel* was a euphemism. On the streets of St. Petersburg, they were simply called *rape clubs.*

And this was the man who ran them. I was panting, now, almost hysterical. Behind me, I could hear Ralavich laugh at my fear. His slow pace made it all the more frightening: he didn't have to hurry. I was trapped like a rat in a maze. "Don't worry, little *suka,*" he said in a sing-song voice. "I'll be gentle."

I could hear a second, much softer set of footsteps behind Ralavich's. *Weiss.* He was using Ralavich the way another man would use a pit bull. I knew he'd listen outside the door, enjoying my screams. Maybe he'd even watch. *Jesus, no—*

I rounded the next corner. *Shit!* A dead end. I backed up against the furthest door.

Ralavich came around the corner and grinned. "Ready for me?"

I twisted the doorknob and almost fell into the room, slamming the door behind me and locking it. When I turned, my heart sank. I was in a stateroom, exactly where he'd wanted to take me. Dark wood. Marble. Soft cream bedding. The outrageous luxury was even more jarring, given what I'd gotten used to for the last few days. I searched but there was nothing that could be used as a weapon and the only door led to a bathroom.

"Why don't you unlock the door?" asked Ralavich. "I can break it...but it's a shame to break such a nice boat. If you make me break it, I'll have to hurt you."

He would, too. I could defend myself, but judo only goes so far. One good punch from his ham-sized fists and I'd be unconscious. *Helpless.*

I checked the drawers, under the bed, hoping he might have stashed a gun there. Nothing.

"Open the door, *suka*. I want to show you how a Russian man fucks."

I could feel tears rising in my eyes: fear and hatred and humiliation. I couldn't believe that, after everything I'd been through, it was going to come down to this....

Then my eyes fell on the porthole. Like everything else, it was framed in dark wood with gold trim. And there was a hinge. It opened.

I walked over to it on legs that had suddenly gone numb and prickly with shock. I couldn't believe that I was even thinking it....

I looked through the glass. It was so dark outside, I could barely make out the churning sea. But when the moon broke through the clouds for an instant I saw: a sheer drop, sickeningly high, into the black, freezing waters. I hadn't realized just how big the yacht was. Waves the height of buses were slamming up against it, making the hull groan and echo. *Jesus, I can't go out there!*

The doorknob rattled.

I took a deep breath and unlocked the glass cover, then swung it open. Immediately, the storm's fury filled the room: a howl that hurt my ears, stinging spray that tore at my face. I leaned out and looked to the left. More portholes, all closed. I made the mistake of looking down and nearly threw up: nothing but slick, white hull and then the massive waves below. *If I fall, no one will even hear the splash.* To my right....

The next porthole was almost six feet away. But it was ajar, probably opened for ventilation and then forgotten.

A *bang* behind me made me spin around. The door was rattling in its frame.

My heart thundering in my chest, I leaned my head out again, then hooked a shoulder out. The porthole was too small for most people but with my small body I could just fit. I crushed myself against one side and gritted my teeth as I hooked the other shoulder through and then started to wriggle out. I couldn't use my hands until I got past my arms. The further I went, the more I tipped down. Soon I was descending almost vertically, head-first towards the water. *Oh Jesus...I should have gone feet-first.* But it was too late now.

Just as I thought I was going to slither uncontrollably out and fall, my hands cleared the porthole and I clung on for dear life, rocking on my waist, half in and half out. I twisted and stretched to the side but I couldn't quite reach the open porthole. I'd have to wriggle out even more.

I kicked with my legs, coaxing my hips through the narrow opening. I twisted, strained, reaching so far out I thought my shoulder would dislocate.

And suddenly I tipped and *slid,* my scream swallowed up by the wind. My fingers brushed the metal rim of the porthole that was ajar and I instinctively clung, but then my full weight was being taken by that arm and I cried out in pain. My body crashed painfully against the metal hull. Then I was lifted and pulled to the side as if by a massive hand, my body twisting and my grip almost breaking free. Cold like I'd never felt raced down the length of my body, so brutal and bitter it made me sob.

I was hanging from one hand from the porthole and the gale was trying to tear my dangling body loose.

SIXTY-FIVE

Boone

I GROWLED as the boat crested the top of another wave, went fully airborne for a second, then slammed down into water that felt like concrete. The boat was way, *way* too small for this weather. And now that we were away from shore, the wind and the size of the waves was going up and up. It was near-suicidal.

But I was a Navy SEAL. And this is what we *do*.

I was lying almost flat, using my weight to guide the boat and stop it flipping over. My hair was soaked and blown back by the wind, each strand feeling like it was being torn out by the root. Every millimeter of exposed skin was being flayed off me by the stinging spray and my whole body was one giant bruise from being slammed against the deck over and over.

But I almost relished the pain because it felt real. She'd brought me back to who I really was, from the shell of a man she'd first met at the airport. And now I was going to save her. I was gaining on them: in this weather, they couldn't get up to their full speed.

I glimpsed movement on the deck just as something zipped past me. *Shit!* They must have someone standing guard. I knew I was almost invisible in the darkness, with my black clothes and camo paint. They must have night vision, too.

I heard the next bullet rip through the rough fabric of my fatigues and then felt burning pain across my shoulder. It hurt like hell but I could still move my arm so it must have just winged me. The next one wouldn't.

I hunkered low and felt another two shots bury themselves in the boat's inflatable rib. Air began hissing out but it would take a while. If I could just reach the yacht before it—

At that second, a wave hit the prow and flipped the boat vertical. I fell backwards into the freezing water and plunged deep beneath the surface: it felt like falling into a basket of knives. I kicked my way back up but a wave was overhead so it seemed to take forever. Just as I finally broke the surface, another wave hit me in the face, making me choke and gasp.

The shots had stopped—they'd lost me in the waves. But the yacht was quickly pulling away from me, disappearing into the night. I'd lost my night vision goggles and the wind had taken my boat: it was cartwheeling along the tops of the waves, already hundreds of yards away.

I struck out for the yacht but I knew it was useless. Even in the storm, they could go much faster than I could swim. And in these waters, my life expectancy was about three minutes: not nearly enough time to make it back to shore.

I was going to die out here.

SIXTY-SIX

Kate

I CRIED OUT as the wind eased and I slammed against the hull again. The next gust would tear me loose.

I was *so...cold.* My whole body throbbed and ached with it, my mind cloudy with it. It would be so easy to just *let go.* The shock of the freezing water would probably make drowning almost painless....

And then I heard Boone's voice in my head. Telling me I could do it. Telling me I was strong. *Weiss is going to win,* he said. *You want to let that happen?*

I set my jaw and heaved with all my strength, levering myself up like Boone had taught me on the cliff face. I managed to get the other hand onto the rim of the porthole but my fingers felt like blocks of ice. I couldn't tell if I had a good grip.

Hanging on as best I could, I leaned forward and used my head to press against the glass until the porthole cover creaked inward. All I could see inside was darkness but I didn't care: it had to be better than the storm. Arms shaking and rubbery with fatigue, I hauled myself upward until I could get my chest onto the rim, then tried to haul myself forward. But there was barely any strength left in me: the brutal cold had utterly drained me. And the wind was picking up again, plucking at my legs, making me slide back out....

I put everything I had into wriggling forward. There was some sort of metal shelving unit to my left and I grabbed it and *pulled,* even though the sharp metal dug painfully into my hand. And then I was slithering through the porthole and crashing to the floor with a bang.

For a moment I just lay there, exhausted. It was cold in the room but, compared to the storm outside, lying on the chilled tiles felt like sunbathing. The wind had stripped every last particle of heat from my body. I wrapped my arms around me and shivered for a while before I could even lift my head to look around.

I realized I was in the galley. All the lights were off and only a sliver of light came from under the door. I climbed to my feet and crept between rows of shelves holding everything from sacks of rice to fresh melons, then emerged into the main kitchen.

First things first: as soon as I saw a butcher's knife, I grabbed it. Then I cracked open the door and looked out. To one side of me was a wall: I was now on the far side of the dead end I'd reached before. I realized the yacht must be divided into an area for the crew and an area for the guests, and by going outside I'd managed to slip around the dividing wall. Listening, I could just make out Ralavich cursing on the far side. He had no idea where I was...but that would change as soon as he broke down the door and saw the open porthole.

I needed a plan and I didn't have one. The only thing I could think of was to find a radio or phone and call the coastguard. I headed down the companionway, trying to go quietly despite my chattering teeth and numb, clumsy legs. But when I passed a porthole and saw dark, rocky land passing by, I cursed. That must be Little Diomede and Big Diomede, the islands that mark the halfway point between the US and Russia. I had to hurry. In another few minutes, we'd be in Russian waters and I'd be out of reach of any help.

At that moment, I heard footsteps approaching from around the corner. I changed course and headed down a set of metal stairs instead. As I descended I could hear voices above me. Angry, urgent voices. They were searching for me.

I opened door after door, but didn't find a radio. The next door I opened led to a big room full of pounding noise and heat. The engine room.

I could hear footsteps coming down the stairs. I stepped inside, thinking fast. If I couldn't call for help, the next best thing I could do was to stop the yacht. If we were stranded, the coastguard might investigate. And if we wound up wrecked...well, at least Weiss wouldn't get away.

I put down the butcher knife and picked up a heavy wrench. The instructions on the controls were all in Cyrillic so my strategy was going to be to just smash everything and hope that that worked.

I lifted the wrench above my head, about to bring it down—

A gun barrel pressed against my temple.

I froze...and turned my head to see Marshal Phillips standing there.

"Drop the wrench," he said with great satisfaction.

I let it go and it bounced off the metal deck with a clang like a church bell. "Weiss is going to kill you," I told him. "You *and* Hennessey."

"I'd better prove I'm still useful, then," said Phillips. "Catching you should help. Come on. Ralavich and Weiss are waiting for you upstairs."

My stomach heaved. I couldn't face that. Better to die here: at least it would be quick. I dropped to a crouch, grabbing for the wrench...but I knew there was no way I could get it and swing it at Phillips before he fired. Before I'd even touched the wrench, he had his gun pointed at my head again and I saw his finger tighten on the trigger—

But the shot never came. Phillips was frozen in place, just as I had been. I grabbed the wrench and stood. That's when I saw the gleam of the butcher's knife pressed to his throat.

Marshal Hennessey stepped out from the shadows behind him, pressing just hard enough with the blade to indent the skin without drawing blood.

I stared at him, wide-eyed. With everyone searching for me, they'd forgotten to keep an eye on him. We'd all underestimated the old marshal.

Hennessey nodded at the control console. "Smash that fucking thing," he spat.

I raised the wrench high above my head and then brought it down on the center of the console. Metal dented but we kept moving. My second swing shattered a dial and there were a few sparks. On the third swing I heard a satisfying crunch of circuitry and the every bulb on the ship blew out, plunging us into darkness. The thunder of the engines quickly died and the deck started to shift under our feet as we began to drift.

"What have you *done?*" croaked Phillips in the blackness. "We're right by the islands. We'll be smashed on the rocks!"

"He's right," muttered Hennessey. "We'd better get topside and look for a life raft."

But even as he said it, I heard boots pounding down the metal stairs. As soon as the engines stopped, the mercenaries had figured out where we were. I snatched Phillips' gun from his hand but we were outnumbered and outgunned. *We're going to die down here.*

SIXTY-SEVEN

Boone

SWIMMING IN A GALE isn't like swimming: it's like climbing. I was hauling myself up the side of each huge wave, clawing at it with my arms as if I was trying to scale a glacier. Then, at the peak, I'd drop down the other side so fast I plunged down under the surface, only to emerge for the next ascent.

My entire body was so cold, I could barely feel anything beyond my torso. My wounded arm was screaming at me to rest, but swimming was the only thing keeping me warm. When I stopped, I was dead. And however fast I swam, the yacht was still easily pulling away from me. I was just delaying the inevitable.

But I wouldn't quit. I kept my arms and legs going through sheer stubbornness, what my old SEAL instructor liked to call *an inability to quit.* Kate was on that yacht and she needed me and by God, I was going to reach her, even if I had to swim all the way to Russia.

On the next ascent, though, I didn't make it all the way to the top, the cap of the wave smacking me in the face. I went under and, on the next wave, it was even worse. I was in a downward spiral, now, arms and legs growing leaden, the sea winning....

And then I saw something impossible. The yacht started to turn to the side and then lean drunkenly as the wind took her. She was drifting.

I had no idea how that could happen. Engine trouble? *Kate?* But I wasn't going to let it go to waste. I put everything I had into swimming for the yacht. Every stroke brought me closer, now. My shoulders were on fire and my hips screamed but I kept on tearing through the water, terrified that I'd see the yacht pull away again just as I reached it—

I grabbed a dangling rope and hauled myself up to the deck. I rolled over the handrail and just lay on the soaking wood for a moment while I recovered. Then I climbed to my feet. I'd lost the shotgun when my boat flipped over so I was unarmed. But I was *mad.* That would have to do.

The guards I'd seen out on deck were all gone. When I crept inside, I heard gunfire from below decks. *Kate?* I headed that way. The whole ship was pitch black—the electrics must have shorted out. I could hear my own breathing echo in the narrow companionways, sense the walls close to my face. It was almost like being back in the coffin.

But this time, it didn't trigger the fear. The memories were still there. They always would be. But they didn't have the same power over me, anymore. Something had changed, deep inside me. I had something new and real to hold onto, something more powerful than any amount of past horrors. I had *her.*

When I turned the corner I saw the first mercenary up ahead, leaning over the top of a stairwell to fire. They must have Kate pinned down, somewhere down there. I could hear the throaty rattle of their assault rifles and the lonely bangs of a handgun in return. I didn't know how many mercenaries there were: three had come to Alaska but I had no idea how many more had been waiting on the yacht.

It didn't matter. I'd wade through an army if I had to.

I crept up behind the mercenary, slammed my fist into his head and then gently lowered his unconscious body to the deck. I took his rifle and crept down the stairs. It was pitch black down there, the only light coming from the muzzle flash each time a gun fired. I glimpsed four more mercenaries clustered around a doorway, firing inside. With them was a tall, overweight Russian in a suit. And beside him—

Weiss.

"Leave her!" I heard the Russian snarl. "We have to go before we're carried into the rocks!"

Then Weiss's voice. "I am *not* leaving without that bitch!"

I growled and ran down the rest of the stairs firing, desperate to draw their attention away from Kate. I managed to take down two of the mercenaries before they could react but the other two spun and shot back. I had to duck back behind cover and, in the flashes of muzzle fire, I saw Weiss and the big Russian flee into the darkness in opposite directions. *Shit!*

I'd worry about them later. I had to save Kate. I waited until the mercenaries stopped to reload and then ran at them, firing into the blackness until my gun ran empty and then just charging at the last place

I'd seen them.

There was a satisfying grunt as I slammed into one of them. I felt the other beside me and grabbed him, hurling him at the wall. And then everything was quiet.

"Kate?" I called through the darkened doorway.

A second's heart-stopping pause. Then, "*Mason?!*"

I felt around on the bodies of the unconscious mercenaries until I found a flashlight and flicked it on, shining it through the doorway. I started forward but I'd barely crossed the threshold when a warm body thumped into my chest. "Oh God," she whispered. "I thought I'd never see you again!"

I clutched her tight to me, wrapping my arms around her and cradling her head on my shoulder. Then I pushed her back just far enough that I could kiss her. The touch of her was like a drug, a warm glow that throbbed through me and drove back the pain and cold. I only broke the kiss when marshal Hennessey stepped out of the shadows, holding Marshal Phillips prisoner with a knife to his throat. "We've got to get out of here," he told us. "Before—"

The whole room suddenly jerked to the side as if an 18-wheeler had slammed into us. All four of us went flying. I managed to land under Kate, cushioning her a little, and sucked air through my teeth as my injured arm hit the metal deck. We all looked at each other. It sank in that we hadn't suddenly moved; we'd suddenly *stopped.*

A groaning, shrieking noise echoed along the wall, coming closer and closer. Then the yacht started to move again, grating sideways against whatever it had slammed into. It sounded like a monster clawing its way along the hull.

"Oh God," whispered Kate. She climbed off me and tried to haul me to my feet. "Get up! We've got to—"

The first rupture brought a paper-thin sheet of water that shot the full width of the room. Then huge rents were being opened up, glistening black rocks ripping through the metal like wet paper, and the ocean roared in.

SIXTY-EIGHT

Kate

THE WATER ROSE scarily quickly: it was up to our knees before we could reach the stairs. And then, with an ear-splitting screech of tortured metal, the yacht started to tear apart, the rear half rotating and opening up a huge hole in one wall. Phillips, who was staggering along beside Hennessey, was swept off his feet and then out into the ocean. He thrashed, hysterical. *"I can't swim!"*

Hennessey cursed. Looked at us. Looked at Phillips...and then dived in and swam after him, disappearing into the black waters.

We had to retreat up the stairs as the water rose, then up another set to the main deck. We met two more mercenaries coming the other way but Boone slammed them against the wall before they could even raise their guns, leaving them in a groaning heap. He snatched up one of their rifles before running on.

As we came out into the open, I had to twist to one side just to breathe, the wind was so strong. It howled past my ears, so loud I could barely think. Between the spray and the water that had rushed into the engine room, I was soaked through and now the wind was stripping the last bits of warmth from my body. Boone wrapped his arms around me from behind to shield me from the worst of it, but I couldn't stop shivering.

When I saw the black cliffs to either side of us, I started to understand what had happened. We'd rammed right into Big Diomede, the Russian island, and now the yacht was breaking apart in the waters between it and Small Diomede, the Alaskan island. With the hull split wide open, it was going down fast: I could actually feel it settling lower and lower under my feet.

I saw movement in the water and caught my breath. The launch that had brought us to the yacht was powering away, piloted by one of the mercenaries...and I could see Ralavich hunkered in the back, glaring at us. Boone raised his assault rifle but the boat was already too far away.

"Son of a bitch," I muttered to myself in disbelief. I knew he was a criminal, but... "He just upped and *left* Weiss?" The yacht was sinking but I was stunned that Ralavich would just abandon his passenger when he was worth so much.

Then the yacht and the sea around us were lit up in brilliant white. I had to shield my eyes to see the source. It was blasting down on us from a point of light in the sky and I could just make out the roar of helicopter blades over the wind.

The US Coast Guard was here. Someone on one of the islands must have alerted them to a ship in distress. That's why Ralavich had fled so quickly. He didn't want to risk being caught.

I breathed a little easier: Weiss must still be on board. Once he was in custody, he wouldn't be able to pay Ralavich. Ralavich would be out for the cost of the entire operation, plus we'd wrecked his yacht. That would end his plans to expand his empire into the US.

But then my stomach twisted. *Only if we get him into custody.* Once the Coast Guard started lifting us off the sinking yacht, it was going to be chaos. I had visions of Coast Guard officers dragging us into their helicopter while Weiss slipped away.

We had to finish this. I had to *know* Weiss was caught. I was frozen and exhausted and running on empty. But I was still FBI and I had a job to do.

I ran down the length of the yacht, staggering a little on my freezing legs. I searched frantically but I couldn't see him anywhere. *Am I too late?!*

I knew I was being stubborn. I was freezing and running on empty and the yacht was breaking up. But I wasn't going to let the bastard get away.

Then, as I rounded the final corner, I spotted him. He was at the bottom of the stairs which led to the bridge, struggling to get a big, orange bundle that could only be a life raft over the rail. *Shit!*

I ducked back behind the corner. Checked the gun I'd taken off Phillips. My hands were shaking, I was so cold. I took a deep breath and stepped around the corner to confront him—

A big hand caught my shoulder. I yelped in surprise as Boone pulled me back around the corner and pushed me hard up against a wall.

He put his mouth to my ear so that I could hear him over the wind. "I've lost you enough times," he growled. "I am *not* losing you again. We'll take him *together."*

I drew in a deep, shuddering breath, my chest pressing against his as my lungs filled. God, he felt good. I nodded.

Boone cocked his assault rifle, I raised my gun...and we ran forward.

Weiss whirled around as we rushed him and I glimpsed the gun in his hand. He fired once and missed, the shot hissing between us. Then he was lifted clean off his feet by Boone's fist. He crashed down on the deck, dropping his gun. Before I could grab him, he was up and pounding up the stair. Both of us sprinted after him but, as we entered the bridge, I relaxed. There was only one door: we had him cornered.

"You're under arrest!" I snarled as the bridge door closed behind us. It was blessedly quiet inside, after the gale, and a little warmer.

"Wait," said Weiss breathlessly. "*Wait!*" He flattened himself against the far wall.

"It's over," I snapped. I advanced on him step by furious step. "Ralavich abandoned you. The Coast Guard's almost here. We're taking you back to the US!" I could hear the helicopter right overhead, now. They'd be here any minute.

Weiss had gone pale. He looked so much smaller, without his goons to back him up. "We can make a deal!"

Boone and I both shook our heads and strode towards him.

"Listen!" snapped Weiss as Boone grabbed him by the throat. "*Listen!*"

I put my hand on Boone's arm to still him, wanting to hear.

Weiss talked fast. "If the US Coast Guard pick us up, it's not just me who's going to jail." He nodded at Boone. "He will, too."

I froze. He was right. They'd hand Boone over to the authorities and he'd be locked up.

Weiss pounced on my hesitation. "*Get in the life raft with me!* There's still time! We're practically on Big Diomede and that's Russian soil! The US can't touch us! You can both start new lives in Russia. *Together!* Nobody has to go to jail. And I'll throw in a million dollars *each.*"

I looked up. The roar of helicopter blades almost drowned out the storm, now. We had seconds, if we wanted to escape. I looked at Boone. It wasn't the money. It was getting him out of the jail term he didn't deserve. *Maybe* I could get him a retrial but what if I couldn't? What if it failed? In Russia, we could live out a quiet, happy life, find someone to help with his PTSD...I closed my eyes for a second, then looked up into his. "It's your call," I whispered.

Boone looked down at me and then shook his head. "No way."

"You'll go to jail!"

He still had Weiss's throat in one hand. With the other, he reached down and cupped my cheek. "I can handle it, now. At least until you get me out."

I clung to his arm. "What if I *can't?!*"

"You will." His thumb stroked my cheek. "I believe in you, Kate Lydecker."

I caught my breath. Something was different in his eyes. The all-consuming fear wasn't there, even when he was talking about imprisonment. I nodded. Then I turned to Weiss. "No deal," I told him coldly. "You're going to jail."

Weiss's face slowly crumbled as realization hit: he'd finally found someone he couldn't buy.

At that second, the door burst open and a flood of men filled the room. I slumped in relief and turned to greet them.

And then I froze. The men weren't wearing the bright orange of Coast Guard rescue personnel. They were in gray and black.

The helicopter overhead wasn't the Coast Guard. It was Russian Navy. These were soldiers.

And every one of them was pointing a rifle at us.

SIXTY-NINE

Kate

ONE OF THE SOLDIERS screamed something at me in Russian. I could hear others yelling the same phrase at Boone. I didn't speak Russian but I got the idea pretty fast.

My gun clattered to the floor. Boone's assault rifle followed an instant later.

One soldier stepped to the front, his rifle still pointed at us, and the others went quiet. He started throwing questions at us in Russian. "Does anyone speak English?" I asked helplessly.

Another soldier stepped forward and stood next to the leader. "I do. A little." He looked at his leader. "This is Captain Yeltsev of the Russian Navy. I am his second in command, Bostoy. We are here to take you into Russian custody."

My blood went cold. Across the room, I saw Weiss break into a grin. *No. No, no no!* As soon as he got to Russia, Weiss would disappear. Between his ability to offer multi-million dollar bribes and his friends in the

Russian Mafia, I had no doubt it would happen. "I am special agent Lydecker of the FBI," I told Bostoy. "This is Mason Boone, also a US citizen. That man,"—I pointed—"is Carlton Weiss, my prisoner. We need to return to the US."

Bostoy translated in rapid-fire Russian. His boss shook his head and spat an order. "The ship is breaking up," said Bostoy. Even as he said it, the deck lurched. "You will come with us. *Now.*"

No. No! A soldier grabbed my shoulder. I wrenched out of his grip and he grabbed me again, more roughly, this time. Boone stepped between us and shoved the Russian back. Instantly, six rifles snapped up to point at his chest.

"*Get out of the way!*" yelled Bostoy.

Boone shook his head.

Shit. They'll kill him! I put my hand on Boone's shoulder and gently shook my head, looking into his eyes as I did it. This was something that couldn't be solved with raw power.

Boone nodded reluctantly and stepped aside. *Okay,* his eyes said. *I trust you.*

I wished I had as much faith in myself as he did in me. I swallowed and stepped forward, trying to make my voice calm and reasonable...and *firm,* despite my chattering teeth. "Please," I begged. "I can't let that man get to Russia." Then I saw something through the yacht's windshield and pointed up into the sky. "Look! *There!*" A second helicopter was approaching and this one was orange and white. "The US Coast Guard's nearly here. *They* can lift us off!"

"You are our responsibility," said Bostoy tightly.

Why was he being so immovable? This went beyond simple laws and jurisdictions. "*That man cannot go to Russia!"* I yelled in frustration.

Captain Yeltsev shook his head again, as if he'd seen enough, and barked orders in Russian. Soldiers rushed forward and grabbed Weiss. "You may wait for the US Coast Guard," Bostoy translated. "But we must take Mr. Weiss with us. We have orders—" He broke off abruptly, as if he'd said too much.

I suddenly saw what was happening here.

Ralavich must have heard on the ship's radio that both US and Russian authorities were converging on the yacht. He'd abandoned ship to save his own skin in case the US got there first but, now that he was safe, he was desperate to ensure Weiss got to Russia so that he got paid. The Russian Mafia had tentacles everywhere. He was screaming into a satellite phone right now as his launch sped him towards Russia. And some Russian Navy commander was in turn screaming over the radio to Captain Yeltsev.

They weren't going to take *no* for an answer. They were going to take Weiss and he'd get away with everything he'd done. Ralavich would get his multi-million dollar reward and expand into the US.

Unless—

I reached down and snatched up my handgun. Then I pushed in front of Weiss and pointed my gun at the soldiers.

There was a rattling sound as every single soldier cocked their rifle and pointed it right at me. *Oh God, Kate, what are you doing?*

"Agent Lydecker," said Bostoy in a strained voice. "You are in Russian waters. You have no jurisdiction here. Put the gun down."

I could hear my boss at the FBI yelling the same thing. This wasn't *the system*. There were *rules*. I was shaking with cold, close to passing out from exhaustion. It would be so easy just to let him go. *It's not worth getting killed over.*

But I'd had enough. I'd had enough of Weiss bribing his way out of trouble. I'd had enough of the system failing, the way it had failed Boone.

Sometimes, you don't need the system. Sometimes, you need justice.

I summoned up everything we'd endured over the last few days, every moment of cold and fear and hunger Weiss had put us through, and I focused that into a voice of iron and steel.

"You tell your boss this," I told Bostoy. "I am an FBI agent. This man is in my custody. Now *maybe* we're in Russian waters and maybe we're in US waters: we're right on the border. But if you want to take this man from me, you're going to have to shoot me and if you shoot a US citizen in contested waters it's an international fucking incident and maybe the start of a war. I know you've got orders. I know someone's telling you to bring this guy back *no matter what* and you're going to catch hell if you don't. But if you kill me you're going to have much, much bigger problems. Do you want to be the guy who started the war? Because that's what you're going to need to do to take this man because he's mine and *he is going to jail!*"

I stared at him the whole time Bostoy was translating, refusing to budge. Then I had to wait while he thought it over. We stood there staring at each other, the rifles still all pointing at my head.

At last, Captain Yeltsev said something in Russian. I looked desperately at Bostoy for the translation.

"He said," said Bostoy, "you have big balls for such

a small woman."

Yeltsev made a gesture and the rifles lowered. I let out a long, slow breath.

The Russians turned and left, heading back to their helicopter. Weiss's smirk died on his face and he stood there gaping as the Russian helicopter lifted away and the US Coast Guard one took up position overhead. A few minutes later, a coastguard officer in orange rescue gear burst onto the bridge. "What the *hell* is going on down here?" he barked. "Ship's breaking up. Russians made us keep our distance and then left without lifting you off. You need rescuing or not?"

"*Yes,*" I said very firmly. Now it was over, the adrenaline was sluicing out of my system and the shaking in my legs was spreading through my whole body. I was freezing and half-soaked and exhausted. I slumped against Boone, drawing strength from his warm, hard body. "Yes, we do."

EPILOGUE

Boone

I knew it was only a matter of time, so I made every second count.

We had to be winched up to the Coast Guard helicopter separately but, as soon as we were on board and Weiss was restrained, I slipped my arm around Kate and hugged her close. I tried to burn it all into my memory: the softness of the side of her breast, the firm warmth of her thigh as it pressed against mine, the brush of that silken ponytail on my neck.

The two marshals were already on board. The Coast Guard had found Hennessey keeping Phillips's head above water a short distance from the yacht, both of them exhausted and half-frozen. I persuaded the Coast Guard to call the Nome police and Kate and I both relaxed when we found out that the preacher had delivered Megan to them safe and sound: she was already back with her parents.

When they unloaded us at the Coast Guard base, I tensed: I thought it was going to happen then. But no:

I was granted another few hours while they took us to hospital and dressed my wounds. Sitting on the edge of a gurney while the doctor worked on me, I told Kate every damn thing I was going to do with her once we were together again. We talked about where to live and where to vacation, about where I'd work and where she'd work. And when it all got too much and the tears started to creep into her eyes, I leaned close and took her mind off it by whispering into her ear all the things I was going to do to her, on the day I got out. I could tell the doctor overheard some of it because the poor guy turned beet red, as did Kate. But the tears stopped.

When they'd patched me up, I knew it would be any minute. So as soon as the doctor left us, I grabbed hold of Kate and pulled her close. I buried my nose in her hair and inhaled the scent of her, committing it to memory. I knew it would be a long time before I smelled it again. I ran my hands up and down her back, wishing I could magic away all the damn clothes, and tried to build a perfect model of her in my mind, one I'd be able to conjure up on long, cold, lonely nights.

I heard boots tramping down the hallway, the footfalls in perfect rhythm.

"It's about to happen," I whispered in Kate's ear.

She pulled back from me. "What?" She looked over her shoulder as she heard the boots, too. "No!"

"It's okay," I told her. "It's time."

She shook her head. "No!" She cast her eyes desperately around. "There!" She pointed. "There's a fire exit right there."

I shook my head solemnly. "No." I wasn't even tempted. Not now. With the fear gone, I could see clearly and she'd been right, back in the mountains. My whole life was waiting for me. It was time to take it back.

"*Run!*" Her eyes were shining with tears. "I'll slow them down!"

That made my heart swell like a goddamn balloon: the tears told me how she felt about me, but she was willing to give me up, to never see me again, if it meant I could be free. "*No.* I've been running long enough."

The boots were almost at the corner of our hallway, now. Kate grabbed my arm. "I don't know if I'll be able to get you a retrial! What if it doesn't work? What if they find you guilty again?!"

I stared into her eyes. "If they do, will you wait for me?"

She gaped at me. "Yes! Yes, of course yes! But—"

"Then I'll be okay," I said. "Now, quick, let me kiss you—"

"But—"

I didn't have time to argue. I picked her up under the arms and just lifted her to meet me, my lips coming down hard on hers. She groaned and shook her head and then gave herself up to it, flowering open under me, and I growled in pleasure as I traced the tip of my tongue against hers and then plunged deep, exploring her warm softness. I slid one hand under her ass and squeezed and she yelped, a hot little pant into my mouth, stubbornness and outrage and urgent passion: everything I thought of as *Kate.*

"Mason Boone?" A hard, no-nonsense voice. I had my eyes closed. I didn't have to open them to know who it was.

I kissed Kate for another few seconds, wanting

nothing more than to just fall into that warm, sweet softness forever. But then I forced myself to pull back. I wanted to end the kiss on my terms, not have them rip me away from her. "Yeah," I said. "Right here." I set Kate gently down on the floor.

She opened her eyes. "No," she whispered, shaking her head. "Please."

I stood up. "It'll be okay," I told her. And then I offered out my wrists so that the military police officers could cuff them. When the steel closed around my wrists this time, there was no triggering. Things had changed. Instead of the coffin being the only real thing and everything else being an illusion, now my life with Kate was real and my imprisonment—however long it was for—was just an interruption. And the coffin? That was on its way to being confined to my nightmares, fading a little each day.

"I'll contact you as soon as I have news," Kate said, her voice shaking.

I nodded. Reached out with my cuffed hands and wiped away the tears that had started to run down her cheeks. Depending on how things went, it might be months or even years before I could see her again. But she was part of me, now, in my head and in my heart. That meant I could survive anything.

They led me away. A nurse was coming the other way down the hallway and she slowed as she passed, staring at my handcuffs. I strode on with my head held high. Behind me, I heard the nurse ask Kate, "What did that guy *do?*"

Kate drew a deep, shaky voice. "The right thing."

Kate

I got used to a lot of phrases. No one gets a retrial. The Navy doesn't do things that way. And in particular, you're wasting your time.

They didn't know who they were dealing with.

For every letter the military ignored, I wrote two more. For every meeting they cancelled, I requested another three. I took all the vacation time I had coming from the FBI and dedicated myself full time to the cause. I didn't give them a choice. I kept at them until they *had* to listen.

The only time I took a break was to fly to Fairbanks and finally track down Michelle Grigoli—the witness I'd been going to see when this all started. She made a positive ID on my suspect which meant all we had to do was catch him again. I was terrified that he'd attack another woman before that happened...but to my relief, we picked him up in New Orleans and put him away for a long, long time.

In the evenings, when I'd done everything I could for the day, I wrote to Boone. I told him how much I loved him and how much I missed him. And then, nervously and with a lot of blushing, I started telling him what I wanted to do with him, when all this was behind us. As I gradually got more confident, the letters got steamier and so did his replies. I'd get one in the mail before work and then have to wait all day to run home and open it because I wanted to be alone when I did.

We finally caught a break when I got a meeting with the DA who was handling Weiss's case. It was a career-making case for him and it wouldn't be happening had I not brought him in. When he heard my story, he started talking to a few retired admirals he knew and they in turn sent ripples down through the Navy. And finally, three months after Boone went to jail, there was a retrial.

***

"All rise," intoned the officer of the court.

I bit my lip as I stood. I was the only non-military personnel at the court martial. The military judge caught my eye as he took his seat, warning me that I was there under sufferance. I'd had to pull a lot of strings to gain entrance.

When I'd first seen Boone walk into the courtroom, I'd had to do a double take. They'd trimmed his long hair down to a more appropriate military cut and he was clean shaven. He looked like a soldier again.

Throughout the whole six day trial, I hadn't been allowed to talk to him. Our only communication was through looks. He gave his side of what had happened on that fateful mission and, when he reached the part about the family and faltered, I caught his eyes and told him he could do it. He told them about how the insurgents had chained and buried him and my eyes filled with tears, and he looked at me and told me that it was okay, that it was just memories, now, that couldn't hurt us. And every day, when he was led into the court as a prisoner, I met his eyes and I damn well let him know that I was his, whether they found him innocent or guilty, and I'd wait for him no matter how long it took because *I* knew the truth.

"Has the jury come to a verdict?" asked the judge. The "jury" was a panel of just three military officers who'd sat, stony-faced and unreadable, throughout the trial.

"We have."

Boone turned in his seat and stared at me. Our breathing seemed to fall into sync, the rest of the courtroom fading away.

"How do you find the defendant?"

I dug my nails hard into my palms, my whole vision filled with Boone's Alaska blue eyes.

"We find the defendant, Mason Boone, not guilty on all—"

I didn't even let him finish talking. I was up and running across the courtroom and throwing myself into Boone's arms and he was hugging me to him, chains and all. The judge banged his gavel and called for order but I didn't care. He could find me in contempt or throw me in the stockade or whatever they did but I wasn't ever letting go of my man again.

One Month Later

I took a deep, slow lungful of mountain air and smiled. I was getting to like Alaska.

Boone tightened his arms around me and nuzzled my neck from behind. His hair was longer and his stubble was back, now. I was still trying to make up my mind about which I preferred: smooth Boone or wild Boone. Both were pretty awesome.

Both of us were naked under the blanket and we were sitting on the porch of his cabin, watching the sunrise, just as we had that first morning after he'd taken me there. Except now, everything was different.

We'd talked for a long time about where to live and what to do. Boone couldn't leave Alaska any more than I could leave the FBI so, eventually, I'd hit upon the idea of transferring to the Anchorage branch. I'd sold my apartment in New York and, with the money, we could afford a pretty nice house in Anchorage and keep the cabin for weekends like this one.

Working for the FBI in Anchorage was very different to working for the FBI in New York, but I was already loving the challenge. With such a big area to cover, it meant a lot of travelling, sometimes for days at a time. But with Boone on retainer as a local guide and expert, he could accompany me most of the time. He was also going to help supplement our income by running wildlife-viewing trips, taking photographers to the best places to see bears, caribou and moose.

I'd heard from Marshal Hennessey. He'd taken early retirement and was spending a lot of time with Megan. Her drawings of bears, Mr. Mason and Agent Kate now decorated the cabin's walls and made the place seem less Spartan, more homely.

Marshal Phillips, meanwhile, had been jailed for his part in Weiss's escape and Weiss himself was behind bars. If he'd just accepted his fate when he was caught back in Nome, he might have wound up in a soft prison for white collar criminals. But in light of the murder of the pilot and his role in the kidnapping of a child and a whole host of other charges, the judge threw the book at him. He was now in a maximum security federal prison and the billions he'd stolen was gradually being returned to its rightful owners.

Ralavich was back in Russia, licking his wounds. Losing the yacht, plus having to bear all the costs of getting Weiss out of the US without any of the payoff, had left him financially crippled. Word had it, the other mafia families were circling him like sharks who scented blood in the water. He wouldn't be able to expand into the US for a long, long time...if ever.

And one more person was suffering some long-deserved justice: Hopkins, the civilian who'd really killed the family in Afghanistan, had been arrested, tried and found guilty. He was just beginning what was going to be a very long prison sentence.

I leaned my head back onto Boone's shoulder and breathed in deeply. I could smell the dew on the grass, pine trees and, carried on the crisp morning air, the heady scent of coffee. I'd brought a big pack of really good coffee beans with me when I'd moved. You can take the girl out of New York....

Boone bent and kissed my upturned chin and I felt his lips twitch against my skin as he smiled. He smiled more, these days, and he was sleeping better. The nightmares still came but we were down to once a week or so. I'd found a psychologist in Anchorage who specialized in treating veterans with PTSD and that was helping: Mason had been reluctant at first but he'd gradually warmed to it when it started to work.

I felt him smile again. "*What?*" I asked.

"When you lean your head back against me like that, I can feel your braid." His voice dropped to a growl. "It's making me want to do *bad* things to you."

He never got tired of that braid. I wasn't completely sure I understood it, but I liked it. I only had to braid my hair and he'd dive across the room at me as soon as we were alone. Sometimes, he didn't even wait that long.

I nestled in even closer. "Soon," I told him. "I want

to watch the sun come up, first."

We settled into a comfortable silence for a few minutes as the sun gradually lit up the valley in pink and gold. When it was fully up, I looked around at the mountains and sky in awe and said in a small voice, "You think this'll work? Me out here?" I was having a sudden pang of last-minute nerves. "Alaska's too big. I'm too small."

Boone wrapped his arms around me even tighter and kissed me. "No," he corrected me, "you're both exactly the right size."

THE END

Thank you for reading. If you enjoyed *Alaska Wild,* please consider leaving a review.

You may also like *Saving Liberty*.

She's the President's daughter. I'm the last guy she should get involved with, a tattooed former Marine with a bad rep. When I see her in danger, the urge to protect her is stronger than anything I've ever felt. I save her life...but when she asks me to become her bodyguard, I know I should refuse. I can't guard a woman I'm this attracted to. But when I see how scared she is, I can't turn her down.

Now I have to wear a suit and call her ma'am when all I want to do is slam her up against the wall and tear her clothes off. Neither of us can resist...but I can't let her get close, not with what's lurking in my past. And the danger is far from over. The White House is under threat...and I'll do whatever it takes to protect the woman I've fallen for.

Saving Liberty is available in paperback wherever you purchased *Alaska Wild.*

CONTACT ME

If you have a question or just want to chat, you can find me at:

Blog: http://helenanewbury.com

Twitter: http://twitter.com/HelenaAuthor

Facebook:
http://www.facebook.com/HelenaNewburyAuthor

Goodreads:
http://www.goodreads.com/helenanewburyauthor

Pinterest: http://pinterest.com/helenanewbury/

Amazon Author Page
http://www.amazon.com/author/helenanewbury

Don't be shy! :)